STUCK

with the

BOSS

To Bobbie Jo.
You've been there for me since the beginning.
Thank you for your support!

ONE

Erin

"**D**id you know that ninety percent of the genes in a cat are similar to human genes?" Dwayne asks, swirling the wine inside his glass, back and forth, round and round.

If I'm not careful, I'll be hypnotized.

I wouldn't normally think something so silly, but I went out with a guy in college who tried to do just that with a cup of tea, so I can never be too careful.

"It's true. Studies show cats have gray and white matter in their brains just like us," Dwayne continues in a low voice.

He emphasizes the last three words too, as if he's trying to seduce me with facts.

Did I tell him I liked cats or something?

As he rambles on about the details of these studies, I can't help getting distracted by the number of cars sinking into the pothole in the middle of the street, or the pigeon shitting on the curb next to us.

Guilt eats at me for being rude, even if it is internally. I wouldn't exactly say it's because those things are more interesting than Dwayne's cat facts. The optimist in me would just point out that I have a lot on my mind.

It might also be because my friend Bree has done most of the chatting on my dating app, and I can't figure out if she instigated this conversation by expressing interest in cats. I've known her a long time, though, and she's never mentioned being a fan.

I wouldn't have let Bree talk to guys under my profile, but ever since I went home with the guy who kept his own hair in the freezer, I had no choice. I can't be left to my own devices.

My trusted friend insisted Dwayne was a decent guy. One with a PhD.

His own place.

He even has his own car.

When it comes to me, those three things are enough to get guys through the door, and since he showed up as the exact person in his picture… well, that's a plus too.

If I had a dollar for each time the picture was faked, I'd be floating in my own pool by now. That's right—I'd have enough money to buy such a luxury apartment in the middle of Manhattan. As it stands, I can barely afford to walk down the sidewalk, let alone anything extravagant.

I swallow my sip of red wine and cringe as I attempt to force it down. When I tried to order a glass of Pinot Grigio—my favorite—Dwayne insisted I try the red he ordered for himself.

So, I did, and even though I told him it's better than I expected in order to make him feel good, it's not.

"Do you have a lot of cats?" I ask, genuinely curious as to why he knows these facts about them. His degree is in math, so I'm not sure how they relate.

As a high school math teacher myself, I thought we'd have more in common, and I have high hopes those things will show themselves.

And hopefully, *soon*.

"I have one. Fred. His name is Fred." Dwayne bobs his head up and down. "His favorite form of connection is sitting in my lap. Did you know that cats have a lot of different ways they show affection? Just another way they're so similar to humans."

"I didn't know that." I lean forward, folding my arms on the table.

Big mistake.

He apparently takes my casual gesture as an invitation to meet me halfway. When his chapped lips halt only a few inches from my mouth, I wince. If this was a fourth or fifth date—not that I ever make it so far with anyone—I'd be more comfortable offering him my ChapStick. I always carry some around.

I imagine Dwayne wishes he could carry Fred everywhere he goes too.

"I wonder..." He uncrosses one of my arms to take my hand in his, and I tense at his touch. "I wonder what kind of affection your *pussy* would show me," he whispers.

I shoot out of my chair and fling the flimsy piece of furniture backward. The sudden ruckus attracts the attention of the other patrons, but it doesn't stop me. "I'm sorry, but I'm going to go. I need some fresh air."

Dwayne peers at the twinkling lights strung along the perimeter of the patio. "We're outside," he states.

"Right. Sorry." I force a smile and gather my purse, along with my jacket, as quickly as possible. Before I storm off, I whip around to him, very aware of all the curious eyes on me. "You don't have a PhD, do you?"

Dwayne shifts in his seat. "Depends on who you ask." I furrow my brows. "What does that even…"

Throwing my hands up, I shake my head and rush toward where I believe the opening in the gate is.

No luck. I'm locked inside this patio, and now I have to walk back by my disastrous date. Is it necessary to cover the side of my face closest to him? Probably not, but I do it, anyway, as I hurry inside.

When I finally reach the sidewalk, I take a deep breath, letting the evening August breeze fill my lungs.

The air is definitely more refreshing out here since Dwayne's creep factor isn't crawling all over me.

When he calls my name, I don't respond, but I do pick up my pace and scurry in the opposite direction. At the crosswalk, I fish my phone out of my purse while I wait for the light to change. I click on the number at the top of my call list, and the second Bree answers, I let out a long, frustrated breath. "Consider this a Bat-Signal."

"What?"

"Mayday. Defcon one. *Mayday*," I whisper-scream into the phone as the woman to my left eyes me.

"Can you speak English, please?" Bree asks. "I need an emergency margarita night. Now."

"*That* I understand, loud and clear." There's a thud on her end, followed by jingling keys. "I'll alert the others on my way."

When I let out a breath, it's full of relief.

I never ask for an unplanned girls' night with all four of us. Bree might come over unannounced every now and then, but we normally save our dirt-sharing version of jam sessions for Thursday nights.

Even though tonight is Saturday, I can always count on Bree, Tessa, and Madison to come to my rescue.

And this situation goes beyond the scope of our text chain.

They're true friends, for sure, and I've always said it's because of how compatible our zodiac signs are. As in, if an Aries, Sagittarius, Pisces, and Libra walked into a bar, they'd order margaritas, laugh until midnight, and swap dating crises like it's their very own comedy special.

This is us, in a nutshell.

I'm damn proud of it too, but I still wish my dating horrors were works of fiction instead of reality.

As soon as I reach the Mexican restaurant and bar that's unofficially been hosting us for over two years now, I spot our table and thank the universe it's available tonight.

There are other tables, of course, but this is the one we occupy every week. Being as superstitious as I am, I don't like messing with things that work.

And this table works for our collective energy.

I'm the first to arrive, and as soon as I'm seated, the bartender—and our friend— appears next to me. "I didn't expect to see you tonight. Are the other ladies coming?"

"Yes," I confirm and follow it up with a sigh. "I need tequila to wash the creepy off me after the date I just had."

Harvey scrunches his handsome features into a grimace, but it doesn't even begin to cover how icky I feel. "That bad, huh?"

"Truly." I shudder and shake off the negative energy that's flooded me since Dwayne made his inappropriate suggestion. "But one of these days, I'm going to march in here with good news and celebrate that I've found a guy who looks at me like you do Micah."

The deep, sympathetic lines between his brow smooth over, and his expression softens into a wistful one. "You deserve it."

My chest squeezes as I pat his arm. "Thank you, but right this moment, I'll settle for a pitcher of your mango margarita."

He knocks his knuckles against the table as if to answer, "Coming right up," and I catch a fleeting glimpse of the tattoos along his forearms. Then he takes long strides to the bar, where the neon sign hanging on the wall casts a red glow across his cheek.

The man is as sweet as the margarita he's mixing but as strong and chiseled as a sculpture. I should've gone to the bachelor auction last May to bid on the likes of him. That's what Micah did, and they're as happy as ever.

"What happened?" The sound of Bree's voice tears my attention away from Harvey and my seemingly hopeless dreams of love. As she sits, my friend's hair bounces on top of her head, where her messy bun is secured with a flimsy hair tie, wavy strands loose on either side of her head. She has zero makeup on her face, and it's obvious she was settled into her apartment for the night before I called.

Like I said—she's a true friend. "Tell me *everything*," she presses.

"Wait for me." Madison slings her tote bag on the back of an empty chair and slides onto the seat, her cheeks tanner than they'd been before she moved to LA. She's only in town this week to check on her salon and her friends, much to my benefit.

As I open my mouth to hash out the details of why I called them here tonight, Tessa plops onto the fourth chair, completing our table of memories, secrets, and margarita spills.

Harvey sets our specialty drink in the center and only has time to wink before he's called to fill another order.

"Why are we having mango margaritas tonight?" Tessa asks and grabs the pitcher. "Are we celebrating?" Her eyes light up when they land on me.

"Is that what mango is for? I forget." Madison tilts her head, inspecting the frozen drink as Tessa fills her glass. "But if that's the case, we certainly didn't have this when Ian and I got back together. What's that about, you bitches?"

"We celebrated when Carter and I got engaged…" Tessa slinks to the side and peeks at Madison through one open eye.

"Like I said—*bitch*," Madison teases and tosses her thick red hair over one shoulder for good measure.

Bree spreads her arms, and I'm surprised it takes her this long to jump in. "All right, all right. I have the answers, as always." She shrugs in her signature mix of smug confidence and good-natured amusement. "We had mango in celebration of the engagement but not for your reunion with the movie star"—she waggles her manicured finger at Madison—"because you didn't return from LA for *weeks*. Do you remember, or has all the sun you've been getting fried your brain cells?"

Madison narrows her eyes. "Need I repeat myself a third time?"

I hold my hands out, quietly requesting the floor. "We're drinking mango tonight because my date went horribly. He might've been worse than the guy who asked me to wear a wig and a skimpy spandex costume because he was obsessed with female wrestlers. I'm also pretty sure the outfit was his sister's."

"Was it Halloween, at least?" Tessa quirks a brow and dips her chin low, causing her thick-framed glasses to fall down the bridge of her nose.

I turn my very serious and sober gaze toward her. "No."

"Ew," Madison draws out.

"*Ew* for many reasons," Tessa adds.

"Wait. What's the celebration for, then?" Bree eyes me as she grabs a chip from the basket and pops it into her mouth.

"For the first meeting of the school year on Monday," I explain and hold my glass up. "Cheers to my fifth year of teaching!"

The girls pause to glance at one another, confusion written all over their faces, but they quickly recover and humor me by joining in my toast.

As I swallow my refreshing gulp, I revel in the sweetness. I usually reserve this many empty calories for Thursday nights, but what the hell? I'll live a little tonight, and besides, it's an impromptu girls' night.

We're laughing and joking and having fun.

It's way better than wallowing and moping around my apartment alone. So sugar and tequila, it is.

"I think I'll focus on my career for now. On yoga and perfecting my nutritious muffins. I need to find a new coffee shop, too, since I constantly run into Barry at my usual place." I shudder.

"Which one is Barry again?" Mads asks.

"The one who slept with stuffed animals?" Bree guesses.

"You're thinking of Tobias." I shake my head. "Barry is the one who was actually really normal, as far as I could tell, but the only things he ever wanted to talk about were vegetables."

"That's what you call normal?" Bree snorts into her glass.

I nudge her with my shoulder. "I mean, I love my lean green machines, but it's just not sexy to compare my legs to stalks of celery and the hair between them to broccoli."

The table grows silent, and the girls all stare at me like I have something on my face.

I pat my cheeks and find I'm clean, then catch up to what they're thinking. "All right. Barry was *not* normal, okay? Is that what you want to hear?" I ask sarcastically.

"Yes, but we would also like to hear what exactly happened on tonight's date."

Bree shifts to angle her body toward mine, and her plaid shacket slides too, barely hanging onto the back of her chair. "He had so much potential, especially considering he has a PhD." As soon as she makes the statement, her mouth gapes, and she wipes the line of margarita trailing down her chin. "Shit, don't tell me his *PhD* stands for something gross."

"Here's the deal…" I relay the details of my date with the occasional optimistic comment to balance out the cringy happenings.

"The food was great."

"The weather was perfect—not too hot or too bitter cold."

"He was wearing shoes, at least."

I get a lot of pointed stares in response to the last one, but in my defense, I've had so many bad dates in the past—how could I not have lowered my standards by now?

As I finish my story, I clasp my fingers in front of me like I would at a parent- teacher conference and nod. "Basically,

I'm going to turn thirty in the spring and not even know what a true orgasm feels like." I suppress the urge to let my shoulders slump forward. Instead, I release a solid exhale to center myself. "But at least I'm healthy and have a good job, where I work with wonderful people," I mumble, reminding myself of all the things I do have to be grateful for.

"You always do this." Tessa gently places her hand over mine. "It's okay to admit that dating sucks."

"And that guys can be assholes," Madison adds.

"But the right ones—the ones looking for a quickie in the bathroom of a bar—are the ones you need to find, because they don't suck as much. Not unless you tell them to, anyway." Bree licks her lips, and a mischievous gleam sparkles in her eyes. "Which means you don't stick around long enough to find out firsthand that they're terrible people, but you get the best parts of them for a few blissful minutes."

"You're so bad." I swat playfully at her and sigh for the hundredth time tonight. "Maybe you're right. I'm just trying too hard to find my forever like you two did." I point across the table toward Mads and Tessa.

"Babe, you know how long it took us to find them." Madison eases my worries with an understanding smile. "Be patient. Your guy is just around the corner."

I inhale a calming breath, and hope fills my chest. Because I believe her.

I might be discouraged every now and then, but after a few seconds of stewing, I get right back to believing there's a new opportunity every time I step out into the world. Into yoga class. Into the grocery store.

Maybe it's the teacher in me, but I believe inspiration and new chances lie in wait, if we stay open to them.

But I meant what I said before. I think I'm trying too hard when I need to be patient. The universe will work its magic. I just need to *chill out*, as my high school students might say.

That's still cool to say, right? I can never tell with them. Trends in their young world come and go faster than trains at Grand Central Station.

Our margarita guru, Harvey, approaches the table again and switches out the empty basket of chips with a full one, then asks, "Do we need another round over here?"

We glance at one another, reading our expressions effortlessly.

"Nah." Bree leans back with an appreciative smile. "This is plenty for tonight."

"Come on, ladies," he urges with a smirk. "Don't go soft on me now."

"Not soft. Just determined not to get drunk three nights in a row." Bree rubs her temples. "I'm human and can only take so much."

"Three nights?" Madison repeats, lifting a questioning brow. I turn to her and ask, "What did you do last night?"

"I have other friends than the three of you," Bree jokes. "But you're my favorite, and although I have other bartenders who serve me drinks, you're my favorite too, Harvey." She tosses a coy glance at him.

My loving but crude friend has let up on her flirting with Harvey since he introduced us to his girlfriend earlier this summer, but she just wouldn't be Bree Finley without the occasional flirtatious wink targeted at the opposite sex.

"Just for the compliment and this bonus night out, I'm bringing you all a round of shots on the house as a thank-you," he offers.

And of course, there's his big heart of gold to add to the long list of awesome things about him and why we've picked this place as *our* spot.

I definitely should've gone to that bachelor auction to find a guy like him. One with a sharp jaw and smoldering gaze.

Mmm…

Before we can object to his crazy kindness, Harvey spins around and races toward the bar.

"One shot won't kill me, I guess." Bree shrugs and finishes her drink.

We continue talking about dating, work, and Tessa's wedding next month. Her bachelorette party is in a couple of weeks too.

I have the best of friends in my life and a lot to look forward to, and I refuse to let any guy ruin it for me.

But by the time the girls and I part ways, I can't shake the nagging defeat in my chest, no matter how many positive affirmations I repeat to myself during the cab ride home.

The high I was riding tonight plummets with each block blurring through the window.

The second I step inside my lonely apartment, I'm consumed by the silence.

I've kept myself busy all summer with teaching workshops, yoga, and volunteering at the Boys & Girls Club, but the silence of my apartment always deafens me at the end of each night.

I'd take a bad date over this torture any day.

Once inside the door, I slip out of my heeled ankle booties and place them neatly next to my other shoes, then go straight to the kitchen for a glass of water.

Hydration is always a priority, but it tastes especially good after a night of alcohol.

Spinning on my socked heel, the clean and organized space I've called home for the last couple of years greets me. There's a record player in the corner, a cart of alphabetized records next to it, and a bouquet of fresh flowers in a vase on the coffee table. The blossoms grace the otherwise bleak room with splashes of color, as does the carefully folded purple throw blanket across the cream-colored couch.

The only living things are the flowers and other green plants scattered on the shelves along the wall.

I've thought about adopting a cat, but after meeting Dwayne, I could never look at one the same way.

Ever.

As I step into the shower to rub the first part of tonight off me, I consider a dog, but as I turn under the hot spray, I shake myself out of it.

I have these urges every summer.

When I'm not volunteering or organizing lesson plans for the year, I contemplate a pet, a new gym, or a new recipe. It's how I fill the void of absent school hours.

But the first faculty meeting is Monday, and next week is the beginning of the school year. This is not the time to go bananas on life changes.

We'll be meeting the new principal at the meeting too, and I'm sure he'll have updates and changes to announce. It'll be enough to keep me distracted.

I haven't met the new guy yet, but I'm positive anyone will be better and more effective than our old, apathetic principal.

There. That's already enough to reassure me this will be the best year yet.

TWO

Erin

"The date this weekend was a bust, huh?" My friend and co-worker Katie sips her coffee and tilts her head sympathetically at me.

"Totally." I inhale the unique smell of our teachers' lounge, which I've oddly missed. With one deep breath, I get my fill of the ghosts of popcorn and other microwavable foods, along with the rich scent of coffee, lingering in the air. "I did find a penny facing up on the way in this morning, though."

"Let me know when that penny turns into a million dollars." Katie giggles as Bobbie, the librarian, joins us in the back of the room.

"Do you guys think this will finally be the year Johanna retires?" she asks.

The vice principal has been on the verge of retiring for three years now because her husband, who's twelve years older than her, wants to move to Florida. They want to slow down and enjoy the beach with their grandkids.

I've always wondered what it's like to date an older man. In Johanna's case, it seems she and her husband are in such different phases of their lives, but even so, she appears to be happy. Would I be happy retiring at fifty, though? Probably not.

Then again, if I had a husband I was crazy about, I'd want to spend every minute with him appreciating the life we'd built.

But I have a long way to go before I contemplate such things.

"It must be, or she's at least getting close," Katie speculates. "Why else would she turn down the principal spot?"

"Have you heard anything about the new principal?" Bobbie asks, then answers her own question in practically the same breath. "I know he's from London and was a last-minute interviewee for the job, but I don't know anything else." She tears a bite out of her bagel and chews quickly as if she's running out of time, but we still have a few minutes before the meeting officially begins.

She does often complain about having to inhale her food—if she has time to eat at

all—since her son and husband keep her schedule so hectic.

"What is he even doing here? Why would he leave London for a job at our school instead of a private one on the Upper East Side?" I wonder out loud, immediately sucked into this guessing game.

Oscar, the physics teacher, cuts in, his accent similar to the one I'm imagining our new boss will have. "It'll be interesting to have another Brit around. I'm tired of being the only futbol fan in this school." Chortling, he adjusts the slim tie around his neck and smooths it against his sternum.

"We'll all benefit from that," Katie teases. "I think Tommy said he goes to the same gym as the new guy."

"Really?" Bobbie peers over her glasses like Katie divulged scandalous information.

My gaze darts between them as the room fills with familiar faces, the last of which is Tommy himself, the PE instructor.

"He has been spending a lot of time at the gym from what I can tell," Bobbie whispers as she gives Tommy a once-over. "Especially after the divorce."

I frown as I recall having heard the gossip from Katie last week. "I feel so bad for him."

"The poor bloke," Oscar laments.

"Not too poor." Katie fluffs the back of her long blonde hair. "All that time at the gym has served him *very* well."

The vice principal enters the lounge, followed by the secretary. Their arrival draws our attention toward the door, but the room still echoes with teachers catching up.

Soon, the new man in charge will enter, and the tone for the year will be set. A more optimistic tone, hopefully. In any case, I'm sure he'll be neater and more organized than our previous, not-so-fearless leader.

Principal Garth—or Principal Crumbs-In-His-Beard, which I secretly referred to him as—was messy in every sense of the word. The man always had stains of every color of the rainbow on his shirt, but more than that, he didn't seem to have a genuine interest in the students.

We might gossip and complain on occasion, but at the end of the day, we care about the kids and their future, even if some of us show it differently than others. We each have our own styles, after all.

The moment the new principal steps inside the teachers' lounge, our noisy chatter ceases. It's like we all see the tall, mysterious man at the same time and freeze—my lungs stop working altogether.

The baby blue dress shirt clinging to his broad chest brings out the aqua of his eyes.

The lines around those eyes are not simply from age, but from wisdom of his years on this earth. I put him at forty years old, given the charming silver hair sprinkled along the sides of his head.

The strides he takes toward the center of the room are long and uniform. I bet if I took out a tape measurer, each step would match in length. How is that possible?

The second I take in every sculpted inch of the new boss, I swallow my freaking tongue, but nothing prepares me for the moment he opens his mouth.

"Good morning, everyone," he addresses us in a deep, throaty voice that belongs to a divine being instead of a high school administrator. "As you all know, I'm Oliver Westbrook."

He pauses while the group murmurs their greetings.

The pinch between his brows deepens as he continues introducing himself in a heavy accent so captivating, I fear it will make me combust on the spot.

"I have a background in English Literature, and I served as headmaster of an independent school in London for the last five years."

In my periphery, I catch the AP English teacher lick her

lips like she's a shoo-in for some contest—except there isn't one.

Teaching the same subject as the new boss doesn't win you special points, Nancy.

"I hope you all had a refreshing holiday. I've barely had a chance to visit anywhere besides the supermarket and a furniture store since I arrived in the city last month," he says in a light tone, but his tight expression doesn't change. "I also hope you're ready to work to make this the liveliest year yet."

I bite my lip and sway absentmindedly to the tune of his words as I try to figure him out.

He hopes we had a good summer, but his tone is dry and almost bored, like he doesn't care at all if I spent my time off by the beach or lying on the couch.

But there's a slight tic in his jaw, too, and it makes me think the right summer story might make him smile.

And what would that look like? More importantly, would my ovaries survive if I witnessed it firsthand?

I'm hot and flustered just by looking at him. God, what's happening to me? "First and foremost, I'd like to discuss updates to our insurance policies." He glances down at what I assume are his notes.

I should listen to the very important announcement. It will greatly impact me— although the changes always get emailed to us, anyway—but instead, I zero in on his large, strong hands. I'm surprised the pieces of paper in his grip don't disintegrate into dust, sprinkling over his black loafers like snow.

I'm sure women throughout the country of England are mourning the loss of such a specimen. That's the only word to describe him.

I went on a date once with someone who was convinced the Empire State Building was Stark Tower from the Marvel Universe. He rambled on for an hour about how superheroes live among us. I thought he was nuttier than the fact that ketchup was sold as medicine in the 1800s.

But as I study the superhuman in front of me, I question my own sanity. Principal Westbrook could be an Avenger himself.

The dreamy accent of Loki, the confidence of Captain America, and the quiet broody air of Hawkeye.

Of course, he has the muscles of Thor too.

He got an extra special and delicious scoop of handsome when he was created. In fact, my new boss suddenly makes me go back on what I said…

I would totally date an older man if he was anything like Oliver Westbrook. "Wow," I mutter, and my eyelids flutter open and closed, bringing my new boss's face in and out of focus.

His tight lips.

Powerful and clean jawline.

His stern glare pointed right at me.

Oh, wait…

"Excuse me, what's your name?"

I place a hand over my thumping chest to confirm he's speaking to me. When he nods, I manage, "Erin Hayes."

Thank goodness he didn't ask for anything more complicated.

On any other day, I can do the most difficult math problem in our textbook without hesitation, but right now, I'm not sure I'd be able to multiply five by seven.

"Ms. Hayes, I'd appreciate it if you could wait until the

end to ask your questions." "Hmm?" I blink and push off the cabinet I was leaning on for support while I—*gulp*—checked out my new boss.

In a room full of my co-workers, no less.

"Please, Ms. Hayes. I'd like to finish my announcement without interruptions. Can I have your undivided attention?" He pins me with a piercing stare harder than meat- eaters stab their forks into a well-done steak.

And I'm most certainly *done.*

I'm burning. On fire. Thoroughly charred.

My cheeks are as hot and flushed as my palms are sweaty.

It's hard to focus as Principal Westbrook moves on to talk about the next item on his list.

"A teacher retreat." He holds his arm up toward the vice principal and explains, "We've been working on the details of an overnight camping getaway to learn, grow, and bond in order to strengthen our team. We'll have more information for you as we finalize everything, but we will give plenty of notice for you all to make the proper arrangements."

The retreat sounds fun. I love being outdoors, whether it's a picnic in the park, jogging in the city, or drinking coffee on my fire escape.

But the main thing I fixate on is the way he emphasizes the second half of *details* because of his accent.

And the fact that he acts unfazed after humiliating the hell out of me. Then again, it is my fault.

I was one breath away from drooling in a meeting, so I can't blame anyone but myself. Except that's the worst kind of embarrassment.

"Dress code," he asserts, jolting me yet again. "I understand they're very popular, but jeans are not appropriate attire for school, and they are prohibited, as is addressed in your handbooks."

"The handbook also says I can't wear sweatpants," Tommy interjects, placing both hands on the hips of his aforementioned sweatpants.

Principal Westbrook squints at his clothing. "And you should abide by the policies outlined in your handbook." He sticks his intimidating stare on Tommy now, and although I feel bad for my colleague, I'm relieved the laser beam he might call a gaze is no longer on me.

"I'm the gym teacher," Tommy continues in his defense and points to the new boss's shoes. "How am I supposed to show kids how to play basketball if I'm wearing loafers?"

"Let's discuss this privately this afternoon, shall we? I have a few more items I need to present." His attention lingers on Tommy for just a moment longer, like he's testing him to see if he's the kind of person who needs to get the last word in.

When Tommy steps back in line with the rest of us, Principal Westbrook makes three more announcements, then ends the meeting by wishing us a good day.

All of it happens in a blur as blood rushes to my ears faster than water through a dam.

"That was *brutal*," Katie whispers.

I take stock of the room as the other teachers pour out the remaining coffee in their mugs and gather their bags. Principal Hot Brit is nowhere to be found. The meeting is over, and I'm still standing here with my freaking mouth hanging open.

"Seriously," I say back to Katie, my voice shaking. "What if I did have a question, though? He dismissed everyone without allowing us the opportunity to voice our concerns, and I could've had something important to say."

"Did you?" She eyes me with those sparkling blue eyes of hers, and the doubt written all over her is a bit overkill but not entirely uncalled for.

"Fine," I draw out. "You caught me."

I met Katie the first day she started teaching here, and we immediately hit it off over the similar polka-dotted shirts we both wore. We've been friends ever since, and I know it was obvious to her exactly what I was thinking while the new boss spoke.

"If it makes you feel better, I was checking him out too. Those glutes? *Wow.*" She fans herself much like Bree does when she discovers a fine piece of man. Actually, the two women have a lot in common. "But of course, I'm totally boycotting him for being so curt with you."

"I bet he's a Virgo. There's too much brooding in that man for him to be anything else." I grab my empty coffee mug and make my way toward the sink to rinse it out before the brown ring sticks to the inside wall. Katie follows as I say over my shoulder, "And you know what? I hope his horoscope predicts a cloudy day for the—"

A throat clears next to us.

When I snap my head in its direction, my gaze starts at the tips of two black Italian moccasins—as my history-loving grandfather would've opted to call them—and rises up the length of pressed slacks to a leather belt around a tapered waist. Then the top of a firmly knotted tie fills my vision until I reach two bright but frowning blue eyes.

Principal Westbrook holds a mug out toward the sink. "May I cut in?" he asks as if we're at a dance.

How much did he hear?

My face immediately heats again. Except, this time is worse than before.

"Umm… yes… of course," I sputter, my tongue suddenly twice its usual size.

I step aside and realize Katie has disappeared, and I'm all alone with him. Even though the room is large enough to fit one orange *Friends*-style couch, a round table, and two vending machines, it feels no bigger than a supply closet now that it's just my new boss and me.

He casually rinses off his own cup, and it's something I'd normally appreciate, especially since our previous principal did no such thing. But I'm too flustered.

I back away, careful not to spook him. I have every intention to excuse myself and run, but he speaks up before I can string another word together, let alone a full sentence.

"You're a math teacher, correct?" he asks, but it's more like a statement. One he doesn't look my way to ask, nor does he turn when I confirm he's right. "I'm surprised you believe in such asinine things as horoscopes and astrological signs. Do you also believe leprechauns magically gave me the arse you and your friend were loudly gushing over?" He finally turns, and I wish he would've kept his back to me.

Because I can't take the way his gaze bores into mine as he leans his hip against the sink. His stance is far too comfortable, like he's settling in and actually waiting for me to answer.

I wring my hands in front of me as my heart nosedives into my stomach, squashing any butterflies that were fluttering there before. "I'm so… so sorry about that.

Completely unacceptable and unprofe—"

"Principal Westbrook, can I grab you for a minute?" Rita, the school secretary, pokes her head into the lounge and hooks a thumb over her shoulder.

His unnerving attention lingers on me for what feels like

eons before he spins on his heel and follows Rita out of the lounge, leaving me frozen in place with my damaging thoughts.

I'm going to get fired.

Oh my God, there's no chance in hell I will keep my job after the first impression I've given him.

I'm more likely to start eating meat again after completing a year as a vegetarian than to keep teaching here.

This is such a big—

The bell rings, and I jump in place, dropping and shattering the mug I forgot I was holding. "Shit," I mutter and fall to my knees to pick up the pieces.

Each one represents what my career has turned into after a single morning with Principal Westbrook.

THREE

Oliver

I lied to the faculty about all the places I've been so far during my time in the US.

It's true that I have been to the supermarket, and I did pick up what I believe is the bluest couch in all of America for my flat. I bought it in part to stand out as a conversation piece if I ever have visitors.

A third item I've checked off on my list of ways to make this city feel like home is a pub.

Every lad requires a good and comfortable pub, and I have found an English one within walking distance of my building.

Still dressed in my school attire, I pass the deep red wall and slide onto a barstool. "A pint of lager, please, Deidra." I wave to the barmaid, and the second she spots me, recognition flashes across her weary expression.

Smiling, she sets a glass in front of me and asks, "All right today?"

"Just brilliant." I nod, but my head feels more like it's underwater as the exhaustion of the day settles over me. "Cheers." I lift the glass up, then tilt it back for a swallow.

Once I set it down again, I lean my elbows on top of the wooden counter, the gloss finish glistening under the dull light.

Deidra walks another pint toward the far end, where a man sits with the tip of his beard grazing the bar. His worn leather jacket is snug around his broad shoulders, and his voice is raspy but hearty, filling the otherwise quiet bar with unique cheer.

She exchanges a few pleasantries with him, and when she asks about his dog, it's obvious she knows him a lot better than she knows me. Of course, she and I have only spoken the two previous times I've been in here, but I suspect we'll become good acquaintances in the near future.

As I eavesdrop on their conversation, I pay particular attention to Deidra's accent.

She's lost some of her English edge.

It's possible I'm still fresh off the plane and can detect any small nuance, but I caught it last week and again today in the way she pronounced "all right." She had less of the tall pronunciation and more of the wide one, which is common for American English.

Will the same happen to me?

If I stay here, anyway.

I accepted the first job I was offered, where I can continue to make a difference for young minds, and although my flat is nothing to gloat over, I have settled in and made it my own. For me, that means minimal décor, which my ex might've referred to as desolate, but it suits me, nonetheless.

I got a blue couch, didn't I? I imagine it absolves me of my decorating sin in my ex's eyes, even though she's no longer in my life.

Neither the job or the flat will matter if I decide to move back to England, though.

The problem of staying or not is rooted in the reason I came here in the first place.

Rebecca hasn't answered any of my calls the last two days, and I'm growing restless.

It's perhaps why I was so hard on a few of the teachers at the meeting today.

The bloke in sweatpants gave me a hell of a time over the dress code. Since we're both members at the same gym, I've seen him outside the school in nothing but some version of those sweatpants—in every color imaginable, in fact. But it's appropriate to wear such a garment to work out in. I do the same.

However, it's not kosher to parade around the school with his plonker on display in such a flimsy fabric.

I could not understand how he or anyone else could disagree with my logic after a single look in the mirror, which I asked him to do. We agreed he'd find—and wear— proper undergarments with his gym attire.

It was a compromise, something else my ex did not believe I'm capable of.

After what some of these folks might call "tough love," I finally dragged the truth out of Mr. Hall. His initial resistance and dismay had nothing to do with the policy at all. Rather, he met with his divorce attorney a few days ago, and he's chest deep in misery.

I was simply an easy target to lash out at. Next week will

be fine, I suspect. On that front, at least.

There's still the matter of the petite math teacher whom I could fit in my pocket, but she could inflict just as much irritation from there as anywhere.

Ms. Hayes.

She peered at me with wide eyes as if I was a large chunk of meat, which made sense after one of the other teachers mentioned she's a vegetarian. The delicate woman must be starving, and I wouldn't be surprised if she believes her desk and everything on it is a buffet.

But it doesn't curb the fact that I'm her boss, and she was distracted, as many women I've come across are. They ogle me with similar fancy as Ms. Hayes did.

The difference between her and the others is that she was rather intriguing. What math teacher earnestly believes in bloody horoscopes?

"Pork scratchings for ya, love?" Deidra reappears and sets a bowl of crisp pork rinds in front of me.

I offer a small smile of my appreciation and grab one, instantly missing London and the bar I used to frequent with my mates in the years after university.

Connor would bet he could finish his pint faster than me, and Eli would challenge the winner. Our other mate Dalton would stand by and call each match as if we were a live sporting event. Afterward, the losers would buy the rounds for the rest of the night while we played darts until we saw three times the number of boards on the wall.

The four of us shared many laughs.

That was before life pulled us in different directions, though. It's why we've gotten together only a handful of times in recent years.

I glance around at the quiet pub and miss the boisterous bunch even more. There's certainly no place like home, as they say, but there are certain perks of

Deidra's place. Mainly, they have a dart board, and there's the familiar scent of beer- soaked carpet with hints of whiskey and musk. It's the exact smell of the one from home, which immediately drew me in.

To top it off, Deidra is pleasant company as well.

"Is this the match from Saturday?" I ask her, pointing to the telly.

She nods, and as she wipes the bar down, she asks, "Are you going to join us for the one this weekend?" "I'll do my best."

I swallow the rest of my room temperature pint around the sudden lump in my throat, then check the time.

If I call Rebecca now, it'll still be early enough to speak with Malcolm. My attempts haven't succeeded all summer, but my wish is that she'll take me more seriously now that I'm in New York.

I settle up and wave to Deidra before I head out. As I make my way down the empty sidewalk, my shoulders are painfully tense, and I make it worse by gripping the phone in my hand as hard as I would a steering wheel while driving through traffic.

I'm eager to ring her.

It's crackers how easily my life has changed since I learned of her existence.

Once upon a time, I walked along the Thames at sunset, the Tower Bridge in the distance, and I raved about my satisfying life there. I was carefree and relaxed—my version of such a notion, anyway.

Then it all came to a screeching halt.

I do believe this will be for the better in the long run, if I can convince Rebecca to invite me into her and Malcolm's lives.

The soft evening breeze wraps around me, and I silently praise the New York weather. London tends to stick to two seasons year-round, and they're awfully similar most of the time.

The end of summer here is much like home, but I'm looking forward to experiencing the four seasons of this city.

I finally near my building, the windows nestled in succinct fashion against the worn maroon exterior. When I reach the entrance, I hold one of the tall glass doors open for a young woman with a poodle. I move out of the way—at least I attempt to—but the small animal lifts a leg and almost tinkles on my loafer.

"No!" the woman screeches and yanks the dog back just in time. "I'm so sorry.

We're still learning the whole potty-training thing."

"It's quite all right." I slide past her, thankful my shoes escaped unscathed. I only brought a couple of pairs since I moved without much notice. I had to pack lightly, so I donated most of my belongings.

Which is why my closet looks as if no one lives there.

This move has to be the rashest decision I've ever made in my life. More so than the tattoo a mate of mine convinced me to get. The damn thing got infected, and my side was sore for ages.

That in itself is the perfect example of why I keep my distance from spontaneity and reckless behavior.

As soon as I enter my flat, I press a thumb to my phone screen to ring Rebecca.

To my relief, she answers right before voice mail. "I've been meaning to call you back. I promise."

My lips twitch, and my chest blooms with the hope that she's being truthful.

Perhaps my numerous calls have made a difference, after all.

"Between trying to get Malcolm ready for school next week, work, and my schedule at the hospital, I've been swamped." She sounds out of my breath, and my heart lurches.

"Does the same babysitter still watch Malcolm while you're working? Evie something?" I ask curiously as I slide my shoes off one at a time and set them next to each other by the door.

"Yes," she says. "I've single-handedly paid her enough to buy her own island." "Why don't you let me watch him, Rebecca?" I blurt.

"Because I barely know you." She laughs. "I mean, you're my brother and everything, but you only just found out about us three months ago. Hardly enough time for me to know if you're the guy I've always assumed you to be—unreliable and rude— or if you're the kind of guy who sticks around. You could also be the kind who thinks kids are *icky*." There's a strong underlying hurt in her mocking tone, and it makes my shoulders deflate.

I'm full of remorse these days, and it seems to worsen by the day.

"I've already explained to you that I didn't receive your letters," I insist, as if that's enough to erase years of pain I caused her.

"As you've said several times. And I want to believe you."

There's a pause on her end, followed by whispering, and I fight the urge to ask if it's Malcolm. To beg her to put him on the phone.

But I've gotten much better at refraining from being so pushy. I did have to learn it the hard way, though. The second time I ever spoke to Rebecca, I demanded she let me speak to my nephew since it was both our rights to know each other.

She didn't speak to me for a week.

I didn't blame her, either, and I apologized on several occasions for my unscrupulous behavior. I'm usually more reserved, with a Herculean grip on my self- control, but I was particularly emotional back then.

After all, I'd just learned I have a sister.

I didn't know it before, but she'd also tried to contact me by sending letters as a child—correspondence my mother deemed unnecessary to share with me.

A door closing sounds on her end as she says, "I mean, I do believe you, Oliver.

I've just needed time to adjust to this. It's a little much, okay?"

I take a deep breath and nod, even though Rebecca can't see me.

I'm frustrated, but the truth is, I understand her. This is all difficult for me too, but on top of the overwhelming situation itself, I also feel a great deal of guilt.

Of course, it wasn't my fault that our mother didn't tell me about her until recently. She would've taken it to her grave, too, a moment she thought was coming sooner rather than later. So, due to a scare from a lump in her lymph node, my mother decided to give voice to the secrets that haunted her.

It's how I learned of my little sister. The entire tale

unraveled over tea as my mother told me she gave birth to Rebecca during a four-year separation from my father. She was staying in New York with a friend at the time when she met Rebecca's father.

Although I'm thrilled that all has turned out fine and well with my mother's health, her confession has left a special kind of disaster in its wake. One that's shaken me to my core, and I have traveled across an ocean to remedy the situation.

I just can't figure out how to stop botching every interaction with Rebecca.

Remaining quiet might do the trick. Under any other circumstance, I could win awards for how good I am at staying silent. This thing with my sister and her son has me out of sorts, though.

"You're the reason I moved to the States," I say into the phone as I retrieve a lager from my fridge. "To the land of hot dogs on each corner, and a subway that smells like the loo no matter where you are."

"Aren't there actual toilets right on the streets in London?" she asks, and it sounds like she's eating. She speaks around obvious chewing as she continues, "I've seen pictures online of some bathrooms enclosed in one-way mirrors."

I hesitate, fighting a smile. "Perhaps…"

"I didn't ask you to move here." Her stern voice fills my flat, and I can't help but chuckle at how similar I've observed us to be during the few times we've spoken.

We've met in person twice since my arrival, and I noticed within the first five minutes that we have many of the same mannerisms—impeccable posture and rigid enunciation, even if our accents are nothing alike.

Our personalities, however, reside on opposite ends of the

spectrum. She's much more expressive, and I imagine she's more open as well. I plan to confirm the latter the more I get to know her.

"How could I learn I have a sister and a little nephew and not come running?" I set my lager onto a coaster on my kitchen counter and stare out the window at my new fate.

"You could've just asked your mother for tips. She's ignored us pretty easily for almost thirty years." She sighs, and it sounds defeated. I detect a hint of an apology as well.

"*Our* mother," I correct her, although I shouldn't. She has every right to be hostile toward the woman who abandoned her.

When I was ten, I was angry with my mum for leaving me with my father in London during those four years she spent here in New York. But I forgave her the second I saw her again. The moment she wrapped her arms around me, I felt so warm and comforted by having my mother back that I didn't care what had happened.

She never returned to Rebecca, though.

Not many people would call me an optimist, but in this instance, I'd like to believe my mother wouldn't do such a thing to her own child without something larger at play. My little sister—*fuck*, I'm still not used to the idea—laughs, but it's not the good-natured sound I've come to recognize. "I didn't have a mother. I did have a loving father and a caring grandmother, so I'm not complaining. If they hadn't been around, I wouldn't have learned how to change my own tire or crochet," she says with genuine enthusiasm, and it warms my heart a little, settling a fraction of the guilt weighing on me.

It's a relief to know she had a good and happy childhood, even without a mother. After a brief pause to sip my drink, I assure her, "You don't know me very well,

Rebecca, but believe me when I say it's not like me to disregard such news. I'm here to get to know you better, and I'd like to know Malcolm too. When can I meet him?"

The silence that ensues eats at me, and I brace myself for what is likely to occur.

She usually gives me some variant of the answer *no* or offers to meet just the two of us. I don't expect this to be different.

Even though I do hope it will be.

"Next weekend. Dinner," she clips. "But I will warn you—the only thing Malcolm knows about England is what he's learning from *Harry Potter*, so don't be surprised when he asks you if you've been to Hogwarts."

I chuckle and wipe the drops of lager off my bottom lip, my mood instantly lifted.

I'm going to meet my nephew and will have the opportunity to shower him with love and gifts and—

"And no gifts of any kind."

I freeze. "What do you mean?"

"I know this is your first time meeting your only nephew, and presents are the easiest way to win over a nine-year-old, but I don't want there to be any pressure on him, okay? He's going to be confused and ask a lot of questions as it is, which is healthy. I want him to process it all, but he won't if he's distracted by shiny new toys. I don't want that," Rebecca says, and although she makes perfect sense, I don't love the idea.

But I respect her and will do as she asks, nonetheless. I'll just have to wait for a later, more appropriate time to give Malcolm the tie I bought him and the quilt my grandmother had made me as a child.

"I mean it, Ollie. No gifts."

I spin the phone on the counter, the speaker button lit up, and sigh. "Your rules are my new rules. Anything else I should know?"

"Malcolm has a shellfish allergy, so if you're planning on bringing any food— which of course, you don't have to— keep that in mind."

"You are cutting me off at the knees with the ban on gifts. Food might be the next best thing, so that's good to know. I don't like seafood, anyway." I hold a finger up as if she can see me and say, "Oh, and are we calling me Ollie now? Have I upgraded from Major Grump and Annoying Wanker?"

This gets a soft laugh out of her. I never thought of myself as comical in any way, but the pleasant sound makes me want to learn a joke or two just to hear it again.

I also love the nickname. She's growing more comfortable and accustomed to me, and I could not be more overjoyed.

"I need to go, but yes, *Ollie* is your new nickname. Happy?" she asks sarcastically, in the way only a sister could tease her brother.

"Very," I respond, and I mean it. I'm going to meet my nephew soon.

By the end of the call, my spirits are much more elevated than they were at the meeting this morning.

I mentally sift through a list of things I could bring to dinner as I take a seat on my couch, facing the telly.

It's a short list since the kitchen is unexplored territory for me, so my thoughts give way to Malcolm. What will he think of me? Will he think I'm no fun?

As I flip the channels, Ms. Hayes's face comes to mind.

At the end of our last interaction this morning, she no

longer viewed me like a piece of meat, but like a villain straight out of a fairy tale.

I shift in my seat, trying to find a comfortable spot, but this cushion hasn't been broken in yet—that's what I blame it on, anyway.

It's not because I'm at all affected by either of Ms. Hayes's impressions of me. I don't regret my actions or stern warning, either. After all, I'm not at this school to play nice or humor any of the staff with their ridiculous notions.

No matter how flattered I am.

After all, it's natural to enjoy the attention of a lady, especially one as young and lively as Ms. Hayes. Her shoulder-length tawny hair was as bouncy as her personality, and it's a compliment to be noticed by someone like her.

It's innocent, and it will remain as such.

FOUR

Erin

Every step I take down the quiet hall makes me cringe. I repeatedly tell myself it's because I'm sore from yoga.

I think I slept with one leg hanging off my bed last night too. I don't even remember going to sleep, or turning the TV on, but I did do both. I woke up with drool sliding down one side of my mouth like a true MVP, and some news anchor on my television was the first to greet me.

None of my discomfort has anything to do with the fact that I'm inching toward my boss's office.

With a firm hold on the container of baked goods in my hands, I come to a stop in front of the glass door, which isn't usually as daunting as it is now. My heart rate picks up, but it's fine. No big deal. It's too early in the morning for Principal Westbrook to be here, so there's nothing to worry about.

Except the light is on, and the growly tower of a man is most definitely here. "Knock, knock," I chirp and practically bounce into his office before he's even looked up from his computer.

He appears larger in the small office chair, one that seemed average-sized when Principal Garth sat in it. The framed degrees, certificates, and awards behind his head are perfectly spaced like the windows of most apartment buildings in the city. The accolades just add to his intensity. Does all the power he wields ever exhaust him?

When he finally lifts his head, I stop in my tracks. Principal Westbrook is wearing eyeglasses.

As in… he's wearing black-framed glasses around his beautiful eyes, and they make him look like a sexy professor.

My mouth dries as I suddenly imagine him sitting me down, spreading my legs open, and teaching me a thing—or twenty—about the perks of being naughty.

At the meeting last week, he clutched the handbook in his grasp as if it was his tether to this planet. Although I found him extremely attractive from the moment he stepped into the lounge, I didn't think of him as being dominating and seductive.

I do now, and it's going to take eighteen showers, a hundred margaritas, and three years before I can clear the images out of my head.

And it is more imperative than a tetanus shot to get these fantasies as far from my lady parts as possible.

No good can come from being this attracted to my boss.

"Ms. Hayes." He holds my stare as he leans back in his chair. "I don't suppose Rita is at her desk, then."

"I don't think she's here yet." Still mildly dazed by my

scandalous thoughts first thing this Monday morning, I check her desk again and confirm she's not out there. "I didn't think you'd be here this early, either, but it works out since I wanted to give you…"

He takes his glasses off in slow motion, but the display of sensuality that I'll be adding to the list of things *not* to think about isn't what has my voice trailing off.

No, it's the annoyed glare he gives me.

I turn from side to side and catch up with the monumental mistake I've made. "Right." Flushed and extremely embarrassed in front of him yet again, I back out of the suddenly suffocating office. "I entered without you inviting me in, and I didn't ask if this was even a good time. I'm so sorry. I'll come back later."

I'm surprised the container in my hands doesn't slip onto the floor, considering how badly my palms are sweating. Tightening my grip on it, I whip back around toward freedom—this was a stupid idea, anyway.

Did I actually think these muffins would smooth things over?

I should've consulted with Bree before I spent half the night baking. This is exactly the reason I've put her in charge of my dating life.

Not that I'm thinking about dating my boss. It's the furthest thing—like light years away—from my mind.

But this just goes to show I cannot be left to my own devices, personally or professionally. Not when my career and integrity are at stake.

"You may come in, Ms. Hayes." I hear him rise from his swiveling chair, which squeaks with the movement. "What can I assist you with?"

I cautiously turn around. Can he see my blush?

And will I ever get used to his commanding presence enough to *stop* blushing? "It's what I can assist *you* with," I start. "Muffins."

I present the Tupperware like it's a million-dollar check, flashing my best smile and everything.

He eyes the container with the same bored expression that Madison gives me while watching my favorite historical documentaries.

"I made them myself," I continue and pop the lid off, the sound muffled by my racing heart thundering in my ears. "They're sugar- and gluten-free, but they're loaded with protein."

"Why?" He lifts a brow and meets my gaze head-on with the force of a thousand suns.

"These are apology muffins." I stand on my tiptoes like the extra two inches will give me the upper hand, but I still don't even reach his chin in height. "I'm sorry for the incident at the meeting last week. And after. And for being so inappropriate. This is a workplace, and I'm a professional. I know that, and I hope you know that I know that too."

He squints, and my sweating has officially reached my ass crack. I repeat—my freaking *ass crack*.

"I meant, why sugar- and gluten-free? Isn't the point of muffins to… indulge?" He slides his tongue across his bottom lip, drawing my attention to the glistening sheen he leaves there like icing on a cake.

On top of that, he says the word *indulge* like I imagine porn stars would say *cock*, and my core clenches.

"I, um… well, I thought healthy versions of food would keep your fantastic glutes intact," I blurt.

He lifts his eyebrows and maintains eye contact for a

longer amount of time than it took the Pilgrims to sail across the Atlantic.

I slink back a fraction, wincing. "Too soon?"

"And here I thought you were remorseful for being so inappropriate," he deadpans, and to my surprise, I swear the left side of his lips curls upward in what I can only assume is the beginning of a smile on Oliver Westbrook.

But it disappears all too quickly, wiping away any evidence of its near existence. Even worse than the moment passing all too quickly is that it's replaced by a brooding grimace found on the likes of the Grinch.

"I'll leave you to it." I secure the lid back onto the container and spin around so fast it makes me dizzy.

"I'd like to try them." In my periphery, I watch him round his desk and hold his hand out. "You went through the trouble, after all."

I make an incoherent sound as I give them over, and then I practically lunge out of there like he's going to throw them at me.

He wouldn't, would he?

Either way, I race out of his office, down the narrow hall lined with blue lockers, and into the safety of my own classroom.

As soon as I shut the door behind me, I let out a long exhale and cross the few feet to my desk. The room is much like the rest of New York City—cramped and dusty. I did what I could to lighten up the space with bright posters of math equations and positive reinforcement quotes. They help, but since the view out of the windows is of the opposite brick wall, little natural light filters inside, which means a dull shadow lingers in here at all times.

Today, the darkness looms extra heavily, and it shouldn't be the case. It's the first day of school. I should be having a mini dance party to kick off the year before the students arrive, but instead, my skin is crawling with humiliation.

The door creaks open, and I slump into my chair with relief when Katie sneaks in. "How did it go with the muffins?"

"Not the way I expected," I say, but it comes out as more of a question.

"Well, you look great. Is that a new Apple watch? This shirt really brings out your eyes." She smiles widely as she halfway sits on the edge of my desk.

"I did get a new watch. Had to replace the one I left on the subway a couple weeks ago." She doesn't look at me as I talk, and I notice a dreamy smile on her lips. I peer down at the silky green blouse she complimented and furrow my brows. "My eyes are brown, not green…"

"I know, right?" Katie rubs the back of her neck, and her expression turns wistful. "What are you thinking about? Because obviously it's not my shirt." I reach over to
nudge her back to reality.

"Tommy and I ran into each other at a bar last night, and we totally made out." She squeals as quietly as possible.

My jaw drops. "First of all—what were you doing at a bar the night before the first day of school? That's ballsy. Second of all—oh my *God*." I draw out the last word. "Making out with Tommy is also ballsy."

"A girlfriend of mine just moved to New York and begged me to go with her. I agreed on one drink, but after I saw Tommy…" She licks her lips and sways from side to side, almost falling off the desk as the bell rings. Hopping off, she claps and walks backward. "I'll give you the details at lunch. You're not on duty, right?"

"Not today."

"Perfect." She shimmies her hips as she throws my door open before disappearing through it.

I can't help my smile, or the way it widens as students file in for a brand-new year. The first day can always be a little redundant by the time we go home. I'm generally an upbeat person, but even I can't maintain the energy needed to repeat the same objectives and schedules for the year during each period.

But it's the beginning of something special.

As I greet my first class of the day, I smooth my now calm hands over my floral skirt and push all thoughts of Principal Hot but Broody Brit out of my head.

Besides, if I can't impress the new boss with my baked goods, I'll let my teaching speak for itself.

Just for the sake of my position here. That's all I'm worried about.

I have young people to inspire and breakthroughs to coax out of them. It will be enough to show the new principal I belong here and should not be fired because of my rambling mouth.

At the end of the day, Katie and I meet outside our doors in the empty hall to check on each other before I head over to after-school detention duty.

The distant chatter drifts from farther down the hall, where students slam their lockers closed and catch up with friends they haven't seen all summer.

We've barely said two words when Bobbie rounds the corner and stops to talk in hushed tones. "I heard Karen gave five of her students detention for not having pencils." She frowns, placing both hands on her hips and tapping her foot on the green square of the checkered tile floor.

I scoff. "Are you kidding?"

"No, and I heard Nancy brought the new principal some muffins this morning. The kiss ass made them sugar- and gluten-free but full of protein." She giggles, but I don't join her.

Instead, my response gets caught in my throat as an interesting wave of humiliation and confusion washes over me.

"Are you sure it was Nancy?" Katie asks Bobbie, flashing her curious gaze toward me.

"That's what I heard." She throws her arms up.

Is Nancy seriously claiming my muffins?

"I need to get going." I hoist my canvas bag higher on my shoulder and shut my classroom door. "I'll see you two tomorrow, okay?"

I scurry down the hall, nearly running, but Karen would probably give me detention if she caught me.

Then Nancy would likely run to Principal Westbrook to tattle on me as if we're in elementary school. But even when I was ten, I knew better than to let bullies get to me.

I roll my eyes and let go of any negativity toward Nancy. She's not worth the burden.

Inhaling, I trudge into the teachers' lounge for an afternoon coffee and granola bar.

I normally make my own bars, but I forgot to do so yesterday since I was too focused on perfecting my muffin recipe.

Too bad they went unappreciated.

I'm one foot from the vending machine when I come to a screeching halt.

He's here.

"You're a lot like how I picture Mr. Darcy to be," I overhear Nancy telling Principal Westbrook as she strokes his arm. "I bet you get that a lot."

"Sure." He gives her a tight-lipped smile and smoothly backs out of her grasp. "Well, you have my number for book club. We're reading *Great Expectations* this

month, and we would *love* for a fellow literature buff like yourself to join." God, she's practically purring.

If only she'd choke on a hairball.

"Thank you for the invitation" is all he says before she saunters out of the room with more sway in her hips than I've seen on a runway.

And now, my hot new boss and I are alone.

I almost tiptoe right back out of here, but I want that coffee more than I don't want to see his ruggedly handsome face.

He rises from his seat to rinse out the special mug he's more protective of than a child is of their stuffed animals. Oscar said the man threw a fit when he caught him putting that mug into the cabinet.

My heart thundering, I insert a few coins and put way too much focus on pressing the buttons for my snack.

A... Five...

"Do you actually get that a lot, or were you just being polite?" I blurt because I just can't help myself, can I? I clamp my mouth shut and steal a glimpse of him.

Principal Tall and Pensive turns the sink on, keeping his back to me as he asks a question of his own. "What would you think of me if I said the latter?"

"I'd commend you for being honest. It's a hard quality to come by." I catch myself. "In a strictly professional sense, of course."

I wouldn't dream of anything different.

Snack in hand, I sidle up next to him to reach the Keurig, and the only acknowledgment I get is a nod—not surprising.

He remains still and relaxed in his natural posture, seemingly content to end our interaction there. I have thirty seconds until my coffee finishes brewing, though, and it's against my nature to sit here in silence, no matter who the person beside me is.

"I thought Brits only drank tea," I say. "But I've noticed you drink a lot of coffee." "And I thought Americans only ate McDonald's and complained about the referees

during football games."

I dip my head and giggle. "Touché. But for the record, we're both guilty of that last fumble."

He makes a noncommittal sound and carries on like I'm not here.

Does he not get the joke I just made? Because it was funny, and I'm really close to patting myself on the back.

"So…" I start again as he uses a soapy sponge to thoroughly wash the mug. "What did you do in England?"

"As I mentioned during the meeting last week, I was the headmaster of an independent school," he states, rinsing off the suds, and my hand itches for a good old- fashioned facepalm.

"Right," I breathe. *Here comes more sweating.* "I remember you saying as much." When I think he's finished, he starts over like it's shampoo: lather, rinse, repeat.

And my God, his hands know how to lather. They're much

larger than the cup, and the scene of frothy soap covering his long fingers does funny things to my stomach, which are as surprising as they are inappropriate.

Who cares that he didn't react to my earlier joke? Sexy soapy fingers are a touchdown in my book.

The Keurig kicks on, and steam rises from the machine as I lean a hip against the counter to face him. To add to his appeal, he's discarded his jacket, and the careful way he's rolled his sleeves up his forearms is done like a professional clothes fold-er.

And I get my fill of ripped forearms.

I might be in a mood to make football puns, but I don't normally keep up with the sport as a hardcore fan might. Now if Principal Westbrook played—whether it were football or futbol—I'd probably put every game on my calendar with corresponding alarms to ensure I never missed a single one.

"What did they call you, Headmaster Strict and Stern?" I ask, my voice light and playful.

He finishes rinsing the mug a second time and grabs a paper towel to dry it, then angles his body toward mine too. "No, they called me sir and were far too skittish to use any mocking tones."

"Oh, I didn't mean…" I push off the counter and stand upright, my spine straighter than a gymnast's.

What the hell is wrong with me?

Right as I'm about to wave a proverbial white flag and announce my departure from his daily life, the most glorious thing happens.

At least I think it's about to.

One side of his mouth tilts up just enough to reveal a few perfect white teeth, and I hold my breath for a full grin from him for the first time. It's so close to happening, but as quickly as the hint of it appears, his lips drop back into place in their usual firm line as they did this morning.

"I'm kidding, Ms. Hayes."

What does his full-fledged smile look like?

He's teased one twice today, withholding a complete grin like Bree does the names of her one-night stands, because in her words, "They're not important."

I stare at Principal McHottie's mouth far longer than is socially acceptable— especially for a workplace—as if I can telepathically make him put me out of my misery.

"Ms. Hayes?"

I snap my gaze up to his crystal blue eyes. "Of course," I squeak, backing away from him and the counter.

"I know I'm not the most comical man on the planet. Rebecca refers to me as Major Grump, but I thought I'd lighten up a bit seeing as how you and I will be working together for the foreseeable future." He lifts one shoulder.

"Rebecca?" I repeat, fighting the urge to double over. He just knocked the wind out of me.

Oh my God.

Does he have a girlfriend? Is that why he moved here?

And I've been getting all warm and fuzzy and insane over him—a taken man.

A taken man who's much older than me, and to make matters worse, he's also my freaking boss.

For the millionth time, I ask myself: what the hell is wrong with me? "I just remembered—I need to go," I say lamely.

Spinning on my heel, I scurry out of the lounge, my laugh high-pitched and foreign to my own ears. I sound like I did when I showed the students of the spring play how to properly project their voices from the stage.

There's a reason I don't do that anymore. I sound more hysterical than theatrical. From behind me, I think I hear the object of my hopeless desires call out, "Wait. You forgot your coffee," but I don't stop until I'm back in my classroom.

My flaming cheeks are so mortifying that even my classroom decorations laugh at me.

I'm even more flustered when the vice principal pokes her head in to remind me I have detention duty.

At least it's not Principal Westbrook, right?

I wouldn't survive facing him again anytime soon.

Time. That's all I need.

I just need a few days and some distance to get over this incredibly stupid crush I have on him in order to regain composure and my dignity.

Assuming I have an ounce of either one left.

I grab my empty mug off the desk and inform Rita that I'll be right back.

All I've done today is finalize the details of our educator retreat and learn of the term "helicopter parent," which Americans use to describe the parents I've dealt with for the last few hours.

I deemed it appropriate to apologize for Ms. Hubanks's unnecessary detention frenzy over forgotten pencils, but that's as far as my leniency reached.

It's not my fault if little Megan and Suzie didn't earn the proper grades last year to qualify for AP Literature. I can't go in and change grades in exchange for a large donation to the school, as one parent suggested.

I then had to explain the problem with their bribe as if

they were toddlers. Beyond the unethical implications, we're a public school and do not accept such contributions. At the end of my long-winded monologue, they asked, "Is that a no, then?"

The audacity of some parents never ceases to amaze me.

While I don't miss the politics of independent schools and the complicated world of private donations, this jungle of public education has its own downfalls. In either case, both seem to have their own versions and levels of entitlements, also known as Hell.

It's only been a week into the first quarter, and I'm already in need of a break. Not from work but from the parents. The retreat can't come soon enough.

The other administrators and I agreed we need to find a balance between productivity and relaxation. The latter was more of a push from the vice principal instead of myself, but I suspect it'll go over well for the other teachers.

The first week has been tiresome and even overwhelming at times, but the routine I've implemented for myself has made the transition to this new life smoother.

Morning workout.

Coffee in my favorite mug at my desk before the first bell rings.

Afternoon walk in the park, or a lager at Deidra's pub before I grab dinner on the way home.

And repeat.

To some, this might sound too monotonous and strict, leaving little room for spontaneity. Unlike me, they might find their life's purpose in living recklessly, but I've seen what such a carefree attitude can do to a person—and those around them.

I learned my lesson before my mother blew up my life with her secret. In fact, I've known the hazards of being thoughtless ever since I cheated during a chess match as a teen. After my instructor found out, he gave me an earful that jostled my very soul.

I tickled the Devil's funny bone once more after that when I got my tattoo, which again, did not turn out in my favor.

It only goes to show that there are always consequences to our actions, even when we don't see them right away.

It's why I enjoy structure and living responsibly.

Some would probably consider my move halfway across the world to be the opposite of my motto, but it wasn't on a whim. My reasoning was incredibly valid, and it'll all come full circle tomorrow night when I will enjoy an evening with my long-lost family.

I enter the empty hallway and glance down the rows of lockers, nostalgia washing over me.

If I would've known about my sister while I was growing up, I would've loved attending school together and having the opportunity to mentor her.

To be a big brother.

I'm not certain what that would've entailed, but I would've figured it out, as I am

now.

"Principal Westbrook." The biology teacher appears in front of me, and I halt,

jarred out of memories I'll never make. "I was just coming to see you." I take in her frantic state and furrow my brows. "What's wrong?"

She takes a deep breath, and it makes the hair at the back of my neck stand.

Bloody hell, this is serious.

"The copier is out of paper," she says through an exhale.

I search her twisted expression and repeat her statement in my mind to ensure I did, indeed, hear her correctly. "Pardon?"

"The copier is out of paper," she repeats.

The woman appears more offended and upset than if her identity had been stolen, although I don't know why. Is paper a rarity around here? No one's mentioned it.

Look at that—I am hilarious, after all.

It's a joke I imagine even Ms. Hayes would appreciate.

"This is always an issue, and I'm constantly the one who has to refill the tray." She waves her arms toward me. "As a fellow rule follower yourself, you don't think it's fair, do you?"

"No…"

"Principal Garth never did anything about it, but I sincerely hope you do." She holds my stare, and right before she turns, she raises a brow as if we're debating the well- being of our students.

Which I'd much rather discuss instead of this rubbish about the copier.

"The workload around here needs to be shared." She delivers the final statement like a closing argument at a trial, and after she storms off, I'm left thoroughly confused and rather insulted to be lumped into the same group of "rule followers" as herself.

I'd like to believe I'm at least an iota of fun, especially since that iota is the only thing I have to win over Malcolm's affections tomorrow evening.

The bell rings, signaling the end of yet another day.

Students flood the hallways and stairs, and I swim through them toward the lounge to rinse my mug. It's the same one I caught Oscar with the other day, and it led to a stern conversation about refraining from touching what's not ours.

When I open the door and close it behind me, locking the ruckus outside, I'm immediately swept into a cloud of sweet perfume. Who's in the lounge again this afternoon? None other than the incorrigible Ms. Hayes.

We haven't run into each other the last few days, and it's been peaceful.

My mind hasn't been filled with exhausting replays of our conversations and concerns of her impression of me or my jokes.

There hasn't been any stirring in my chest, either.

I did eat the entire container of muffins she gifted me, though, and I even licked my finger for any crumbs like a fucking Neanderthal.

Not that I'd ever tell her I did.

I shouldn't have accepted the baked goods to begin with. I should've stood firmly on my side of the line, but I'm not a monster. Who says no to muffins?

"How are you today?" I ask, purposely avoiding eye contact as I wait for her coffee to finish brewing.

Her bowed lips part, and I suppress the sudden urge to stare at them. I study anything else in the room, which isn't a grand idea, either, since I land on her outfit. Rather than a patterned dress or skirt, she's wearing solid forest green trousers today. The slim-fitting pants tie above where I imagine her belly button to be, and I'm surprisingly fascinated by the way the fabric hugs her toned legs.

What kinds of workouts does she do?

I'm a fitness enthusiast myself, so that's the only reason I'm thinking about it. Naturally.

I take a deep breath and glance up at her. "Well? Everything all right?" She tilts her head. "I said it's just fine."

Did she? I stare blankly back at her, thoroughly confused.

"Was that a trick question or something?" she asks. "Was I supposed to answer in more specific detail?"

"Of course not. That would be absurd." I fidget with the collar of my crisp black shirt.

How long does coffee take to brew in that contraption?

"I'm not the tyrant you might think I am." My lips twitch as she visibly relaxes against the counter, her guard taking a break, no matter how brief it might be.

It's too soon to tell.

"Then why did you snap at Oscar for using your coffee mug?" She stares pointedly at me.

"My name is clearly written on the side of it. What's the reason to label our possessions if it's just going to be a free-for-all?" My jaw tics. "Also, I did not snap. I kindly asked him not to use it. It's a special gift from my sister, and it's mine."

I turn the sink on and busy myself with washing the aforementioned mug, taking great care not to drop and break it. It's not enough to keep me from stealing glances at her, though.

Animated, she holds both hands up in surrender, but it doesn't stop her from raking her curious gaze over me. "Don't tell me you're one of those grumps who pretend not to be home on Halloween, or God forbid, hands out floss and toothbrushes. I don't know which is worse." She cringes.

"We don't participate in such archaic holidays."

"You don't have Halloween in England?" she asks, her pitch a higher octave, as if I told her I kick puppies in my spare time.

Which I don't. I would just prefer they don't piss on my

loafers, and that's not a crime. Even someone like Ms. Hayes would agree with me on that.

Dear God, this strange woman has me questioning every little thing now. How is it possible?

"More and more people celebrate it nowadays than they used to, but I don't consider myself to be part of the outrage." Once I set my clean mug to the side, I rub my temples in an attempt to curb the headache I know is coming from the swirling thoughts she's elicited. It's been a long day, and this is the opposite of what I need. "Many younger folks combine Halloween and Guy Fawkes Day into one, dressing up as witches and ghosts while hosting bonfires and shooting fireworks. I, however, don't like changing traditions *willy-nilly*, as you might say."

Internally, I roll my eyes at such a ridiculous phrase. I'm surprised I even had it in my vocabulary, to be honest.

She blinks like I'm an alien from outer space. "I have so many questions."

"I think I liked it better when you were afraid of me."

Her laughter gets caught in her throat. "I was never afraid. Just… intimidated."

"And now?"

She visibly tenses as she studies me.

I'm not sure why I asked—nothing good can come of it—but I desperately want to know the answer, nonetheless.

"Curious," she says.

I sigh. "All you need to know about me is that I like order. Consistency. Control." She rolls her tongue against her cheeks, seemingly mulling over my revelation. It shouldn't be too interesting to begin with, but she watches me like I'm a mystery novel, fighting the urge to flip to the end.

That's the difference between Ms. Hayes and me. I'm the type to turn to the final chapter to avoid surprises, while she insists on whimsy and unpredictability.

Why else would she rely on the stars and clouds for guidance?

At last, she drops her arms. "More control over something leaves less room to adapt and grow."

I cock a brow.

She smiles, and it surprisingly softens the tension in my shoulders. "My grandfather would tell me about the Wright brothers. He was a huge history buff. It's why I watch so many documentaries. They're fascinating in and of themselves, but mostly, they make me feel close to him."

This woman just blurts anything that's on her mind, doesn't she?

"Anyway, we'd often talk about how the brothers first started building their planes. They used unstable material in order to allow them more control when they piloted each aircraft. They couldn't tame an already controlled beast."

My finger freezes halfway to the paper towels I need to dry my mug, and our eyes collide as she divulges an intriguing revelation of her own.

"Something to think about." She shrugs like she didn't just reach into my chest and tug.

"I most certainly will." I nod and suppress a grin, although I can't help the twitch in

the corner of my eye.

From our first meeting, I haven't known what to make of this perky young teacher. She's a ball of wild energy, but she's also clearly wise. I'd like to metaphorically flip to her last chapter in order to figure her out faster, but I have to admit that getting to know her more slowly has been… fun.

Endearing, even.

Ms. Hayes spins around and puts her hands on both hips. "It's nice to see you in such a good mood. I just wish I could figure out the reason for it."

It's a statement, but she leaves a wistful question in the air as well.

"I'm meeting my nephew tomorrow night for the first time." I dip my head and feel lighter than ever, not just because of the big dinner, but also because it's a relief to tell someone about it.

Her mouth forms a small *O*.

"I'm actually a bit nervous," I blurt, and we both freeze as my admission floats in the space between us. We watch one another like we're in the middle of a chess match. Although I'd like to be the first to make a move and run off before I tell her anything else too personal, she beats me to it.

As she takes a seat, she says, "Tell me about him."

I shift my weight from one foot to the other, then relent and sit beside her at the round table. I have no one else to share this with, and she seems genuinely interested.

She's also the type of person who would appreciate the sentiment and significance of such an event.

So, I settle in too and cross my foot over one knee. "He's called Malcolm, and he's nine. Evidently, he loves Hogwarts, but that's basically the only thing I know about him." I slide my hands down my trousers.

"Why are you just meeting him now? I figured you'd say he's three months old or something." Her eyes dart all over the room, and she appears to be solving a math problem in her head.

My nerves rattle more wildly.

"Is that why you're in the US? For Malcolm?" she inquires.

I blink, and a soft chuckle dances its way up my throat. Ms. Hayes is rather candid, indeed.

"I'm sorry. I did it again—I overstepped. It's none of my business." She waves her arms around and starts to stand, but I reach out to stop her.

"Yes. My sister, Rebecca, is his mother, and they live here in New York," I confirm, purposely leaving out the bit where my mother did not disclose their existence until recently.

That's for me to know and deal with.

"Rebecca?" She tilts her head back, and her mouth falls open as she repeats the name with more understanding in her tone.

"Right." I nod. "And my sister forbade me from bringing Malcolm a gift."

The young teacher sets her elbow on the table between us and rests her chin in her palm as if she has nowhere else to be. Her kind, deep-set eyes are a brilliant shade of chocolate brown, and they peek up at me with amusement flitting about like blinking lights.

From this close, I can practically count the scarce freckles dusting her pert nose. If I had my glasses, I'd make them out more easily, but it doesn't stop me from trying as I get sucked into her aura.

"Is that because she knows you'd bring him accounting software or a tie?" Ms. Hayes giggles.

I cringe. "What if I *did* get him a tie?" "You didn't!"

"I'm certain he has plenty of toys and such. A tie would be a whale of a time."

"Does the tie have whales on it? Because that's the only way this would be a cute gift."

I slink in my chair, suddenly—and confusingly—embarrassed and vulnerable. "It's
a plain navy-blue tie."

"I am not surprised you chose one without fun animals on it."

"It's practical," I defend myself.

"Nine-year-olds don't care about *practical*." She pats my forearm, and my gaze drops down to her dainty hand on me.

Her fingers rest right below my elbow, where my folded sleeve meets my skin, and instantly, a drunken shiver jolts up to my shoulder faster than those death traps at amusement parks.

"Listen, I'm just kidding around." She gives me a warm smile, and her eyes flash brighter, a cheeky gleam sparkling in them. "Malcolm is going to be thrilled to meet you. Kids love meeting new people, especially when they're family. You don't need toys or silly clothing to win him over, I promise."

I tear my focus away from our physical connection and try to listen to her advice, but it's difficult with the shift in the air.

Since when is the lounge this humid?

"I must warn you, though. The excitement will wear off. I mean, kids' attention spans are shorter than the laces on my running shoes." She sweeps her tawny hair over one shoulder, still seemingly content to be chatting so openly with me. Truth be told, the more we discuss, the more at ease I am as well. "When that happens, just ask him to tell you about the things he likes and dislikes. If he wants to play a game, or if he plays any sports. Kids love talking about themselves, and eventually, when he's more comfortable, he'll ask about you too."

I nod as I take mental notes, but when the unfortunate realization hits me, I frown. "I don't play or keep up with anything but futbol…"

She grimaces. "Then you're in trouble." I scoff.

"You might as well just learn to love American football. It would save you both some time and pain."

I cover my laugh behind my palm, and even though I thought she'd laugh too, her face falls.

Is that disappointment? Does she care about football that much? Or is it something else?

As my own grin falls, we blink at each other like we've just recognized one another, and panic replaces the peaceful feeling, which was just settling in.

"Thank you for… this." I hesitate as my heart rate quickens, the initial rush similar to riding a bicycle down a hill—exhilarating and joyful, but there's a twinge of uncertainty if the bike will ever safely come to a halt.

I've been spilling secrets of my personal life to someone who works for me. We'vebeen sitting here so closely together for far longer than I expected, and we're crossing boundaries that shouldn't be toyed with.

"I should be going." I stand and deeply inhale, which is a mistake, as her lovely perfume invades my senses yet again.

What is it? The sweet smell of roses?

I'm halfway to the door when she calls out to me, "You forgot your bag."

When I face her again, she watches me expectantly as she dangles my rectangular leather messenger bag between us.

Can I afford to re-enter her atmosphere just for my laptop

and important school documents? I desperately wish the answer was yes, but I can't.

I retrace my steps and accept it, but she turns at the same time to swipe my keys from the table, mumbling that I forgot them too.

The enchanting young woman doesn't let go of the strap when I tug on it, and it brings her along with it like she's losing a game of tug-of-war.

Before I comprehend what's happening, her soft lips graze the corner of my mouth. As in, she's… kissing me.

With the heated contact, I get a better whiff of her fragrance as well. It's definitely roses with a mix of honey and fruit.

Charming and bewitching, just like her.

My intake of breath is sharp as my body hardens all over. *Fuck*.

I shouldn't have this kind of reaction to her. It's far from innocent—the opposite, rather. I'm her boss, and this goes against my rules and principles.

I can't enjoy her this way.

It's inappropriate… but she's positively intoxicating.

She gazes into my eyes, an unreadable expression in them at first. It quickly transforms into one of heat, though.

I may not know her really well, but I know desire when I see it.

And it resides in the microscopic line of her irises, which only grow darker by the nanosecond as we continue standing like this.

I take another deep breath to compose myself.

I don't know what changed between us from the moment I walked in until now, but I need to get a grip of the situation before it takes us both down.

For heaven's sake, we're at work, and anyone could walk in and misconstrue things.

I don't want to be characterized as the perverted new boss. Even if her reaction does please me beyond measure.

"Listen," I start and clear my throat as I put a safe distance between us. "I appreciate the chat, but I didn't intend to give you the wrong impression. I wish to keep things between us professional since I am your superior, and I'd prefer not to complicate matters."

Her shell-shocked expression worsens, and it's not long before her cheeks turn rosy. "Of course," she whispers, and it's followed by a gulp louder than the echo of a scream in a cathedral. "It was just… an accident."

"I'm well aware of the effect I can have on ladies, and the way you looked at me during our first meeting is much the same as you are now. It's how many women look when they have a little crush. As long as that's all it is, I'm flattered, of course, but…" Now I'm the one with rosy cheeks. The heat in them becomes worse than if I were inebriated.

Am I actually having this conversation with one of my teachers?

This doesn't feel like we're a boss and employee, though. In fact, our entire conversation before this one felt natural and very unlike the ones I've had with other colleagues in the past.

All the more reason to nip whatever this is in the damn bud.

"That's not at all what's happening," she insists and holds her hands up, palms out.

With each word, her enunciation improves as the shock wears off.

Any lust I glimpsed in her eyes before completely disappears as well.

She scoffs. "And to be honest, it's pretty arrogant of you to assume everyone has a crush on you just because Nancy does."

"It's not arrogant if it's the truth, Ms. Hayes, and you've partially proven my point.

The number of times I've had to deflect another woman's advances is staggering, and I want to make it perfectly clear that nothing can come of—"

Her sharp inhale is muffled by one of the other teacher's intrusion. "Erin, aren't you on detent—" The art teacher, Ms. Katie Bumble, cuts herself off as her surprised gaze bounces between us. "I'm sorry to interrupt, but the students are waiting in the library for detention."

Ms. Hayes blinks in the direction of the doorway and brushes past me without another word or glance backward.

I'm left alone with the low hum of the vending machine and my nerves bloody rattled.

The woman is infuriating.

So much so that I find myself still curling my hand into a fist for the rest of the afternoon.

My fucking trousers are tight, for Christ's sake.

The way she looked up at me in challenge was… arousing, for lack of a better term.

And God, do I wish I had a better term, because I'm crossing so many lines even thinking about someone I work with in this manner.

But we don't just work together. She works *for* me. I'm her superior, and whatever exists between us goes beyond the realm of a workplace.

Which is absolutely unacceptable.

I drag a hand down my face and grind my teeth. I need a proper shag, that's all.

With the family drama and the stress of moving, I haven't been intimate with anyone in months. That's a reasonable explanation for this reaction I'm having to Ms. Hayes.

It has nothing to do with the vibrant, yet adorably skittish math teacher, who just called me arrogant.

I shouldn't appreciate it so much, but I do. It was refreshing as hell for someone to speak their mind when it comes to me.

My ex wasn't always so forthcoming.

On the contrary, Ms. Hayes might be quirky, but she's confident too. And it's dangerous to admit, even just to myself, but I like that.

SIX

Erin

'm normally in bed by ten o'clock on a school night, but I make exceptions on Thursdays for the girls.

Especially when certain British pigs rile me up worse than when I watch the episode of Ross and Rachel's breakup—the first one, anyway.

I barely see or hear the crowd and bright colors of the Mexican restaurant as I storm into the establishment like I'm on a rampage.

But it's no one else's fault that I continue to make an ass of myself in front of my new boss, or that he, himself, is an ass.

Seriously, a crush? What are we—in high school?

I expected a more sophisticated response from him, given his nature and the fact that he's about ten years older than

I am. But his presumptuous accusations were more like the ones I'd expect from the teenagers I teach.

I'm not sure if I actually recognize my friend or if I just feel her presence. Either way, I sink onto a chair at our usual table with a huff, lost in my spiraling thoughts.

"He thinks he's so fancy and educated because he pronounces classroom with so much *kla-us*," I mimic Principal Hot but Frustrating Brit. "At least I'm not the one stalking around like I freaking own the place and looking down on us mere peasants, who are just trying to do our jobs, by the way."

"Whoa, slow down." Bree signals for Harvey, and when he gets close, she asks for a strawberry margarita—or a sassy strawberry, as we refer to it.

"Good call." I nod.

She wiggles in her seat, obviously getting comfortable, then leans forward. "Start from the beginning, babe."

"I kissed him," I confess. "And that's not even the worst part."

"That's *not* the worst part?" Her jaw drops, elongating her usually round face. "Oh, God."

"Oh, God, what?" Tessa appears, and her confused expression matches Bree's. I quickly note her styled blonde bob, one side of her hair expertly tucked behind her ear. She looks too fancy for our margarita night.

"What's with the flawless makeup and silk skirt? Where have you been?" Bree asks, voicing my exact question as she gives our friend a once-over.

"Carter and I went to happy hour with some of his co-workers." She shoots Bree a playful glare. "You're not the only one with friends outside of this foursome."

"You wish your life was half as exciting as mine." Bree

wiggles her eyebrows and shifts in her seat, her impish smile full of naughty implications.

Sometimes, I'm curious to know every last detail of her wild nightlife, but at the same time, I know it's for the best that I don't. I can't keep up, anyway. She's far more experienced and better versed with men than I ever hope to be.

But in an alternate universe, I'd love to have even a fraction of her finesse. That way, I probably wouldn't be in this crazy predicament with my boss.

"Will your fourth be joining you tonight?" Harvey asks, pointing to the empty chair and setting a fresh pitcher of frozen heaven between us.

"Madison is back in Hollywood, kicking ass and enjoying life on freaking movie sets." Bree rolls her eyes, amusement gracing her features. "Can you believe her?"

"If she does hair and makeup like she shoots back tequila, then I definitely believe her," Harvey teases, ending on a low chuckle before he's summoned back to the bar.

"So? What's going on, Erin?" Tessa pries as she pours us each a glass.

"I kissed my boss," I say in a rush, as if saying it faster will erase the entire embarrassing thing.

But nope.

It happened.

I kissed the broody Brit and then got my ass handed to me.

How easy is it to move to Alaska? That's far enough away from him and this humiliation, right?

Tessa gasps at the same time as Bree cuts in, "But apparently it's not even the worst part."

They both look questioningly at me, and I sigh. "After

the incident, he lectured me on keeping our relationship professional, like I was coming on to him."

"And kissing him means you were *not* coming on to him?" Tessa asks and slowly crunches on a chip. She could be either really confused, buzzed from happy hour, or both

—I'd bet on the latter.

"It was an accident," I emphasize the last word so hard that drops of margarita fly out of my mouth. And here I thought Bree was the messy one.

What is happening to me?

My skin is hot and crawling with nervous goose bumps like fire ants treating themselves to an all-you-can-eat buffet.

"I did well to avoid him for a week, especially when I found out about Rebecca." I dab at my mouth with a wad of napkins, flustered and riled up.

Bree grips my arm. "Who's Rebecca?"

"Well, I thought it was his girlfriend, so I avoided him until I got a handle on my little attraction. But it turns out, Rebecca is his sister, which was a huge relief for me, even though it shouldn't have been."

Tessa practically sings through her shit-eating grin, "But it was, because you totally have a crush on him."

"Yes!" I clamp my mouth shut. "Wait. No… not exactly. I mean, my *feelings* are purely physical."

Bree and Tessa lock eyes and snicker while I groan into my palms. "Okay, okay." Bree shakes my shoulder. "Tell us about the kiss."

Straightening my spine, I swipe the hair out of my eyes, although I should be hiding behind the thick strands for this story. "I tried to hand him his bag because I'm a nice freaking person, but he yanked it from me because he's a damn brute," I clip.

My mind races as I replay the scene in my head like it's a horror film—it's my nightmare, all right.

"Why would I even flirt with him? The man is so *not* my type. He's cold and brash, and his energy is more negative than any of the greedy money-grabbers on Wall Street.

Seriously." My stomach curls in knots as I continue rambling. "Plus, he's so much older than I am, so that's just not realistic."

Tessa gasps again, and Bree covers her mouth with both hands like she does when she reads juicy gossip magazines.

"What?" I hold my drink up, then take a sip to wet my suddenly dry throat. "You definitely *like* him!" Bree squeals. "And it's way more than just a crush." "That is not even... You could not be more mistaken, ma'am," I stammer, nearly

choking on my margarita. The hard flakes of ice are hard to swallow as they sting the walls of my throat. "The only thing I want from him is his respect as... as an educator. That's all."

"Oh my God." Tessa leans forward, and her eyes flash with a gleam brighter than her engagement ring. "You do! You're all hot and flustered, and—are you blushing?"

My hand flies to my cheek, which is undeniably warm.

Bree dances in her seat like she did over the summer when we flew out to LA for Ian's shindig—a beach party with an array of Hollywood stars. I thought my friend was going to have a heart attack from the invitation alone. She was so excited and awestruck during the party that Tessa and I each had to hold one of her arms to keep her grounded.

But this moment comes close as she taps away at her

screen, her lips moving as she mumbles to herself with glee.

I love seeing her this happy, but not at my expense.

"What in the world are you doing?" I ask, swatting at her phone.

"No fucking way," Bree manages around the big *O* her mouth forms. "You have totally been holding out on us, you little bitch."

Tessa reaches across the table. "Let me see!"

I keep grabbing at the phone, although I don't know why, and when Tessa's eyes light up further from what's on the screen, my curiosity gets the best of me.

I jump up and snatch the phone. "You guys…" I whine as I glimpse the school's website.

None other than the principal's picture stares back at me, and my body—my whole, traitorous body—shivers.

The picture is a good one. He's not smiling, but Principal McSteamy Douche stares at the camera like he's peering into my soul—and panties.

"He is *hot*." Bree scoots her chair closer to the table and takes her phone back. "God, I'd let him and a British friend Eiffel Tower me in a second."

I cover my mouth and fight a giggle—I can't help it. Not when it comes to these girls.

"Is the British version called Big Ben or something?" Tessa asks, amusement in the twitch of her margarita-stained lips.

"Good question. Let's ask the expert." Bree turns to me. "I'm sure you've learned a thing or two from hiding this hunk all to yourself."

"This hunk is my boss, so no, I didn't ask what they call two guys doing the same woman at the same time." I roll my eyes and pick up my glass, toying with the straw before I take a sip.

"What are the chances he's done it? I bet he has. There's a specific look in his eye in this picture." Bree points to her screen again for us to study it more closely.

Instantly, the image of us in the lounge earlier today slams into me.

I made him laugh, but he covered what I'm sure was a glorious grin, like maintaining a rigid façade is more important than letting me know he is capable of letting loose.

And I won't even get started on Principal McSchmexy in glasses. I seriously—and very shamefully—picture him in those thick rims while he gives morning announcements. It's become a problem for my lady bits. I mean, how much teasing can they take before I explode?

It's only week one, and I'm in the danger zone, for sure.

I shake my head and desperately try to sound convincing when I say, "It's a headshot for the school website. There is no sexy look in his eyes, especially since he was probably thinking about the weather or something equally boring while he posed for said picture."

"Says the woman who teaches math, the most boring subject in school." Bree blinks sarcastically in my direction.

"Math is a necessary subject."

"The weather is too," Tessa chimes in.

"I'm telling you—this guy has a dirty side," Bree insists. "One that would make even the likes of me blush."

"Is that possible? Because I'd need to see it for myself to believe it," I say.

"I bet he's hiding a huge dick in his knickers."

It's a miracle I don't choke or smear the table and floor with frozen margarita. My friend has a heart bigger and more genuine than anyone I know, but she can be a crude mess too.

"I think *knickers* refer to women's panties," I correct her.

"Have you been studying British dirty talk?" Bree says, her tone accusatory as she narrows her eyes.

"No," I draw out. "I'm pretty sure I noticed it from *Bridgerton.*"

The truth is—I have no idea if I saw it on the historical romance show, but I did come across the distinction while I looked up a little British slang. After I found out they don't celebrate Halloween, I naturally got curious.

I was only researching the language to avoid accidentally saying something offensive to the new boss, anyway. I figured arming myself with such information would stop me from further embarrassing myself at school.

If Oscar was better about teaching us the differences, I'd already be equipped with such knowledge. He's spent the last ten years in the US, though, and he doesn't seem to openly notice the nuances himself.

"I wouldn't blame you for researching sexy British things." Bree waggles her eyebrows at me. "I can see him using that tie of his in the bedroom. Phew!"

She fans herself with exaggeration, and Tessa and I shake our heads while our other friend's filthy imagination grows fishnet-clad legs and runs wild.

I almost suggest she gets a room, but I'm caught up in my laughter.

Once it subsides, I sigh. "Even if he wasn't my boss, I'd never actually date a guy like him."

"Why the hell not?" Tessa twists her lips. "He's smart, responsible, reliable, and definitely not bad to look at. What would be the problem? Hypothetically speaking."

Bree groans. "The fact that he is your boss, and it's taboo, makes it so much fucking hotter—and I'm *not* being hypothetical."

I chew on the inside of my cheek and lean forward. "I don't know how to date a real man like him. I'm used to immature boys who pick me up an hour late for a date and name my breasts Beavis and Butt-Head."

Bree snorts. "Are you serious? I haven't heard about that last one."

"No, you haven't, because I've been too embarrassed to tell anyone, but such is my life. I might as well own it. It's *humiliating*." I bury my face in my hands again, my shoulders slumping forward with the force of a thousand bad dates. "As if what happened with the principal wasn't mortifying enough, we're going on a teacher retreat next weekend, and I'm crossing my fingers and toes that word of the incident doesn't get around to the other teachers. Otherwise, I will never hear the end of it."

Bree bursts into laughter. "I'm sorry—I am—but this is freaking gold. I can't believe Madison is missing this." Bree snaps her fingers. "We need to FaceTime her right this second!"

"We don't. There is nothing to tell her," I hiss as I reach for her phone again, but Bree just holds my face away like a wrestler might hold back an opponent.

After a brief pause, she groans. "No answer. That was going to be epic and would've totally cheered her up, because you know she misses this." Using her free hand, Bree waves around the table.

"And we miss her." Tessa leans her elbow on the table next to the basket of chips and blows out a loud breath. "I specifically asked her to cut my hair last week before she left, even though I didn't need it. I just wanted to sit in her chair like old times."

We all sigh, and Harvey interrupts us. "Whoa. Why aren't you three the loudest table in here right now? I figured you'd be rowdy as hell performing a ritual to curse whatever son of bitch is the reason for the strawberry margarita tonight." He leans on the empty chair, and we all stare at it.

"We'll get right back to your question as soon as we quit missing our fourth—it'll be a while." Tessa clasps her hands on the table and forces a smile.

Harvey offers a sympathetic grin of his own. "What can I do to cheer you up?"

"Don't you ever get tired of being so great?" Bree asks teasingly.

Before we can come up with anything, a young blonde woman in a poodle skirt and a scarf tied around her neck rushes up to our table, offers us a greeting, then grabs Harvey's arm.

His girlfriend, Micah.

She works at a fifties diner, and she must've come straight from there. As adorable as she is no matter what she's wearing, I can't help but picture the comical ride over here in this particular outfit.

"I thought you were going home after work." Harvey furrows his brows. "Everything okay?"

"Oh, yeah." She smiles up at him. "I just forgot to grab my key from you earlier, so I'm locked out."

Harvey mutters a curse under his breath. "I'll be right back to check on you," he says to us as he walks backward toward the bar, his hand in Micah's as she uses her free one to wave goodbye.

The three of us watch them with dreamy sighs—young love.

They just moved in together, and they could not be cuter if they tried.

"You know you want what they have," Tessa interrupts my thoughts. "You just need your own Harvey, or Carter, for that matter. Someone to buy you sparkling new shoes and take care of you."

"In every sense of the notion," Bree adds with a slurp of her nearly empty drink.

Then she grabs the pitcher to pour the last of its contents into her glass.

"I swore off guys, anyway, remember?" I remind them. "I need a break from the disappointment."

Bree and Tessa exchange a look I can't decipher, and before I can ask, Bree speaks up. "In the meantime… how do you know if you want to be Eiffel Towered?"

Laughter bubbles out of me, and I cover my mouth with my hand as Tessa says, "I figured you of all people would definitely be up for it."

"Right? But I just don't know if I would." Bree shrugs more casually than if we were talking about purchasing a rug for her apartment.

"Oh, you would know if you really wanted it," I blurt.

Two pairs of eyes shoot in my direction, shocked. It's not easy to render Bree speechless, but I shouldn't be surprised. A lot has happened the last couple weeks that are out of the ordinary.

There must be a full moon I didn't know about.

"What?" I shrug. "I once heard one of the women coming out of the porn director's apartment talking about it."

I hadn't thought about my dad's old neighbor in a while, especially since those run- ins were the reason my mom hardly ever let me visit him right after their divorce.

The fact that I remember any of it now is extra bizarre.

There's definitely something strange going on in the universe. The stars are out of whack, or the upcoming season change has caused a shift in the natural balance of things.

Is Mercury in retrograde already?

If so, this does not bode well for me.

I need all the good juju on my side if I'm expected to get through this teacher retreat and beyond.

At least during the week, I can avoid the principal more easily. I don't have to go to the teachers' lounge, which seems to be the driving force of our unfortunate meetings.

What is up with that, anyway? I haven't seen Oscar or Tommy in there but once in the last two weeks. But Principal Hot Ass? Now him, I can't seem to get away from.

No matter. All I need is to stop thinking about him or the way the corners of his eyes crinkle when he's on the cusp of a smile.

Or the way his voice reaches deep into my soul.

Or the fact that I'm now wondering if Bree is right about his… dirty side. Why did she have to go and give me those ideas?

Now that she's put them in my head, they're all I can think about as I crawl into bed after margarita night.

Well, they were already in my head, but I blame *her* for making them worse.

It has nothing to do with the tingle I still feel on my lips from when they were on my boss's warm skin.

SEVEN

Oliver

Trying to sleep last night was an asinine idea.

All I could think about was how humiliating my conversation with Ms. Hayes was after the accidental kiss on my face. The more I thought about it, the more I felt like a complete arse for telling her how attractive many women find me.

I didn't even mean it in such a pompous way as she obviously took it, but I was too ruffled to explain myself. If I would've seen the spirited young math teacher today, I would've explained as much. I would've tried to fix our delicate situation—I wanted to.

But by the time the last bell rang, I was relieved I didn't see her. It wouldn't have benefitted me in any way since I spent the last half of my sleepless night dreaming of her gentle fucking lips on me.

Accident or not, the contact elicited more pleasure than I care to admit, and I despise my reaction.

I use my free hand to knock on the unfamiliar door and shake the tension out of my shoulders as I wait for my sister to open. During the silence, I turn in place to take in the fairly quiet neighborhood. I was happy to learn my sister lived in Queens and not right in the middle of bustling Manhattan.

At first glance, this is much more family friendly than parts of the city I've experienced, and it gives me peace of mind for Rebecca and Malcolm's sakes.

I can't imagine my nephew growing up with the metro as his playground. The clean park I passed on the way here appears far more ideal, and I made a mental note to go there together sometime.

It all depends on this dinner, though.

Behind me, the door creaks open, and Rebecca stands to the side to invite me in. "Hi," she says, and I'm relieved she's home.

I half expected her to have canceled without notifying me due to some emergency at the hospital, or because she'd changed her mind.

"I brought cupcakes," I announce as one might the score of a match, but I have much less finesse. My heart thunders in my ears at a dangerous rate.

"Thank you." She accepts the white box of sugary treats.

"Thank *you* for having me over. It's lovely." I gesture toward the box again. "I wasn't sure which ones you two would enjoy, so I lived on the edge a bit and picked out a flavor myself. I hope you like it." I teeter on my heels at the top of her stoop as she studies me.

"I'm sure these are great," she says without looking inside. "Besides, Malcolm doesn't say no to sugar, so there's no worry there."

I let out a calming breath. I've never been so flustered like I am when it comes to my new situation with my sister and nephew.

In secondary school, I was a candidate for student body president, and I was a wreck for weeks before the election. It was the first time I'd ever put myself out there, which was obvious when several fellow students stopped me in the halls to tell me they'd never heard of me until that race.

I lost, and when nothing terrible happened to me as a result, I vowed not to let such insecurities get to me—a trait I've carried with me like a suit of armor ever since.

Until the unknown was thrown my way. Is there even a right way to handle this sort of thing? If there is, I haven't figured it out quite yet, but I'm determined to do so tonight.

"Come in." Rebecca waves me inside, where we exchange a few pleasantries, during which she delivers a quick briefing regarding her noisy neighbor, Mrs. Lincoln. "She pokes her head out every time a freaking cat meows. If she's not too busy yelling at her husband to turn the TV down, that is."

Chuckling, I move inside the warm living room. Her home is modest and uncluttered. My first reaction when I step from the neutral-colored welcome mat over the threshold and into an open floor plan is that this is the kind of place I'd live in myself.

I don't have children, but from what I've gathered from visiting friends with little buggers, I expected the place to be littered with toys, crumbs from various snacks, and school memorabilia. On the contrary, everything seems to be put in its place and tidy here.

"Malcolm," Rebecca calls, and my stomach curls with nervous anticipation as hurried steps echo from the hall.

A young, lanky kid rushes around the corner and comes to a halt in front of me.

He has my sister's almond-shaped eyes, and the shade of bright blue matches hers as well. I might even be so bold as to say both of theirs are similar to my own.

My chest tightens at the thought.

"You must be Sir Westbrook," Malcolm says in a British accent.

A smile cracks through my rigid exterior, and I bend down to meet him at eye level. "And you must be Sir Lewis," I say, mustering as much gusto as my animated nephew.

This is all so new to me, but I hold my breath and hope for the best.

To my delight, his cheeks split into a wide grin, and he hooks a thumb over his shoulder in the direction he came from. "Want to see my room?"

I peer up at Rebecca, who leans on the wall next to the telly, a picture of the two of them hung on the wall to the left of her head. "Would that be all right?" I ask her.

She nods, and I follow Malcolm's quick steps toward a white and red room. A stack of *Harry Potter* books sits on a wooden nightstand, and two posters of superheroes are proudly displayed above his bed. Along one wall, rows of action figures are lined across staggered shelves, and below them sits a large chest.

When he opens it to dig inside, he presents more action figures.

Malcolm shows me his toys and other knickknacks one by one, in order of his most to least favorite. As he does, it helps me solve the mystery of how tidy the rest of the place is. I suspect he and his mum cleaned up the main rooms just for my arrival.

In the middle of his spiel about a burly gentleman he refers to as Thor, Rebecca pokes her head in to let us know dinner is ready.

When I make my way back toward the kitchen, I notice the plush couch in the quaint sitting room, a sturdy coffee table with drawers surrounding it, and a few framed photographs of a man whom I deduce to be Malcolm's father.

Rebecca's never really mentioned him. The only thing I know is that he passed away unexpectedly a few years ago.

The urge to ask about him is always compelling, but there doesn't seem to be a good time to do so, especially not once we sit at the table to eat. Asking about such a thing in front of Malcolm doesn't feel appropriate.

None of us speak for what feels like an hour, although in reality, it's probably only been five minutes.

I've resisted the urge to check my watch to find out for certain so as to avoid offending Rebecca and Malcolm.

My family.

I can't afford to disrespect them at such a lovely dinner—the first of many, I hope.

If only I can salvage this awkward silence.

"Thank you again for the invitation to join you this evening." I clear my throat of the cobwebs its accumulated over the last half hour.

While I was in Malcolm's room, I didn't speak much, opting to take Ms. Hayes's advice to listen to my nephew and learn about him. It worked too, but we're regressing now.

"You're welcome—again," Rebecca says as she slowly chews a green bean.

I take careful bites of my meatloaf, even though I want to follow Malcolm's cue and devour it. I'm not much of a cook myself, so home-cooked meals are as rare for me as acne at my age.

Malcom eyes the macaroni and cheese with great zeal. I was told it's his favorite when I first arrived. As he licks his lips, he stabs a forkful of the creamy pasta and stuffs it into his mouth.

I study him to ensure he doesn't choke. The kid is smaller than I imagined, and as he continues to take enormous bites of his food, I worry for his safety.

More so than I worry for the failure of this dinner.

We were off to such a wonderful start. Malcolm talked nonstop while we were in his room, and it was easy to hang out with him. Of course, it was simple since he was rather thrilled to tell me all about his action figures. Out here, we don't have such subjects to focus on.

It's so quiet I can hear Mrs. Lincoln yelling at her husband next door. This could be because she's merely that loud, as Rebecca warned me when I first stepped inside, but my paranoia doesn't leave room for such optimism.

I'm keenly aware of Rebecca's eyes on me as I continue to slowly chew.

Clinking his fork against the bowl—a sound that echoes across the small kitchen— Malcolm scoops up the last of his pasta coated with preservatives, and I make a wish for him to grow out of his obsession with it before his arteries are clogged with the fake cheese.

"Malcolm, honey, why don't you go into the living room and set up a board game for us to play?" Rebecca suggests, and my ears perk up.

But once she and I are left alone, it's not exactly the conversation I thought we'd have.

"You can relax," she tells me. "We don't bite, and obviously, you don't, either.

Malcolm was very excited to meet you." "Really?"

"He's talked about you nonstop." Smiling, she sets both hands on the table, nudging her plate to the side. "And he's having a great time. I appreciate the effort you've put into listening to him, even when he's describing every one of his action figures in specific detail like you can't see them for yourself."

I bring my napkin to swipe at my chin and chuckle. "I know I've been hard on you, and I'm sorry."

"Don't apologize. I was hard on you at first as well, for which I apologize. I absolutely understand and respect your caution. I'd do the same."

"Still. I'm sorry I called you a wanker because I wanted to hit you where it hurts in your own slang." She takes a sip of water, and I can't help but laugh again.

My sister has quite the personality, and I appreciate it now more than ever as her candor puts me at ease.

"I'm also sorry I thought you were like her. I kept worrying you only wanted to meet us to ensure we're doing fine so that you could curb some sort of guilt. Then you'd take off," she says solemnly.

There's no need to clarify whom she's referring to—I already know it's our mother—but the last part twists my gut with agony.

"It's my fault she left you, though, and for that I am guilty," I whisper, the words hard to force out.

Rebecca vehemently shakes her head.

"I'm sorry," I say, nonetheless. "Had I not begged her to

return home, perhaps she would've stayed with you to be the mother you deserved."

"Stop." She waves her hands. "It wasn't your fault, and you have nothing to feel guilty for. I don't blame you."

I drag my hand through my hair, my stomach swirling with overwhelming emotions. Most prominently, I'm surprisingly relieved to get all this out in the open.

"I appreciate you saying as much." I give her a tight-lipped smile. "It's not why I'm here, though, and I reassure you I will not be leaving. You and Malcolm are important to me."

She tilts her head, possibly aware there's more I'd like to say, and she's giving me the space—and ear—to give voice to what's going on it my crowded head.

"It's hard to be without family," I start. "I've always had my parents, but we were never the same after my mother returned from New York. We didn't laugh or play as much, and I didn't realize just how terribly I missed being close. Not until I learned of you."

I swear I note tears in her eyes, but she blinks all too quickly. After a few long beats, she gives me a small smile. "The more you've nagged me, the more I've realized that you're genuine and kind. You know, beneath your brooding, hard exterior."

"I appreciate you saying that—even the last part." A lightness infiltrates my aforementioned tough exterior, and hope floods my chest.

The air shifts. Instead of being filled with uncomfortable tension, the energy steadily changes to one of peace and gratitude.

"I guess you can stick around." She shrugs sarcastically, but I know she truly means it. "But you don't have to keep thanking me for the food or the invitation, nor do you have to keep eating as if you're afraid of it. Just tear into the damn meatloaf like you mean it already." She sets her fork down, and the amused glimmer in her eyes evaporates. "Unless you don't like it. In that case, you're more than welcome to help yourself to

Malcolm's mac and cheese or the takeout menus in the drawer."

"Rebecca, this meal is fantastic. I can honestly say it's the best I've had in weeks." I wave around the colorful spread she's made and laid out on the table between us. "It's much better than anything I've had at Deidra's, and I've practically tried everything on the menu."

"Not much of a cook, huh?" She asks the question, but her tone indicates she knows the answer before I confirm it. "Well, you can—"

"Ready!" Malcolm bursts into the kitchen, waving his arms for us to follow him into the other room.

"One minute, buddy. We're almost finished." Rebecca turns back to me. "If you want to come by for dinner more often, that would be… great." She lifts her sober gaze to meet mine, and the weight of her offer settles into my chest.

The breakthrough we've made tonight isn't lost on me, and for the first time since I arrived in this country, I let out a breath so relieving, I'm almost dizzy.

This is what I came here for. To earn my place in my sister's life. To play with my only nephew and become a person he can count on.

I can do so now.

My sister is extending an olive branch, and I don't hesitate to grab onto it like a lifeline.

"So it's not just Malcolm who enjoys my arid company, then?" I crack over the lump in my throat.

"I definitely enjoy it too. Being around you widens my vocabulary with words like *arid*, and I already feel so much smarter," she teases right back.

Smiling, I hold her gaze and nod. "Thank you." I set my fork aside and add, "That's the last time I'll say it, I promise."

She rolls her eyes, and I lean forward as an urge too severe to ignore presses on my vocal cords. "And if you'd like to discuss… her, I'm available," I offer hesitantly.

As she chews, she stares over my shoulder, but there's an emptiness there. It's obvious she's not looking at anything in particular, and I grow uneasy again.

How many more rises and falls remain on this roller coaster of a dinner?

"Even if there was anything to say, we're not there just yet," she says with a tight- lipped smile around a bite.

"Of course. But I've been known to nag a bit, so I'm confident I'll eventually wear you down," I say playfully.

"No casual observation gets by you, does it?" "It is a gift, just as my nagging is."

"I'll say. Seriously, you were starting to remind me of my high school boyfriend who would call me repeatedly every time I didn't answer. Just promise me one thing— you will not harass all my friends if I happen to miss one of your calls, okay?"

"I'm not a monster."

We continue talking and eating like this until both of our plates are empty, after which we meet Malcolm in the sitting room for the game.

They have to explain the rules to me since I've never played Sorry! Neither of them is surprised.

"Is it because you're old, or because you're British?" Malcolm asks, and it sounds like it's partly a genuine question. Either way, he still bursts into laughter, and it barely reaches the decibel of Rebecca's.

As I join in their good-natured laugh, I revel in the fact that they've already gotten to know me well enough to playfully tease me.

We may not be ready to dive into the pain of the past, but tonight still feels like the beginning of something big. Something wholesome and special and warm.

I could always feel the love from my mother and the respect of my father, but I haven't had a particularly *warm* relationship with either of my parents in quite some time. Being here with Rebecca and Malcolm makes me realize how damaging it's been.

But not anymore. Not if I can continue to make such strides with my newest family. And the only person I want to share this with is Ms. Hayes.

Her sweet smile pops into my mind like an electric shock, quick but powerful. As kind and caring as she is, I have no doubt she'd share in my excitement over the success of my first family dinner.

But I shouldn't.

I'll do anything to keep earning my place in my new family's lives, which is why it's a necessity to push all thoughts of the young woman out of my mind.

I cannot afford to jeopardize my career and the life I'm building in New York. I've hardly cracked the surface of this new relationship with Rebecca and Malcolm, and I'll be damned if I let a foolish attraction get in the way of it.

EIGHT

Oliver

To answer, or not to answer?

This is the question I ask myself as I stare at my mother's face on my phone screen.

She's ringing me for the first time since I announced I was moving. What could she possibly have to say after all this time?

Is something wrong? Is it her lymph nodes again? Perhaps there's an issue more dire than we previously expected.

The thought alone and the growing concern in the pit of my stomach is the reason I set my bowl of oatmeal onto the coffee table and swipe to answer.

"Oliver?" her voice fills my apartment. "Can you hear me, darling?" "Yes, Mother." I work my jaw back and forth. "Are you all right?"

"If you call worrying about my son all right, then yes," she quips. "Have you come to your senses yet?"

I don't dignify her question with a response, because if I do answer her, it won't be respectful in the slightest. No matter what she's done, she's still my mother, and I will honor that.

"When are you coming home?" she presses.

"Mother, how are you feeling?" I ask, purposely ignoring her question and the misplaced warning in her tone.

"I'm well, Oliver. But if I wasn't, would you come home then?" "Don't toy with the fragile thread we have bonding us."

Her frustrated breath comes out in a long, exasperated puff of air.

"I'm not returning to England," I assert. "Things have taken a lively turn with Rebecca and her son, and I want to stay here with them."

Tense silence commences, and I squirm on the couch, a mix of annoyance and impatience pricking my nerves.

When she still doesn't speak, I snap, "Are you ever going to ask me about them?"

There's yet another pause, and I stand to pace, the muscles in my back stiff and angry after this morning's workout.

I continue as if she gave me the go-ahead. "I finally met Malcolm. He's brilliant, and his curiosity is much like mine when I was his age. Rebecca's a good mum. She's done a lovely job of raising him on her own after her husband died a few years back. I, for one, am enjoying being here for them, and—"

"Stop," she snaps. "I know what you're doing, and it's not going to work. You'll never understand, Oliver, because you've never made any mistakes in your life."

I sit back down on the couch and stare at my oatmeal. The bland breakfast is decorated with various berries, but at its core, it's still brown mush with no flavor. I eat it to stay strong and healthy, and this internal conversation is better than the one I'm having with my mother.

"Do you recall the day you had surgery to remove your appendix?" This time, she catches me by surprise.

"Of course."

"You and I went for ice cream afterward," she says wistfully, her tone less stern than before. "I got whipped cream on my upper lip from my sundae, and you laughed so hard, your stitches almost popped right out."

"What does that have to do with our situation?"

"I'm just trying to remind you that I'm not the wretched goon you think I am. The situation with Rebecca is more complicated than you're imagining."

I swallow, but my throat is drier than summer in London. "I need to go, Mother," I say, my voice hoarse.

After we end the call, I take my oatmeal and dump it into the trash, then grab a banana and eat it while I pack the rest of my bag.

I have thirty minutes to spare for a shower before I need to arrive at the school for our departure.

And I will not allow my mother to derail this weekend.

I've worked diligently to organize our itinerary for the retreat, and I will enjoy it.

The board meeting also went well this week, so it'll be a bit of a celebration for the administrators—one they definitely deserve.

It's not easy to welcome a new member to the staff, logistically and otherwise.

Especially with the rumors going around about Nancy's very obvious and childish *thing* for me.

Fortunately, nothing of my incident with Ms. Hayes has surfaced. I assume she hasn't mentioned our discussion to any of her teacher friends, either, since no gossip of it has made its way to my office.

And Rita is certainly my eyes and ears at the school, relaying every large and small tidbit to Johanna and me. Just yesterday, she guffawed over toilet paper stuck to Karen's shoe, so if she hasn't mentioned anything related to Ms. Hayes with it being so significant, then the story isn't circulating.

Unless…

Could Rita know something? Perhaps she's simply sparing my feelings.

I grip the edge of my bathroom counter and lean forward with a curse as bitter as a bad apple on my lips.

There's no need for further dissection of the episode with the math teacher, anyhow.

It was an accident, and I shouldn't have opened my stupid mouth afterward.

I made it worse by addressing the situation, given I didn't do it for her benefit to start with.

But for mine.

I didn't trust myself, so my need to draw a firm line between us overshadowed my duty as her boss. I should've simply accepted her apology and walked away. Instead, I foolishly let my emotions get the best of me and further mucked up our professional relationship.

It hasn't helped that Ms. Hayes has been avoiding me.

I haven't caught even a glimpse of her eccentric floral and polka dot patterns or easy smile all week. The lounge has failed me too, no longer spitting her into my line of sight as it often did before the incident.

During our after-school meeting to discuss the retreat and chaperones for the homecoming dance next month, she never made eye contact—not once. When I concluded the meeting, she bolted out of there faster than if I were chasing her on a horse during a polo match.

I wish to God it didn't bother me as much as it does. That I didn't care what she thinks of me.

That I could simply focus on doing my job and being a strong and guiding presence in Rebecca's and Malcolm's lives.

Instead, as I yank my stuffed bag off the bed, all I can bloody think about is the quirky teacher who's gotten under my skin and how we're going to be off campus together for an entire weekend.

"Good workout this morning, buddy," Tommy says and offers his fist for me to bump as we stand by his vehicle.

I stare at his closed, expectant fist, then glance up at him. Dropping his hand, he shifts his stance. "How you feeling?"

"Perfect." I give him a tight-lipped smile and immediately feel guilty for being short with him.

It's not this man's fault that I'm in a sour mood.

Tommy did blast terrible country music the entire drive up to New Jersey, and he maneuvered the roads along the lake toward the campgrounds like a pissed-off maniac. It didn't seem he'd ever heard of a speed limit.

It's not even that he insists I call him by his first name instead of Mr. Hall because "We're gym bros now," as he put it. Aside from our shared interest in fitness, I suppose he also feels close to me after our heart-to-heart, as some might call it, when we first met.

Since then, no matter how hard I've tried to maintain the line of professionalism, he's put forth twice the effort to break through it. I can no more cement my boundaries than I can turn water into wine at this point.

But none of that has anything to do with why I'm so tense, although it hasn't helped.

To be honest, accepting Tommy's offer to work out alongside him this morning was rather brilliant. I found it more challenging than usual, and it was the kick in the arse I needed. It also reminded me of the workouts the boys and I would destroy during the days of university. I hadn't felt a sense of camaraderie in a while before the gym teacher convinced me to exercise together.

On top of that, it temporarily distracted me from my hormonal frustrations. I just wish Ms. Hayes wasn't the reason for those frustrations.

Why couldn't I be captivated by anyone else? There are plenty of fine women I come across in the gym who would be much less complicated, and we'd actually have something in common.

But of course, I drive myself fucking mad with the one woman I can't have.

I peek over at the object of my torture. Again, she hasn't awarded me even a single glance today.

To make matters worse for me, she's wearing tight jeans, and they hug her sinful figure like a glove. The thin fabric of her loose shirt is also dangerously close to falling off one shoulder and exposing more of her creamy skin.

Tearing my eyes away from seeing the end of that show, I reach out and stop Tommy from leaving. "I appreciate the assistance this morning. I was certain our last set of deadlifts would be the end of me," I say, forcing a smile through my peace offering.

"A real rush, huh?" He claps, his spirits obviously lifted. In fact, he's been in a rather pleasant mood ever since the first day of school—nothing like the grief he gave me over the dress code a week before that. What could be the reason? Maybe he could teach me his tricks. "Right when you think your lungs are going to collapse, you complete the final rep and can stand a little taller. I love it."

Normally, I'd respect the passion and intensity over describing fitness with similar enthusiasm as one might a rare wine or exotic creature, but I'm not in the mood.

"Exactly," I mumble as my attention drifts over to where Ms. Hayes laughs with two of the other educators.

"They look like they may need help with their bags," Tommy says as Ms. Bumble tries to drag her oversized suitcase out of the trunk.

The thing is twice her size, and the seams appear ready to burst. Did she pack enough for an entire month?

Tommy jogs ahead of me and reaches for Ms. Bumble's bag, but instead of walking away with it, he remains in place, staring down at her.

And she twirls her hair.

Are they…?

On second thought, I don't want to know. Not unless whatever their involvement is interferes with work.

Scratching the back of my head, I make my way over to the group, my steps far less eager than Tommy's.

Is Ms. Bumble why he's been particularly chuffed lately? If so, never mind on learning his tricks. Sleeping with a teacher is the exact opposite of the answer I'm searching for.

As I approach, I hear their conversation more clearly, although part of me wishes I hadn't.

While the other, more sly half of me is glad I do.

"You know all about terrible dates, though," Ms. Bumble says to Ms. Hayes, then places her hands on her hips and shares a knowing smirk with Tommy. "You're like, the queen of bad dates."

Ms. Hayes keeps her back to me as she says, "What gave me that title—the guy who wanted to dress me up in his sister's clothes, or the one who didn't believe in showers?"

"What reasoning would someone have..." The librarian glances up at me, but the others don't.

Ms. Hayes snaps her fingers and says, "Oh! There was also the horrific experience with the guy who made his own red wine. Remember him? The liquid was way too thick and looked more like blood, and I have to be honest—I think it might've been."

"I hope you didn't drink it," I blurt.

The petite math teacher jumps a whole meter to the left and almost twists her ankle, while her other two friends gasp. They move with their arms out, seemingly to ensure Ms. Hayes is steady on her two feet, but I beat them to it.

"Didn't mean to startle you." I pat her shoulders, and as soon as I confirm she's all right, I yank my hands away.

It's best not to touch the employee who's been haunting my thoughts since our first meeting.

"You did," she sputters, clutching her heaving chest. "If you keep sneaking up on me like this, I'm going to have to insist you wear a bell around your neck."

"Like a cat?" I fight a twitch in my cheek, and behind me, Tommy's offer to assist the others with their bags is muffled.

"Yes, and before you get offended, you should know… I recently learned that cats are very similar to humans." She holds up a dainty finger. "Actually, ninety percent of the genes in a cat are similar to ours."

"Is that so?" I furrow my brows.

What an odd turn this encounter has taken. It's possibly stranger than the bloke with the homemade wine.

She squirms in place, then peers over my shoulder as the chatter grows louder. I turn to find the rest of our group have arrived, and when I turn to say something else to Ms. Hayes, she's no longer next to me.

Instead, she's joined her friends.

Unfortunately, Nancy is quick to replace her. "Beautiful day," she breathes and arches her back in a suggestive stretch, and it makes me wince. "Every time I see a dock like that, I imagine a flashing green light at the end of it."

I hum.

"Like in *The Great Gatsby*." "Of course."

"It's so romantic, isn't it?" she gushes.

While I appreciate a cheeky reference from a classic, I don't like the way Nancy bats her eyelashes at me.

I force a smile as I admire the wooden dock. It expands far into the tranquil lake, and I do wish I could openly discuss the whimsy of such a scene with someone who'd appreciate the literary symbolism of it.

But alas, I'd much rather dive into the frigid water than fake niceties with this flirtatious teacher.

"Since we're all here, I'd better make the announcements." I nod and step around her as if she were poison ivy, careful not to accidentally touch her.

I find the vice principal, and together, we gather the others for a quick welcome and to pass out cabin assignments.

Once we're finished, I involuntarily steal an eyeful of Ms. Hayes as she bends over for her bag, and the back of her shirt lifts.

I tear my gaze away and bite my knuckles, willing myself to think of anything but the sliver of skin that peeked out, the perfect curve of her backside…

Christ.

"You okay, boss?" Tommy slaps my back, and immediately, something happens to my cheeks.

They're burning.

Dear God, I'm… blushing.

My face wasn't even this hot after a week at summer camp as a painfully shy and awkward eight-year-old.

"Fine. Thanks, mate." I tilt my head toward the path that will lead him, Oscar, and me to our quarters for the next two days.

I'll be heading to my own individual cabin, and I'm so close to the promise of much-needed solace I can barely stand it.

While we walk, they reminisce of their time in Boy Scouts, and I quietly walk behind them. It's not that I don't want to join the conversation, not that I could—I was never in the Scouts.

Normally, I'd take a moment to cherish the fresh air and listen to the birds chirping. But right now, their melodious singing only grates on my nerves.

Because I'm irritated with my behavior, and I was almost caught admiring a teacher's body like some creepy peeping Tom.

As soon as this weekend is over, I'm going to get out after hours, and not just to Deidra's. I love the pub, but the only other patrons are gentlemen in worn leather jackets and the occasional mates from the local university. It's not a place to meet ladies, which is what I desperately need before I lose my mind altogether.

It's imperative that I meet someone other than the people I work with. Someone who doesn't have a soothing voice or petite frame.

A woman my age.

In other words, anyone other than the math teacher.

"Tommy and I will definitely be making out in the woods at some point this weekend," Katie declares as she hops onto the bottom bunk bed.

Bobbie follows behind me into the cabin, and we both look knowingly at each other. "I already suspected as much," she says with a snort.

Standing to one corner, I take in the sparsely decorated space. The cream walls, plaid comforters, and lone lamp between the bunk beds and single twin.

It reminds me of summers spent with my grandpa at his lake house as a kid. He let me hang up my drawings in my room, and I plastered every inch with as much pink as I could manage.

He did draw the line at glitter, though. I threw a minor tantrum, but looking back now, I know it was the right call.

The buyers after he passed away would never have been able to get that shiny shit out of the house.

This cabin is nothing like the vibrant house of my memories, but I feel a hint of peace to be doing stuff like this again.

It's been far too long since I've been camping or to a lake, and I get both this weekend.

"So, since Katie's obviously claimed that one, do you mind if I take this single one?" Bobbie already moves toward it. "I'm afraid of heights. I mean, I'm getting dizzy just looking up there."

I smile sympathetically. "Of course."

I set my bag down by the wooden ladder, unzip it, and dig for the charger to my Apple watch but come up empty. "Shoot," I mutter under my breath.

I must have forgotten it at home. I'm generally an early riser, but I was extra disoriented this morning. It was probably from the late night of watching *The Lost Symbol*.

In any case, I must've overlooked it in my frenzy. day.

I check my watch and find I have enough battery left to get me through most of the Katie sits up and asks, "When is the first event?"

I pull out the itinerary we were each given when we arrived and run my finger up to the first line. "There's a welcome snack bar in twenty minutes, followed by a keynote speaker."

"Who's the speaker?" Bobbie asks at the same time Katie asks, "What snacks do they have?"

"No details on the snacks, but the speaker is some education guru from NYU."

"We had to come all the way up here to get lessons from an NYU professor?"

Bobbie lifts an eyebrow. "We could've just taken a field trip for one day to the campus instead of making all this fuss."

"I like it." Katie kicks her feet, sweeping the heels of each along the scuffed floor like she's on a swing. "This place makes me feel calm already, and we haven't even gotten to the yoga session yet."

"That's what I'm most excited about." I smile and reach into my bag for deodorant. "Yes, well, neither of you have to deal with incessant texts from a frantic husband."

Bobbie rolls her eyes and taps at her phone screen, then turns it toward us. "Seriously, I've been gone for a few hours, and already, he's sent me twenty-two texts."

"Is something wrong?" I ask, thoroughly concerned. "Is your son okay?"

"Of course." She scoffs and clicks her phone off. "One of the messages asks me where I hide the pancake syrup. *Hide* is the word he used, like I intentionally keep it a mystery just to annoy him. I don't have that kind of time!"

"Maybe I'm glad I don't have a husband." Katie snickers and leans over to high- five me.

"What about Tommy? Aren't you two a thing?" Bobbie asks in the same teasing tone teenagers use when prying into the romantic entanglements of their friends. I wouldn't be surprised if my affable friend breaks into song about Tommy and Katie sitting in a tree.

"Ha!" Katie shakes her head. "His divorce has been finalized for like, five minutes.

Tommy is not thinking about jumping right back into something serious, which works out well for me since I'm not, either."

Just another way she and Bree are so alike.

"That's what you think, but before you know it, you're knocking boots, and he's knocking you up. One year later, you're living in a studio apartment with a crying baby that gives you minus one minute of peace, and you're never having sex again." Bobbie makes her way to the door while Katie and I are stunned into silence. She painted quite the picture, didn't she? Glancing over her shoulder, Bobbie says, "Oh, it didn't happen to me like that, but it did to a friend of mine who enjoyed one-night stands like they were a roller-coaster ride. Fun for the moment, but the rush never lasts."

"I'm not sure that helps," Katie says sarcastically as we make our way to the main hall.

The path along the lake leads us past a few trees, which hover over a gazebo and a couple benches set up in front of it. The leaves and grass are in the middle of changing colors with the loving touch of the upcoming fall, and the air is fresh and free of the city's waste.

This is the kind of clean air that's as great for my soul as it is my sinuses. It makes me wonder what the hell I'm breathing every day in Manhattan, but now's not the time to sink into that rabbit hole of negativity.

Once we reach the main hall, we join many other educators, along with the ones from our school, and exchange pleasantries. The large space is brimming with sharp, innovative minds and determination, and I'm immediately swept away in it.

I mean, is there a better place to gain encouragement and reinvigorate ourselves than this?

The open room is illuminated from the bright sun beaming through the windows lining one wall. A brick fireplace stands next to it, and round tables are set up side by side across one half of the room. The other half consists of a stage and two long tables in front of it, each topped with a colorful assortment of meats, cheeses, and fruits like charcuterie for giants.

The setup is pretty extravagant and nothing I would expect, given the bleak colors and scarcity of the cabin.

Not that I'm complaining.

In fact, checking out the snacks makes me realize how starved I am. Avoiding meat for a year has made it difficult to reach the same level of satisfaction when it comes to feeling full. As I stare at the slices of salami, I can't even remember the reason I gave up the food group in the first place.

I lick my lips and am almost putting my tongue back into my mouth when I look up to find Principal Westbrook staring right at me.

Instantly, goose bumps line my forearms, and my cheeks heat like I've embarrassed myself yet again.

But I didn't even say anything this time!

The man has the worst timing and tends to appear out of thin air only when I blurt something super mortifying, but even when I say nothing at all, I still feel like I'm standing naked in front of a room full of people.

How does he do that?

I duck behind Katie and Bobbie to escape his weird mind games.

"Is it appropriate to be the first in line to fix a plate, or do we have to wait for a direct go-ahead from someone in charge?" Katie asks.

Bobbie searches the room for what I assume is an answer. "I think it's better manners to wait."

The *riveting* debate is interrupted by someone on stage and the announcement they make through a headset.

We're instructed to grab a plate and take our seats, which we don't hesitate to do, but when my two friends start to walk toward Tommy and the principal's table, I steer them away at the last minute.

"What're you doing?" Katie hisses. "I had every intention of playing footsie under the table with Tommy during the speech. You're ruining my dirty hopes and dreams."

"Just sit," I order in the sternest voice I've ever used on her. Usually, I reserve such a tone for my students when they misbehave.

As much as I love them and hate to get onto them, it's a necessary evil for maintaining order.

And now, it's absolutely necessary so I can stay far away from Principal Piercing

Gaze.

Except when I sit, I still feel his eyes on my every move.

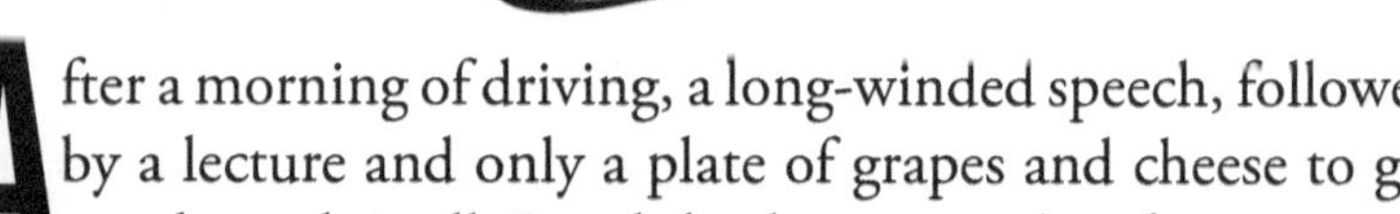

After a morning of driving, a long-winded speech, followed by a lecture and only a plate of grapes and cheese to get me through it all, I rush back to our cabin for a granola bar before my favorite event on the schedule—yoga.

I really need to move and stretch my body, but I'm also excited about yoga by the lake. The beautiful scenery will take me to a whole new level of zen, and the idea alone sends a boost of endorphins to party in my body.

As I scarf down my snack, I take quick steps toward the spot by the lake where we were told to meet. I only stop along the way to take a few pictures with my phone, and I share a couple of the good ones to my Instagram Stories. Breathing in a lungful of air, I walk until I find the rest of our faculty and yoga mats spread on the ground in neat rows.

"Ms. Hayes, I presume?" the instructor asks me, and all heads turn in my direction. "Present," I joke—I'm a teacher, after all.

But it doesn't quite land, as indicated by the number of frowns I receive from the others. I'm going to blame it on the fact that it's overused, and not because I don't have a single comedic gene in my DNA.

"You were the last one we were expecting, so let's get started," the instructor says, clapping her hands and nodding to the rest.

Or, that's why.

Everyone was waiting on me.

"My name is Azalea, like the flower," she starts, and I check my watch as I inch toward Katie and Bobbie.

"I'm not even late," I whisper to them.

Katie gives me a shrug as if to say, "What do you do?" and Bobbie groans when the instructor asks us to find a partner.

"This is a team building activity, so we will do a few exercises together to strengthen the bonds between you. To learn to trust one another. To lean on one another," Azalea says in a soothing tone as she circles us, until she stops next to the principal and vice principal.

"Administrators, you spend a lot of time together as it is." She smiles and points from them to the rest of us. "Get out of your comfort zones and choose a teacher as a partner."

I barely comprehend her as I glance between my friends, instantly panicking that I'm going to get stuck with Karen. She'll probably complain about everything from my hair to the color of the lake water.

I would agree with her if the water were murky like some lakes, but this is actually pretty clear.

In my periphery, I see Nancy's shoulders slump, and I'm going to assume it's because she already snagged Tommy as a partner and has lost her chance of putting her hands on the principal.

Katie grabs Bobbie's arm and grimaces toward me—the traitor. "I'm sorry, but I've been to yoga with you. You're far too advanced, and I don't need that level of negativity in my life right now."

I purse my lips and turn toward Bobbie, who raises her hands. "What she said.

Seriously, if I was as limber as you, my husband would never keep his hands off me, and I'd have twenty-five kids by now."

I roll my eyes and place my hands on my hips as I search for an available partner, feeling like I did as a kid when I was always picked last for group projects or games in PE.

Even Karen is taken since she's paired up with the instructor—she's every bit the teacher's pet, so I'm not surprised.

But I quickly wish she could be my partner when my gaze lands on the only person left.

To my absolute horror, it's Principal Westbrook. And he's walking right toward me.

"Let's get started with some seated meditation." Azalea lowers herself onto the mat, crosses her feet at the ankles, and places both hands on her knees, her back against Karen's. "Sit back to back with your partner like this."

"After you." My partner holds his arm out.

I blink at it while I try to figure out if it's too late to

fake food poisoning or claim that an alien life force has commandeered my brain.

"Ms. Hayes?" He searches my gaze as his unreadable expression remains intact. I prefer his visible annoyance over this mystery.

Sighing, I move toward the mat and sit, resigning to whatever torture awaits. "We are about to get up close and personal, so you can call me Erin," I mumble.

When the wall of a man sits behind me, he rests his brawny back to mine, and I have to suppress a sharp inhale, especially when he mutters over his shoulder, "In that case, call me Oliver."

I squeeze my eyes closed and try to focus on my breathing and on Azalea's instruction.

But when she calls out, "Take a moment to connect with your partner," I involuntarily stiffen.

His back is so muscular, with grooves and planes far too extraordinary for a high school principal, although I can understand why he pursued this path.

He's great with kids.

At the assembly on the first day of school, he commanded the entire auditorium from beginning to end. In the past, we've always had to escort at least a handful of students out for being too loud and disruptive.

Every time I see him walking down the hall, many students greet him, and some even high-five him.

It's how I know that Principal—erm, *Oliver*—was perfectly fine when he met his nephew. I'm sure the man was nervous, and it's understandable since it was the very first time. But I have no doubt the two of them hit it off.

Not that I've asked him or said anything else to the puzzling bane of my professional existence.

"Match your breath—inhale for inhale, and exhale for exhale—with your partner."

Azalea's voice cuts through my thoughts.

But Oliver is still distracting.

It takes a moment to sync our breathing, and when we finally get it, we're instructed to do the opposite. An inhale for an exhale, instead.

When Oliver's back curves into my arched posture, it's hard not to get dizzy from the waves of heat rolling off him.

I swear electricity passes from him, cuts through the fabrics separating our skin, and jolts me into a chaotic state of hypersensitivity.

Breathing exercises usually calm me and put me in the right headspace. But by the time we stand, I'm experiencing the exact opposite. I've never felt more tense and overwhelmed.

I'm so far away from my center that my brain might as well be in Area 51—I'm totally lost in the unknown here.

"Please face your partner on the mat and stand a couple feet apart." Azalea's voice carries over us as she walks us through the next pose, which will serve to open our shoulders.

Oh, God, he's about to touch me. With his hands.

The fingers that turn me on without coming anywhere near me are about to rest on my bare shoulders. Why did I wear a freaking tank top?

I bend at the waist and stretch forward to get into position, accepting my fate as my thoughts run wild.

My body is in overdrive the closer I get to where I think he'll be.

Right when I think I've reached him, the top of my head bumps his, and I jump upright.

"Sorry!" I say at the same time he says, "My apologies."

"It's okay, you two," Azalea calls out to us. "That's the reason partner yoga is so important. It teaches us to work together and improves our joint flow."

Gulping, I adjust my top, pull my loosened ponytail into place, the ends tickling the back of my neck, and give myself a pep talk.

I can do this.

Yoga takes up literally ninety percent of my time outside of my job. No hot boss of mine will distract me from the benefits of this session.

We successfully get into position, but it's a short-lived victory. Because my breathing hitches the second Oliver slides his palms up my arms until he rests his hands on both my shoulder blades.

They're rough, like the kinds of hands I'd expect from a guy who lifts a lot of weights.

He also has long, thick fingers, and they're probably very… skilled.

I keep my head down as my eyelids flutter, and a breeze nips at my flushed skin. I move my hands to mirror his position until they rest on his shoulders, the stretch in my lower back and upper body a distant memory.

Instead, I get lost in the hard contours of his rear delts.

I've never found a man's shoulders to be particularly sexy, but damn—the mountains my hands roam over are the hunky stuff of legends.

I chew the inside of my cheek to keep a moan from escaping, because it would not only be highly unprofessional, but also extremely embarrassing.

And haven't I done enough of that already?

I let out a long exhale as we're told to stand upright again and prepare for the next pose.

The rest of the session goes much like the beginning, where I actively avoid

meeting Oliver's gaze as much as possible. In between, I try not to like his touch too much.

But I do. I really do.

How can I not feel heat trickling down my spine when we get into the extended side-angle pose? My ass is to his front, and our hands grab each other in the middle, for crying out loud!

Azalea said we didn't have to do the hand-holding challenge, but we could try if we felt adventurous.

Evidently, Oliver and I were.

And I couldn't decline when he asked, "Fancy a go at it?"

Of course, I pictured him referring to something else entirely—something a lot more sinful—but I like a good challenge, anyway.

How have I gone all my life practicing yoga without realizing how sexual it really is?

Then again, I've never done partner yoga with someone like Oliver.

I'd expect someone of his size and muscle mass to be less flexible, but he's pretty limber.

Which only serves to bring my ovaries closer to combusting.

By the time we're finished with *Savasana*—the final step in every yoga sequence I've experienced—my mind is filled with several conflicting thoughts.

Aside from the very shameful feels he gave me, he actually helped me get a deep stretch in my inner thigh that I've never reached before.

As I stand and wiggle my legs out, I feel looser than ever. *Damn him.*

I slip my flip-flops back on and turn to face him, noting crimson signs of exertion across his chiseled cheeks. Coupled with the gray T-shirt and navy sweatpants he's sporting, my boss looks far more accessible than usual.

More at ease.

Sexier.

"*Namaste*, Oliver." I nod. "Thank you for, um, being my partner."

"I hope I was a decent one." The firm lines around his mouth and eyes are more relaxed than when we started. "My back is so sore from a workout this morning, and I didn't think I'd make it through some of those poses."

I scoff—because what else can I do? If he was that flexible with a tight back, I'm impressed as hell. "I didn't notice at all."

He finishes putting his shoes on and stands tall, towering over me.

"I have some essential oils with me. They might help with the soreness." I hook my thumb over my shoulder to point in the direction of my cabin. "I also have an apple cider vinegar drink recipe that works every time, but unfortunately, it is pretty rough on the taste buds."

Oliver smirks. "I don't believe essential oils can reach into my muscles to break apart the lactic acid, so I think I'll stick to my routine of bananas, hydration, and stretching."

I purse my lips. "Those work too," I mumble, and I've never felt so defeated after yoga.

"I just don't buy into the whole thing."

"How silly of me," I deadpan, my heart sinking as I back

away from him in hopes the small crowd remaining is enough to make me disappear.

Maybe I'll just hide in the woods until we leave tomorrow.

"I didn't mean it like that." He lunges forward, his arm outstretched for me to stop.

But I don't. Instead, I skip to follow Katie and Bobbie back to our cabin for a change of clothes.

As we make our way down the path, I berate myself for thinking he and I could be anything more than colleagues.

The girls were right—I like him.

I don't just want him to respect me as a teacher, but I want him to *like* me in the searing way a man of his caliber likes a woman. I imagine it would be passionate and intense. Something akin to a spiritual experience.

Which is ridiculous and dangerous.

I've been naive numerous times in the past, but this tops any stupid thing I've ever talked myself into believing.

The old me would probably be more optimistic and make excuses for his hurtful behavior to work in my favor, but it's time I accept the truth.

Romance is not waiting for me around the rough-and-broody corner of Oliver Westbrook.

TEN

Oliver

It's been over seventeen hours since yoga.

We've completed a canoe race, which was meant to be friendly competition but grew out of hand when one of the other schools threw a fit over the winner.

There's been another lecture, I've met with one of the principals from another school, and the sun has set and risen since I had my hands on Erin Hayes.

This weekend has given me a wealth of knowledge and networking opportunities. It was supposed to be relaxing as well. But I'm more tightly wound than when I arrived.

All because of yoga.

Nowhere on the brochure or itinerary did it say partner yoga. It also didn't mention beforehand how sensual it is.

I have half a mind to sue the damn retreat organizers.

"Fantastic weekend, boss," Oscar says and shakes my free hand as I exit my cabin. "Were you on the rowing team at university or something? Because the way you crushed us at the canoe race leads me to believe you have experience."

"You're just jealous because of those shrimpy golf balls you call biceps," Tommy teases as he joins us.

"That's not what your mum called them last night." Oscar shoves him to the side, his similar accent to mine a comfort, even if he is a little rough around the edges.

The bloody mug stealer.

"Are jokes about one another's mothers still a trend?" I lift a brow, and the two stop messing around like teenagers attending an actual summer camp.

Perhaps I should take this into account for future trips—camping at a remote location could cause teachers to lower their levels of maturity.

While I might not actually go through with that, I will definitely be striking off yoga.

This juvenile interaction is also why I didn't assign myself a roommate for the night. I didn't want the other instructors to get too comfortable with me and start making asinine jokes about my mother. We've certainly bonded, but I still need to be cautious of the glue that holds this teaching ecosystem together—the boundaries.

Besides, I did not want to subject myself to what I'm positive was a sleepless night between Tommy's snores and Oscar's commentary on every single plant outside.

I might have been lonely, as I've noticed over the last year of living by myself, but I'm confident I made the right decision in staying alone this weekend.

In the parking lot, I drop my bag by Tommy's car and turn in place until I find Erin walking up with the others.

The way she said my first name during yoga yesterday made my knees fucking buckle.

She's back to calling me Principal Westbrook now, and I hate it. But not more than I hate the fact that she's barely spoken to me at all since then.

She's avoiding me again, and although I should be cheering—and back to referring to her as Ms. Hayes—I can't stand it.

What the bloody hell is the matter with me?

One second I'm complaining about the lust-filled way she gawks at me, and the next, I love it.

One minute I'm enjoying the feel of her backside against me, and the next, I'm hating myself for liking it.

The woman is driving me mad.

The sooner we get out of here, the better.

I secure my shoulder bag across my body and wait to put it in last, so it's on top.

Can't have my laptop smashed to bits so soon after the start of the school year.

We put the rest of our bags into the boot of the car, and the parking lot slowly fills with other attendees packing up theirs. When I turn, Erin is no longer standing with the others, and she seems to be the only one missing.

"Where is Ms. Hayes?" I ask the group.

Ms. Bumble points in the direction of the cabin they shared. "She forgot her watch and ran back to get it."

I lean my hip against the car and check my own watch. We're supposed to be pulling out right about now, and I wouldn't mind being a couple minutes behind schedule had I not promised Malcolm I'd take him to the park this afternoon to kick the ball around.

Turns out, the boy loves futbol, much to my relief and joy.

After a few more minutes, there's still no sign of her. Is tardiness a quality of hers?

She was late to yoga yesterday as well. If this is a common occurrence for her, she doesn't seem to let it affect her work. I've never received a complaint of that nature, anyway, and it's something Ms. Hubanks undoubtedly would've brought to my attention.

The others have started a game of throwing rocks across the lake. They're getting restless.

I make my way over to them and clap to call for their attention. "Why don't I check on Ms. Hayes while you all get going?" I offer.

On my way back to the parking lot, I tell the vice principal to go ahead as well since I know she usually spends Sundays with her family, and I wouldn't want her to miss any more of it than she has to.

I throw a finger up for Tommy to wait a moment, then take long and measured strides toward Erin's cabin.

But when I reach it and look inside, she's not there. If I weren't so agitated, I'd appreciate the way they left the space so impeccable with each bed made and tidy.

Shutting the flimsy door behind me, I glance to my left and right, but I still don't see her. She couldn't have gone far, right?

From the poorly constructed and squeaky porch, I spot more people with bags over their shoulders and peek over their heads toward the main hall. Could Erin be in there?

If she forgot her watch, maybe she thought she left it there this morning during our "Bye Bye Breakfast." I change course and walk up the steps to the large building, where I pull the double doors open and peer inside.

One gentleman drops a trash bag and waves. "Can I help you?"

"I'm looking for a young woman about *yay* tall." I hold my hand up to my sternum to indicate Erin's height and hope for a satisfactory response.

To my dismay, he shakes his head and continues cleaning up. "Sorry. Haven't seen her here."

"Thank you." I close the doors and keep searching the grounds. My grip grows tighter on my bag the longer I come up empty.

She's not by the gazebo or on the dock. Perhaps she went back to the parking lot— it's the only explanation.

This is getting ridiculous.

With the birds playing overhead and the leaves rustling in the soft midmorning breeze, I head back toward our cars. As I pass the main hall once again, Erin pops out from behind one of the trees.

"There you are!" she says.

"Dear God," I mumble and jolt backward.

"See? It's not nice sneaking up on someone. I am sorry to scare you, but it was just to make a point." She sways and bites her goddamn lip.

And my blood pressure rises.

"I've been looking for you everywhere." I place both hands on my hips and take a deep, calming breath. "Where on earth were you?"

She holds her wrist up and presents a square smartwatch with a gold wristband. "I couldn't remember where I left this and had to look in several places before I finally found it on the bench in the gazebo."

On a sigh, I ask, "Why did you take it off in the first place? Isn't the point of those things to wear them at all times, even including the shower?"

"I forgot to bring my charger for it, so there was no point in wearing it." She shrugs. "It's dead."

"How—never mind. Let's go." I brush past her and say over my shoulder, "Everyone's waiting on you."

I hear steps along the gravel behind me as we reach the edge of the parking lot, and I let out an exhale.

Only to have it get caught in my stomach. Because I don't see our rides anywhere.

"Didn't they park…" I rub my chin and spin in place, but none of the remaining cars appear familiar.

"What're you stopping for?" Erin asks and comes to a halt next to me. "Because either our cars turned invisible, or they left without us," I bite out.

"There's no way. I'll call Katie." She whips out her phone as another car leaves its spot.

The taps on her screen are quick and purposeful before she brings it up to her ear. I wait expectantly as she mumbles that there's no answer and tries Bobbie.

Then Tommy. Then Katie again.

When she tries Tommy a second time, he finally answers, and she puts him on speaker. "Tommy," she starts. "Where are you?"

"On the interstate back to the city," he answers slowly like it should be obvious. "Have you guys left yet?"

"No," Erin draws out. "Where are Katie and Bobbie? Or Karen?" There's a pause before he says, "Aren't you with them?"

"No, we're not," I cut in. "Tommy, I thought I asked you to wait a moment. You took off without us?"

There's another pause, then, "I thought you were both going in Katie's car. She said she'd wait for you."

"Oh my God," Erin mutters. "I need to call her. Bye." She doesn't look up as she rings Katie again.

The parking lot is empty now, and I'm not certain anyone else is left here. Not that they'd do us any good. Educators from all over the area—some from farther north—were here all weekend, and I don't think they'd be happy to go three hours out of their way to take us home.

Bloody hell.

"Katie!" Erin says into the phone. "Where are you?"

"What do you mean? We're driving back to the city." She sighs and cuts us off. "I'm sorry we're making you ride back with the guys, although you and the principal are cozier than ever now. What's a few more hours snuggled up to him in the back seat, right?"

"Nope. Not *right*. That's not…" Erin's jaw drops.

I'm momentarily speechless myself, and I almost forget our predicament.

What in God's name did she tell her friend about us—another teacher, no less? Are there rumors about Erin and me? Rita most certainly has been holding out on me.

"Anyway, Bobbie had to leave right away. She got a call from her husband with an actual emergency because their son has a fever and is throwing up, so she needs to get back." She blows out a breath. "I hope he's okay."

"I hope so too, but Katie, um… you kind of left me at the camp." Erin's blushing cheeks slowly pale as panic visibly sets in.

"Aren't you with Tommy?" Katie asks. "He left!" she screeches.

"No way. His car was definitely there before we took off." There's mumbling on their end, and all I catch is Bobbie swearing a blue car like Tommy's was still sitting in the parking lot when they left.

But she also admits she could be mistaken, given the distress her husband's phone call put her in.

I miss the rest of what they're saying as I try to think of another plan.

Erin clicks off the call and tries Tommy again. "You have to turn around and come get us," she asserts before he even finishes his greeting.

"What?"

"Tommy, you left us at the campgrounds!" she hisses, and the veins in her neck are currently thick and threatening.

"Are you serious?" Tommy murmurs in the background, then says, "We'll turn around at the next exit. We're quite a ways, so it might be a minute."

"You couldn't have gotten that far."

"Maybe Karen hasn't, but she doesn't drive more than fifteen over the speed limit like I do…"

"Tommy!" She scowls, and it's probably a good thing he can't see her.

Even I'm seconds away from cowering.

This is yet another curious side of the normally bubbly woman. "You're not a state trooper, so I don't have to explain myself."

"Just hurry," she insists, then clicks off and snaps her fingers. "I'll call Karen." But she doesn't answer, either.

"Her phone is probably on the *Do Not Disturb* setting

since she's driving. The woman never breaks a rule," Erin sings with sarcasm. "What if we call an Uber?"

"They'll take the same amount of time, but they'd likely be longer, especially with us being in the middle of nowhere."

"You don't know that." She crosses her arms over her chest. "They could have their own secret roads to take to get here faster."

"Are you listening to yourself?" I pinch the bridge of my nose.

"I don't hear any decent ideas coming out of you," Erin throws back.

"Here's one—there are no secret shortcuts that Uber drivers keep for themselves." My jaw tightens as the reality of our situation sinks in, and my blood further boils. "We'll wait for Tommy, even though he won't be here for at least another hour, and that's *if* he's not caught in traffic or gets a flat tire."

She gasps. "Don't jinx him. You better knock on wood or—"

"Bloody Christ." I run both hands through my hair. "You're right. I should go knock on a tree trunk and ask a woodland fairy to erase this whole disaster. Better yet— why don't I check my star charts for a way back home?"

"Oh, that's right. You think I'm insane," she shoots back, her sarcasm even heavier than before.

"Not insane, but what math teacher believes in hocus pocus remedies and answers in the sky?" My nostrils flare as I step toward her and try not to stare at her heaving chest, although it's achingly difficult.

Now is not the fucking time.

"Would you like to know what I believe?" I ask.

She narrows her gaze, and instead of letting her answer, my emotions get the best of me.

"I think you chose math because it actually makes sense, and you're desperate for an inkling of truth in your life."

"So?" Erin spreads her arms and takes a challenging step in my direction, her chin jutted high. "Of course I want some logic in my life, but it doesn't mean I'm not open to the unexplainable. Maybe you should stop and ask yourself why you ever became an English teacher, because it seems to me that you crave subjectivity and creativity yourself."

"English requires evidence to support an interpretation," I argue. "There's a difference between making a case of symbolism in *Wuthering Heights*, for instance, as opposed to debating my mood based on the angle of Earth's axis."

I wipe my mouth from the intense enunciation, unable to discern if it's from my passion or drool. The woman has a way of reaching into my head and jostling my brain.

"You think you're just so fancy and intelligent." She waves her arms around. "Look at me—roses are red, violets are blue, I'm Oliver Westbrook, and I have nothing to *do* but torture teachers with exasperating *poo*," she mocks, then straightens into impeccable posture. "There. A poem for you to analyze to death while we wait for our ride."

Did she actually just say *poo*?

And I'm supposed to take her seriously…

"I think I need another look. Might I find the fantastically riveting piece in the *Times*? Or is it more likely to be scratched into a bathroom stall at Legoland?" "You are so—" She cuts herself off and stops a couple inches from me, her attention on my mouth.

"Don't leave me on the edge of my seat," I deadpan.

She's clearly unnerved, and I'm aware I should be the one to diffuse the tension.

However, I can't help myself.

I'm stuck at a camp with the one person who's as perplexing as she is enchanting.

She makes me dizzy—in the best, yet most confusing, way.

Erin is also extremely close, and the gravity pulling me toward her cannot be ignored.

She shakes her head and laughs, but it holds no gram of humor as she composes herself. "That's it. You take the cabin over there, and I'll take this one," she announces and points to opposite sides of the camp.

I place my hands on my hips and glare, but it doesn't stop her in the slightest. Then again, what did I expect? I've given her yet another reason to dislike me. Many reasons, actually, and to be honest, I'm not my own biggest fan at the moment, either.

Especially when I catch the vulnerability in her eyes and the slump of her shoulders before she spins on her heel.

I've wounded her.

She marches up to her side of the camp, her strides heavy like she's angry at the dirt, and calls over her shoulder, "This way, you and I don't need to speak at all, and there's no need to think I'm *flirting* with you because of my so-called *crush*."

I grind my teeth, and red spots fill my vision.

"We can hang out on our own until Tommy shows up to rescue us."

She says *rescue* as if she's in danger. As if being stuck out here with me for another second is so horrible.

And I can't bloody take it anymore.

I take off after her, sweeping my feet through small piles of leaves and throwing them backward as my heart rate spikes.

Overhead, the sky darkens and brings with it thick clouds. If I was ever going to make the case for symbolism, this would be the perfect example to show how my head and temper are mirrored in those rain clouds.

But now is not the time.

"Where do you think you're going?" Erin turns around but doesn't stop walking.

She merely continues backward with wobbly steps. They're dangerously close to making her fall.

With labored breaths, I lunge after her and call out, "You've been avoiding me all weekend."

This stops her in her tracks, but she's turned her back toward me again. "You've barely made eye contact. In fact, you went so far as to fake a sneeze

yesterday in order to escape a conversation with me." My volume rises with each word, and my grimace deepens too as I reach her. "Why?" I press, stepping in front of her and forcing her to meet my eye.

"I thought you liked it better when I didn't talk to you. I'm just trying to give you what you want," she retorts and folds both arms across her chest again.

While I try not to stare.

She's gotten color in her cheeks with all the nonstop sun over the last day. She's radiant and beautiful, and it tears at my fucking heart that she thinks talking with her isn't the best part of my day.

Even though I don't know much about her.

I just know the way she makes me feel is special. But it shouldn't be.

I shouldn't crave to be in her presence, but she has a magnificent way of getting inside my head and making me feel things I never have before.

Erin starts to move past me, but I hold on to her forearm. "That's not what I said, nor did I intend to make you think I don't enjoy your company. The reality is… I want you to think of me as…"

She lifts her brows.

"To think of me as more than a cat," I blurt, and alarms go off in my head, my ears ringing.

The firm edges of her frown soften, as do her eyes. "A cat?"

"Right." I drop both arms to my sides, breaking our connection as sweat skips down the back of my neck and over the ridges of my tight shoulder blades. "I'd like you to view me as your boss. As someone you can come to at work. That's all."

She studies me, and I fear she sees right through me, especially when her eyes crash with mine.

I'm on display, but instead of running to hide like I should, I continue standing here and staring right back.

After a pause, she loosens the tension in her arms and asks, "Is that really what you want—for me to think of you as *only* my boss?"

My nostrils flare, and the desire to tell her the truth threatens to escape. The need to tell her I'd like the opposite is more powerful than a shot of Balkan 176.

But even without an outright confession, it's obvious Erin knows. She wouldn't have asked me to confirm it if she didn't.

Nonetheless, it would be irresponsible to answer her honestly. "Yes," I rasp, clinging to the pretense for dear life.

Her eyelids flutter closed for a slow blink, and my gaze

lingers on her wispy lashes fanning out above her charming pink cheeks.

A vibrating text interrupts us, and as she reads it, there's no indication in her expression of what it might say. "You truly enjoy my company?" She sneaks a glance up at me, but I'm still confused. Is that Tommy?

With a tic in my jaw, I nod.

Her frown isn't what I expect for the answer I give her, nor am I prepared for what she says next. "Good, because you're going to get a lot of it since it'll be a while before anyone gets here."

ELEVEN

Erin

I knew something was up with the universe.

And the dirty bitch is probably patting herself on her bony shoulder for this stunt.

There's nothing like getting stuck at a camp with my very hot British boss to make me rethink my beliefs in the power of the cosmos—aka, my very existence.

The only other person we noticed left a few minutes ago to get home in time for his daughter's birthday lunch, and I was so close to begging him to take me with him.

That's right—I was ready to hitchhike just so I wouldn't have to spend any time alone with Principal Broody Brit in this gorgeous place.

Especially after he said he does, in fact, enjoy my company.

It was the revelation of the century, and I wanted to leap

into his arms once he said it. Those bulky, capable arms that held me during yoga yesterday.

What is wrong with me?

The only explanation is that I've gone out with too many jerks lately, so now I've fallen victim to them and pine after the worst of the worst.

A bird caws above as if it disagrees with me, and the truth is, Oliver isn't actually the worst of the parade of jerks in my past.

Sure, he's rude and judgmental. Stringent, too.

But he also has a big heart, and it's not cold and black like I originally thought at our first encounter. On the contrary, he's caring, especially when it comes to his nephew and keeping his promises.

My stomach growls, and I drop my hand from where I was idly playing with my necklace and wishing it was Oliver's hands on me.

I clutch my midsection and squeeze my eyes closed. Breakfast was scarcer than panties at Victoria's Secret at the end of their semi-annual sale event. The number of vegetarian options were even fewer, so I walked away with my appetite less than satisfied.

Gulping, I stuff my hands into the pockets of my sweater and take small steps toward the gazebo as more clouds roll in, painting the sky with raging puffs of gray. I didn't see rain in the forecast for today, but it's very well possible.

My horoscope also said the universe would be in the mood to lend a helping hand, but I wouldn't say my current situation—plus the fact that Tommy is trapped in a line of cars from an accident—fits the bill.

I pull my phone out to text Bree and Tessa with my

whereabouts, so someone other than Tommy knows I'm stranded here.

> **Me:** Carter wouldn't happen to have a helicopter flying around New Jersey, would he? #notaskingforafriend

> **Tessa:** No...

> **Tessa:** What's going on?

> **Me:** The teachers left me at the campgrounds, so I'm stuck for a while.

> **Tessa:** OMG! Are you okay? What do you need? Carter and I are out of town, but maybe Bree can come get you?

> **Tessa:** BREE!!

> **Bree:** Is someone yelling for me?

> **Me:** I'm fine. I'm actually with Oliver.

I blink at my phone, but there's no indication that either friend is typing. I click it off and on again, waiting for a new message, until my phone finally vibrates.

> **Bree:** So you're stranded at a pretty lake with your hot as fuck British crush?

> **Me:** I wouldn't use those exact words, but... yes. Basically.

> **Bree:** I don't understand the emergency.

> **Me:** Are you kidding? THIS from the woman who thought watching the new season of *Love is Blind* the night it premiered was an emergency!

> **Bree:** I couldn't NOT watch it the second it premiered. That would be like finding a mole and not getting it checked out asap.

Me: You're insane!

Bree: Isn't that why you love me?

I roll my eyes and send a few more texts back and forth—some responsible ones from Tessa to confirm we do have someone coming to get us, and even more ridiculous ones from Bree.

Mainly, Bree describes very specific and dirty things I should be doing with Oliver in the lake.

Or against a tree.

Bree: You should be breaking the bunk beds from too much sex right now instead of texting your friends!

"Again, my apologies, Malcolm." Oliver's voice drifts over to where I sit on the bench inside the gazebo.

I quickly click my phone off like he's standing over my shoulder and reading the crazy messages from my friends, then stare out at the water, feigning innocence.

My freaking boss already overheard Katie mention how cozy he and I have gotten. What must he think about that? If he's affected by his staff making cute jokes about him, it doesn't show, and I hope to every divine being out there that he doesn't try to talk to me about it like he did the infamous "crush."

"We'll play soon, I promise," he says into the phone as he gets closer. "Cheers."

I peer over my shoulder at him as he stuffs the phone into his pocket. This weekend is the first time I'm seeing Oliver in anything other than slacks, and I must say, these light-colored jeans are working for him.

And me.

They might actually be my favorite pair of pants he owns.

His polo is still on brand for him—neat and tucked into those jeans like he's halfway ready to go to the golf course—but he's more loose here.

And easy on the eyes.

I clear my throat. "How did he take it?"

He leans on the opening of the gazebo. "That I wouldn't make it back in time to keep my promise to play futbol? Just fine." He hangs his head, and it's obvious he's disappointed. "It doesn't bode well for me with Malcolm, nor his mother. I'm trying to win their trust, which they don't give easily."

Guilt eats at me. This is my fault, after all.

If only I wouldn't have forgotten my damn watch.

"I'm sorry," I offer and kick my feet out in front of me, sweeping the worn wooden floor with the heels of my shoes. "I know it was silly to forget my watch, but in my defense, I didn't think they'd seriously leave us here. I mean, that's the kind of ridiculous thing that happens in a movie."

"I thought you believed in the unexplainable," he tosses back with an underlying smug tone, and when I glance up, I note the tic in his jaw like he's fighting a smirk.

"I do," I argue. "But it doesn't mean I'm not surprised or confused by it on occasion."

He nods and shifts his weight, averting his gaze to the lake instead of me. "My apologies for being so hard on you before."

"I get it." I rise and slide my hands down my leggings. "You had plans, and I ruined them."

I trudge down the two steps and onto the ground across from him, tilting my head back. For a moment, we stand in silence as the clock ticks, and the world continues.

Squirrels race up the tree behind him, and the occasional

breeze coasts through the grass, taking with it the flowers around the perimeter of the gazebo. The petals tilt off their axes, and it's exactly the way I'm feeling as I stand here with Oliver.

My boss.

The one I have a crush on, and it's not the kind I had on Nick Carter of the Backstreet Boys when I was young.

"How is it going with Malcolm?" I ask, the question rushing out of my mouth before I let my rampant thoughts run their course.

They were not headed in a good direction, but how can anyone blame me?

The man exudes power and sensuality. Even in silence, heat radiates from him as if to whisper, *Come hither*. I don't like tanning beds because of the temperature, but I'd gladly trap myself with him in an enclosed receptacle.

The burn—and panic attack from the claustrophobia— would be so worth it. "It's fantastic." His features soften as he angles himself toward me. "He's intelligent and full of energy. And you were right with your advice on ways to bond with him. It's been really lovely."

"Glad to help."

"How do you know so much about children? Do you have any?" He stands upright, and his wide eyes instantly fill with apprehension. "I'm sorry to be so intrusive, and—"

"I don't have kids," I say with a smile to hopefully put him at ease. "I'd have to go out with an eligible guy in order to even get close, and since that's never happened to me before, I have no kids."

"Ah, yes. The queen of bad dates." He chuckles, and he doesn't cover his mouth.

I get the full effect of his grin, and my lungs cease functioning. They shrivel up faster than fruit I toss into my food dehydrator, and although I can't breathe, I long for this moment to last a while.

Because Oliver's smile is surprisingly easy and charming, and it loosens his rigidity.

It took a joke at my expense, but it's totally worth it.

"I volunteer at the Boys & Girls Club, so I spend a lot of time with kids of all ages and backgrounds," I whisper.

"That's very noble of you," he says, and he seems to mean it. Which makes my chest bloom.

"Were you married?" I blurt.

He flashes his shocked gaze toward me.

"There's a rumor around school that you were, and it's why you moved." I chew on the inside of my cheek, then ramble, "Because of a nasty divorce."

"You know I moved here for my sister and nephew." I shrug. "There could be more than one reason."

"I've never been married." He gives me a tight smile, and the veins in his neck protrude more than if he were setting a deadlifting record. "Let's go for a float." He points toward a canoe by the water with a thick and sinful finger, the skill of which has lived rent-free in my filthy imagination for far too long.

We walk together in silence, and once we reach the handful of canoes, I kick my shoes off and wiggle my toes in the cool sand.

At the edge of the water, I push in one end of the canoe, and he wades in knee deep to pull it the rest of the way. While he holds it steady for me, I climb in with wobbly legs and crawl up into a sitting position to wait for him.

"Careful," I say, grabbing the edge on either side of me

like it's going to defy the structure of this tipsy thing.

It'll help about as much as telling him to be careful will.

"All right?" I ask, having learned by now that's how British people ask if they're okay.

"Smashing." His lips curl as he settles into the seat across from mine and faces me. The wooded area expands behind him like a fall painting, one that's breathtaking and beautiful and might belong in a Soho art gallery.

Even Oliver—control freak, unyielding Oliver—looks like he belongs out here in nature, especially in those casual jeans.

He was so irate when we first realized we were stuck here. His words have never been so enunciated, and his eyes turned the darkest shade of blue I've ever seen.

But his fury has obviously worn off. He's so relaxed now. Here, he actually seems to be enjoying himself, unlike at school where he's as formal and professional as his expensive slacks and pressed dress shirts. He's stoic with the teachers, anyway, since he seems to reserve his relatively fun side for the students.

It's like we're in a scene right out of *The Notebook*, for crying out loud. All we need is rain and a dramatic confrontation on the dock.

A second one, anyway, because the one we had right after I talked to Tommy was pretty heavy.

"Have you ever been in love?" I whisper, and my heart pounds in my head.

He pinches his brows together like I asked him to prove whether he wears boxers or briefs, à la Bree.

I clear my throat. "I just mean—"

"I shared a flat with a woman for two years," he answers, and his shoulders relax.

Victory!

I suppress the amused smile tugging at my lips. "You didn't exactly answer my question."

"I think I did." A sparkle graces his eyes as he takes hold of the two oars and grunts into the rowing motion, the shirt sleeves hugging his biceps like they're swaddling him. "What about you, Ms. Hayes?"

"I thought we were past the formalities." I quirk a brow and continue fidgeting with my fingers in my lap as the boat dips and rises with the small waves.

A shadow crosses his features when he pins his stare on me. I hold my hands up in surrender. "No."

He hums as he takes in the stretch of water and continues his back-and-forth motion to move the boat. But he slows his pace with each row.

"What happened with you and the woman?" I press, desperately curious to know more about him.

"We didn't work out." He shrugs like it's a tale as old as time, and there's nothing to unpack.

But I don't let it end here, although I probably should.

Besides, who knows when Tommy will arrive to take us home. We could be here all day, and it's not in my nature to let his vague answer pass without an explanation.

Smiling, I insist, "There has to be more to the story. It's not like you woke up one day, had coffee, and buttered your toast. Then somewhere in between, decided you didn't want to be with her anymore."

Oliver rests the ends of the oars on his impressive thighs and cocks a brow. "That's exactly what happened, except it was over crumpets, and she ended things with me. I'm certain I would have done so eventually, though."

I gulp.

His heavy sigh mixes with the soft whistle of the wind. "My mates were all settling down and having children—one moved off to Spain to be with his wife—so it felt like it was time for me to do the same. And we made sense at one point. Julie and I were generally compatible."

I lean forward and literally sit on the edge of my seat for him to continue. He's mesmerizing.

"But as time progressed, she wanted more of me. More spontaneity, more grand confessions of the heart, more excitement to have dinner with her mates. And I didn't know how to give her those things, nor did I want to pretend to be someone I'm not."

"Wow, her friends must've been really boring," I tease.

And it earns me a low chuckle from him. It's gruff and raspy, yet full of happiness. "It sounds like you two did the right thing," I offer seriously. "My parents divorced

when I was eight, and it was painful at the time. But in hindsight, it was for the best." "I'm sorry," he says, and I feel his eyes on me as I tear mine away from him.

I picture my parents when they were married. The loving way my dad would kiss her cheek when he got home. The ease of every conversation, whether they were talking about stressful bills or a fantastic cruise they wanted to book.

Our family co-existed in harmony. Until it didn't.

"My parents eventually got caught up in their careers and everything but each other. I figured it was just a rough patch. That they'd get through it. But I knew something was wrong when they stopped doing the little things for each other. That's what it's about, I've come to believe—the little things. Whether it's taking out the trash or holding hands during a movie in the living room."

"I thought you've never been in love."

I grin. "I haven't, but I never said I haven't witnessed it. My mom and stepdad seem to be the real deal now. The little things just look different for every couple."

"What does it look like for them?"

"Going to shows, taking cooking classes, and making pottery." "Those sound much more significant than taking out the trash."

I swipe my hair from my forehead, and my smile grows wider. "My stepdad hates all of it, but he knows it's important to my mom. She, in turn, listens to old country records with him. Give and take."

Oliver picks up the oars again and rows, his back toward the edge of the lake. But his eyes remain on me.

"I think if you're with the right person, you'll do anything to make it work," I whisper. "And it wouldn't make you miserable in the process. Seeing the other person happy would trump all that."

I lose myself in this moment with a man who makes me flustered. And hot.

He's confusing, yet enlightening, and I can't get the feel of his hands out of my memory. My body remembers how firm and confident his grip on me was, and I want more of it.

I ache for more of him.

His circling motion slows again, and I'm not sure we're still moving, or even swaying.

Our surroundings fade, and I zero in on Oliver like I'm seeing him through a window.

Blood roars in my ears as I push off my seat toward him, but the second I get close, his peaceful expression transforms into one of panic.

"Erin, wait." He holds his hand up, and somewhere seemingly in the distance, an oar drops into the water with a splash.

Oh my God.

I misread the situation.

Abort! Abort!

I try to sit back down, but I lose my footing. The canoe wobbles, and then it rocks onto one side, flipping into the water and tossing us both overboard. I yelp as I hit the frigid lake, my mouth hanging open, perfect for a mouthful of water.

Except I'm more worried about what an idiot I just made of myself.

Did I seriously try to kiss my boss? Why in the hell did I try to kiss him?

Instead of responding to Oliver's cries to help me, I take off toward the shore, my extreme embarrassment fueling me to swim faster than all the sea characters in *Aquaman* put together.

When I come up for air, I hear splashing behind me, but I don't stop until I'm crawling up the sandy shore. Once I get close enough, I place both hands on the edge of the dock and haul myself into a standing position.

"Erin!" Oliver's voice sounds from close behind me, and a few seconds later, he's grabbing me by the arm and spinning me to face him.

Dear Holy Spirit and Lady Gaga—a put-together Oliver isn't fair, but a dripping- wet, shirt-sticking-to-each-hard-ab Oliver? Now that is just cruel, especially during this humiliating crisis.

"You misunderstood me," he says between labored breaths.

I shake my head. "It's fine. We don't have to talk about it. In fact, let's pretend it didn't happen. After all, you want to remain professional, and I was being so freaking silly," I babble and try to wriggle free from his grasp, but no such luck.

"The canoe…" He waves over his shoulder, where the stupid thing is flipped upside down and freely gliding over the water.

I scoff, thoroughly ashamed but also angry that he's more concerned about losing the canoe than what just happened—or rather, *didn't* happen. I mean, I know I said let's forget about it, but how is it so easy for him?

"Yes, I can see it, and I'll go get it. No big deal. It's not like it's going anywhere."

"Of course not. The lake isn't like a moving river or stream. It's stationary water."

He looks back at me, water droplets hanging off his eyelashes.

But that's not why my jaw drops. "I know. I'm not totally incompetent, and I don't even know why we're—"

"The canoe was about to flip when you stood up, and I was only concerned for your safety," he says quickly.

"Oh." I shrink back a fraction as a burning blush heats my cheeks.

"I wanted to kiss you." He inches toward me with those measured steps of his that I've come to find comfort in.

But I'm not comfortable right now.

I'm turned on and wet—and not just from the dive in the lake.

My core is weeping with glee. For once, I'm not crazy and naive in thinking a guy feels what I do.

"You did?"

He nods and drops his focus to my trembling lips.

"Then why have you been giving me such a hard time? I didn't think you liked me at all before today."

"I do, though." *And another step closer.* "I just couldn't tell you. Our situation… The rules frown upon any involvement between us." *One more step.* "It's complicated, but I'm finding it harder and harder to resist this temptation. Not when my feelings for you are as all-consuming as they are."

I quirk a brow, my heart humming in my ears as I manage, "Are you telling me you pulled an elementary school stunt of being mean because you like me, so to speak?"

He bites his smiling lip in an uncharacteristically boyish way, and my heart lurches. "Not my finest moment."

"And what is?" I whisper as he closes the remaining distance between us. "This," he rasps and presses his wet lips to mine in a dizzying kiss that has me

holding on to him for balance.

My eyelids flutter closed, and I'm equal parts light-headed and grounded in the most glorious mix of pleasure.

As he kisses me, his hands slide up my damp arms until he's cupping both my cheeks in a firm and possessive way. It makes my toes curl into the grass, the thin blades tickling my feet like the prickling goose bumps along my arms.

I'm aware of every sensation he elicits, and when his tongue seeks entrance between my lips, I gladly open and wrap my arms around his waist to pull him closer.

None of it is enough.

How is he so warm? I'm freezing from the water, but he's holding on to his heat like a boiling cup of hot cocoa.

The peppermint kind.

His taste is minty and spicy, and I instantly thaw, melting into him as his hand finds the back of my head, cradling me to angle my face where he wants it.

I kiss him back with fervor and aching desire.

This man…

He pulls back abruptly. "All right, then," he says and spins around to march back toward the water.

I stare after him, blinking rapidly through the whiplash he prompted.

What just happened?

I bring the back of one hand to my forehead and note the warmth of my skin. Am I clammy? Is that why he marched off?

Oliver dips into the water and wades in a few feet to retrieve the canoe as if he's completely unaffected.

Once the shock wears off, I storm toward the shore, my chest heaving with annoyance.

Oliver Westbrook has irked me for the very last freaking time.

I thought we were past the mixed signals, but evidently, we're only getting started. And I will not stand for it.

I reach him right as he lugs the traitorous boat safely onto shore, his back muscles magnificent as they effortlessly roll with each movement.

Black spots fill my vision.

I am not in the mood for distractions, back muscles. Not today.

"Are we going to talk about what just happened?" I ask, searching his unreadable expression for any sign of what he's thinking.

He angles himself toward me, and his thin lips form a tight line. "It was pleasant," he says evenly.

"Excuse me?" I stand back as if he slapped me, which is basically what his description did.

I mean, *pleasant* is how I would describe holding the door open for the person behind me or helping someone with their groceries.

It's not exactly the word I'd use to describe the heated kiss we just shared—one that basically split the ground open and swallowed me whole.

I open my mouth to tell him as much too, but no sound comes out.

Instead, my vision blurs, both knees buckle, and everything goes silent and dark.

TWELVE

Oliver

I pace beside the bed as she finally stirs.

Erin's eyes flutter open, and she lets out a soft whimper, a dazed glow about her like she was having a lovely dream.

Which puts me at ease.

"What's going on?" she says with a raspy edge in her voice and clears her throat. "Thank God, you're awake. You fainted. I was two seconds away from ringing an

ambulance." I sit by her ankles, and most of my body hangs off the tiny bed.

"They'd at least get here before Tommy." She digs both hands into the mattress and hoists herself upright until her back rests against the headboard. "Did you carry me in here?"

"I had help from the woodland fairies I mentioned earlier," I say in an attempt at a joke, but she frowns. "Right.

My apologies. You just… You gave me a scare, is all."

"I'm sorry." She pushes the heel of her palm into the side of her head.

"This is the first time I've ever charmed a woman into a coma," I try again, and it seems to work this time.

Her expression transforms into a touch of amusement, and even though she's unusually pale at the moment, the smile lights up her features brighter than a Christmas tree.

And I'm damn happy to see her in better spirits.

She shifts on the bed, and the cabin fills with a third presence. At least, that's what it sounds like when her stomach's angry growl echoes around us.

"Well, there's the answer to my question regarding the cause of your episode— you're starving." I rise from my position and start to help her up, but she pinches the fabric of her shirt between her thumb and forefinger, peering up at me.

"Did you change my clothes?" she asks.

"I did." My heart thunders in my ears. "There were camp T-shirts in the closet, and yours needed to dry after our unscheduled swim in the lake. I also, um… hung your pants over there to dry."

She follows the thumb I've hooked over my shoulder to where her leggings, sweater, and socks are draped over the chair, across the desk, and on the ladder leading up to the top bunk. "This looks like a scene out of a horror movie."

"Does that make me the serial killer?"

"You'd definitely be a suspect, given how ridiculously neat you always are." Her gaze drifts lazily over me, and I worry she's feeling faint again.

I lunge to her side and grab her hand. "What is it?" "I just realized you changed shirts too."

I stretch my arm to the side and show her where the sleeve cuts into my bicep. "Didn't have my size. Evidently, grown men don't attend summer camp. I'd be relieved of that fact during any other time."

She covers her mouth as she laughs, and the sound fills the dusty cabin with a special kind of energy.

Her presence is so unique and joyous, and it's actually making me start to believe in absurdities like cosmic energy. How else would I explain the way we fell into each other's lives other than fate? I wouldn't be surprised to find myself reading my horoscope tomorrow.

But right now, I need to feed her.

She accepts the hand I offer to help her up and lets the sheet fall from her waist as she rises. Immediately, I turn away to avoid catching even a glimpse of her knickers for fear I'll be the one to faint next—from lust and supernatural restraint.

I haven't been this aroused by a woman since I was a teenage boy, daydreaming of my math teacher in Year Ten.

Have I always had a thing for math instructors?

I hand Erin her damp pants and keep my back turned to her, grinding my teeth. I know what she tastes like.

My mouth was on hers just a few minutes ago, and I wanted so much more but was overwhelmed by my attraction to this intriguing woman. I wanted to scoop her into my arms, throw her over my shoulder, and spank that taut arse of hers for taunting me since we met.

The fear of coming on too strong stopped me, and I needed to cool off. To take things slow. To be careful since we are in a rather precarious situation. It's why I submerged myself in the lake.

In hindsight, I should've told her it was better than

pleasant. For God's sake, our kiss deserved far more than such an inadequate description.

Of course, I didn't have a chance to correct myself. Not since she collapsed and instantly turned my heated desire for her into a frozen panic.

"I didn't peek at any of the goods, either," I announce and stand a bit taller with pride.

"The goods, huh? What am I, a produce stand?"

When I assume she's fully dressed, I face her again and find a splash of color has returned to her cheeks.

"All I'm saying is, I was a perfect gentleman, even though it was hard to resist the red lace of your… thong." I clench my jaw and feel heat drifting into my cheeks.

"I thought you said you didn't peek." She sways in place, goading me. Her curious eyes travel down the length of me, and the wild glimmer in them is anything but innocent.

"I didn't," I insist, but it's weak.

I'm weak for this woman.

I have been since day fucking one.

"I left my bag at the gazebo," I manage. "I have a couple snacks in there to settle your stomach until we can get out of here for a proper meal."

Instead of heading out, she continues studying me, and the silence is as deafening as her scrutiny is disconcerting.

I'd be more at ease if I were on the edge of a cliff.

Because when Erin looks at me in such a way, the only thing I want is for her to see and accept all that I am, which is more terrifying to someone like me than jumping off a tall rock.

Whatever this is between us is far stronger than I previously suspected, and the realization forms knots of excitement in my stomach.

This woman turns me to mush without any intention of doing so. It's positively miraculous. Although I hated it before, I'm starting to warm up to the idea of being someone more exuberant and light.

She finally nods and heads for the door, saying over her shoulder, "As long as it doesn't have meat, I'll eat it."

My steps falter as I follow her out into the open. "That's right—I forgot you're a vegetarian."

"Uh-huh." She holds her chin up with pride like she just swam across the English Channel, and in a way, she has.

Giving up meat is a special kind of Hell.

I tried it once in order to impress a Greek girl I fancied during university, and it was customary to give up all red meat during Lent.

I lasted two days.

As I follow behind Erin, I try not to stare at her peach-shaped arse, although it's more difficult than stopping myself from breathing.

How can I resist a peek?

I'm a jumbled ball of anxious nerves by the time we reach the gazebo, where I scoop my bag up. As soon as I unzip the pocket, I feel it.

A raindrop.

"Ah!" Erin squeals as she rushes past me. "Hurry!"

Rain falls in large drops, like tears from the Statue of Liberty back in the city, which is where we should be right now instead of running in the storm.

I take off after her until we reach the closest cabin. It's the same one I carried her into after she fainted like a chivalrous knight saving the day.

My actions might be described as respectable, but my thoughts of her now are the exact opposite.

I blame the red lacy panties.

"We can't catch a break." She squeezes the ends of her damp hair, and small droplets scatter across her shoulders. "I—"

She sways again, and her eyelids grow heavy. I catch her in my arms, but she doesn't collapse this time. Instead, she gazes up at me, her mouth forming a small *O*, and I burn to capture her lips with mine in another kiss.

One that would lead to more. But first, she needs nourishment. *Chivalrous knight.*

I need to be a chivalrous knight right now, and a devilish brute later. "Sit down, and I'll see what I have in my bag."

She hums in response and sits on the edge of the bed while I cross the room and hope like hell that I have something other than meat products to offer her.

"Have you always been a vegetarian?" I ask. "Only for the last year."

"Why did you make the change?" I bring my bag over to the bed and dig into it, glad I reached my computer in time to avoid losing it to the rain.

I'd be more glad to find a suitable snack for Erin, but I'm not having any luck.

"I went out with a guy who insisted we watch a documentary. I only agreed because I thought he was talking about a history one, which I love, but it was a video on the horrors of slaughterhouses. When I asked to turn it off, he told me to wait for the good part." She tilts her head to the side and shudders. "It never came."

"Is that a dirty euphemism of some sort?" I grimace.

"God, no!" She waves her arm. "I meant, um, no good came of the movie or the date, for that matter, other than a cold hard lesson."

"How romantic," I deadpan, and after a heavy pause, I sigh in defeat. "I'm sorry, but I have bad news. The only food left in my bag is beef jerky."

Her face falls.

"I had packed dried fruit snacks and protein bars, but Tommy must've sniffed them out like a Rottweiler. The man consumes more food than I thought possible for a human being. I'm surprised he left anything in here at all."

She giggles, but it's short-lived. "I'll just wait for him to come back. He should be close, right?"

I grab my phone off the desk and check my messages and calls. "No updates yet." Off to the side, I ring Tommy and hope for good news.

Although I don't want to cut our time alone together short, I have to get Erin some food soon.

But after a brief chat with the lad, it doesn't look like that'll be happening anytime

I rub my sweaty palms down my damp jeans and lose myself in the uneven ticking of the rain against the windows, the music of nature.

Which is not on our side.

"We have a problem—" I spin around to find a stick of beef jerky hanging out of Erin's mouth. "What are you doing?"

She jumps to the other end of the bed, her eyes wide like she's posing for a mugshot. "I'm sorry!" Erin throws her hands up, and the rest of the meat falls out of her mouth and into her lap. "It just smelled so good. And I'm *so* hungry. If you think about it, this perfectly compacted cow saved my life."

I hang my head and chuckle—I can't help it. The woman is adorably absurd.

"Have you no self-control?" I tease and sit next to her on the bed as lightning strikes, illuminating the cabin through gaps in the window blinds.

It seems as if it's sealing my fate.

Because the moment I settle beside her, I'm very aware of the fact that we're sitting on top of a mattress together.

Alone.

No one around for miles.

Erin slows her chewing, then pops more into her mouth as she watches me. "I'm not the only one with no self-control."

"Pardon?" I blink.

Did I say anything incriminating out loud? I kick myself for merely thinking inappropriate things while she's in this condition. It's not chivalrous or noble at all.

She tilts her head until her temple nearly rests on her shoulder. "I said, it's a little late to ask about self-control."

"Oh." I nod.

I'm off the hook and completely absolved since she has no idea that I'd love nothing more than to lay her back and make her feel better myself.

To touch her in a way that would make her forget she's ever been on a bad date.

Out here, it's even easy for me to forget we're a boss and an employee. A much older boss, at that.

So much is stacked against us. Yet, I can't stop my imagination from running wild.

Not since I've gotten a taste of her.

And knowing she wants me in return makes it nearly impossible to keep my hands to myself.

"Oliver?" Erin peeks at me and crinkles the plastic in her hand from the finished snack, the sound like an aluminum can being crushed in her grip. "Do you need some beef jerky too? Because I feel much better after that, and I know you would too…"

I shake my head from side to side, slowing my movements as time stands still.

Her sharp inhale makes my entire body hard, especially when flashes of our kiss slam into me.

Hungry. Warm. Sensational.

Kissing her before was better than quenching a naughty thirst. It was like savoring an exquisite cocktail of lust, passion, and poetry.

Would it be like that again?

Only one way to find out.

She licks her lips like she's imagining my taste on them too. "When did Tommy say he'd be here?" she asks, her voice weaker than before, as if she couldn't care less about his arrival.

As if she no longer needs to be rescued.

"He's dealing… with a flat tire."

Her eyebrows rise into her hairline. "So, you jinxed him. Didn't I warn you about that?"

"How can I make it up to you?" I narrow my gaze at her.

In a flash, she leaps into my embrace and plants her mouth on mine with urgency. I topple to the side, one foot hanging from the bed, and she almost falls too. Her clumsy eagerness is endearing, to say the least, and I revel in it.

I wrap my arms around Erin and pull her fully onto the bed without breaking our vigorous kiss. Then I roll over until I'm on top, my weight pushing her farther into the mattress.

Her brilliant yelps and moans echo in my head, and she awakens something long dormant inside me.

My heart hammers away with anticipation. Hot blood pumps with enthusiasm too.

Arousal pricks my skin, especially at my fingertips as I run them down Erin's arms to the waistband of her leggings.

They're still damp, and if I reach inside, I'm sure I'll find she's wet as well. Both her legs are trapped between mine, though—something I need to remedy.

I thrust my tongue farther into her mouth, and she writhes beneath me, her hair fanned out and untamed as she hums with pleasure.

She hasn't seen or felt anything yet.

"Open for me," I rasp into her mouth, then run my tongue along the inside of her bottom lip.

Erin shivers against me and opens her mouth wider. I tsk. "Not what I meant, love."

I show her exactly what I meant and grip the outside of her thigh, which quivers in my grasp and drives me mad. When understanding—and need—colors her features, I shift onto my side and allow her room to spread her legs.

For *me*.

A caveman-like hunger shoots through my nervous system and overwhelms me.

Chasing more of that high, I ruffle her shirt up and kiss her stomach as my fingers glide over her skin with minds and intentions of their own.

She licks her lips, peering down at me as she threads her fingers through my short hair.

Dazed and enamored by this woman, I lose myself like I

never have before and pull the middle of her waistband down to expose the teasing red lace of her knickers.

And I place a heated kiss at the top.

"Yes, yes," she pants, and goose bumps erupt along her skin as if she's cold. But I know she's feeling the same elation of what's to come as I am.

"What do you want, Erin?" I ask in a low, scratchy voice and lean up to cup her between the thighs. "What do you want me to do to you?"

"I want… you to… take both our pants off." She rises onto her elbows and nods toward my bottom half, where my pants tent between my legs.

No matter how badly I want to bury myself inside her, this is not the time or place. But that doesn't mean we can't have our fun.

"I asked for what you wanted me to do to *you*," I emphasize. "For *your* pleasure." She gulps, and the sound is heard above the storm outside.

"Because as much as I want to fuck you, I'd rather wait to do so after a proper date.

To be a gentleman before I show you… a different side of me."

There's a rather impish warning in my low voice, and I sense she picks up on it like the cheeky devil she is.

Erin quivers beneath me, and the whimper she lets loose is equal parts breathy and needy.

"Do you like the sound of that?" I toy with the top of her panties, and my knuckles brush the skin below her belly button. When she nods and arches into my touch, I dip my hand inside to further tease and turn her on. "Or do you like it when I say… fuck?"

This earns me a sharp gasp, and her eyes fly open. A dark shadow passes across them, and it urges me to do bad things to her—in the best way.

"Both. Everything," she mutters, pure sinful lust dripping from each syllable. "Oliver, please…"

At the sound of my name, a primal growl escapes me, and I yank her leggings down, leaving no time to savor the way the tantalizing material slides down her smooth skin.

And I don't stop until her glistening heat is staring back at me, mine for the feasting.

As I lower my head between her legs, I feel her curious eyes watching me, wicked anticipation pooling in the depths of them.

All I want is to exceed expectations. To bring her more pleasure than any wanker before me. It's what she deserves, and I want to be the one to give it to her.

I take a deep breath, inhaling the smell of her sex, and it further arouses me, making me hard and reckless. Instead of starting slow, as I probably should, my snapping resolve takes over, and I open my mouth wide enough to cover her whole.

She bucks her hips off the bed, and I use both hands to hold her down as I continue my relentless—and clearly welcomed—assault.

I lick upward from one end to the other, enjoying the sweet taste of her and the fact that she's dripping wet.

I lap it all up, suck on her clit, and start over again, growing more and more ravenous with each swipe of my greedy tongue.

I'm feverish and wild.

It's not long before she writhes and thrusts her hips upward to the rhythm of my movements until she's riding my face like a bull, holding my hair tightly to steady herself and stay on as long as possible.

"Shit… Oliver… yes," she moans, each mumble a mix of incoherent sounds and gasps and pants.

I suck on her swollen clit, and she tenses, ready to explode.

Right when the walls of her heat tighten, I pull back. "Not yet, love. That was just the appetizer." I climb over her and give her a roguish grin. "Time for the next course."

She nods with enthusiasm and clings to my shoulders, her small hands seeking as much of me as they can grab onto.

"Hold on." I start from the beginning, only instead of my tongue, I use my hand.

Hovering over her, I insert my pointer finger first, stretching her as her legs fall wider open.

Erin bites her lip as if she's trying to hold in a scream, and I tsk. "Be loud, Erin. Scream for me. Cry. Let me hear how good this feels." I peer down between us, where my hard cock rests against the outside of her thigh, screaming enough for the both of us.

But I want to hear it from her. And I do.

She practically howls my name, and the beautiful sounds she makes drive me to work her over more thoroughly.

I fuck her with my finger, thrusting a second inside her, and she squeezes her eyes closed, her face flushed with pleasure as she alters from yelling to mumbling and back to crying out.

"That's it." I lick my lips, and the taste of her still lingering there is more delicious than any dessert I've ever had. "Time for the third course," I whisper gruffly and lift her shirt over her ample breasts.

Her bra holds them high and proud, and I ache to cup them each.

Her pleasure drips down my fingers as I continue thrusting them in and out of her, and she rocks into me with more passion than before, eager for release.

Desperate for me to drive her over the brink.

"You're absolutely brilliant," I say, rising onto my knees.

She shudders as I bring my free hand to pull her bra down, exposing a bouncing breast that's begging for my attention. Quickening the pace with my fingers, I clamp my mouth around her hard nipple.

Simultaneously, I curl my fingers inside her and swirl my tongue around her nipple until I'm sure she can't take it anymore. "Come for me, Erin," I mutter around my mouthful of her breast.

"Oh, oh… oh!" Her labored breaths transform into one long scream as she comes, her climax spilling with ferocity down my palm.

But I'm a rapacious bastard and don't let her stop there.

I use my thumb to apply pressure to the overly sensitive bundle of nerves above her clit and chase another release. It nearly bucks her off the bed.

I catch her and hold her in place, letting go of her tit with a cheeky pop. Her mouth hangs open, her chin nearly reaching her chest.

The muscles in her stomach remain clenched as she rides out wave after wave of ecstasy.

And the mattress under my knee is soaked.

She's complete perfection in this state of undeterred bliss with her inhibitions abandoned, and I'm captivated by her.

I'm positively charmed by the math teacher.

THIRTEEN

Erin

The orgasms he just gave me have left me dizzier than any fainting spell, or ride on a roller coaster.

His tongue. His fingers.

Oliver is as sexy and skilled as he is tender and loving.

I might've fantasized about experiencing such an awakening, but the real thing exceeded every dirty possibility my imagination could've summoned.

I shift onto my side to face him, still flushed and tingling from the way he worked my body. He wraps his arm around my naked waist, and I sigh into him, my skin hot and my satisfaction high. We barely fit on this twin bed, but I'm not complaining about how small it is.

Not since it's Oliver smashed against me.

"I've never experienced that before," I blurt. "I mean, I've had orgasms—I've had sex before too—but nothing like what you just did. I felt so… good."

"Thank you." He runs his hands through my hair and kisses my temple like it's more natural than the sun rising in the morning.

Peering up at him, I furrow my brows. "I was going to say thanks."

"Why? It's a compliment toward me." His grin turns smug, and when I nudge him in an attempt to pull an explanation out of him, he immediately understands my question before I've asked it.

How are we so in sync already?

"A noble lad takes care of a woman," he says, his tone sober and confident. "Besides, the fact that you didn't lump me in with the other wankers you've dated in the past is a compliment in itself."

I bury my face into his chest and giggle, my bra-covered breasts rubbing against his tight shirt with the movement.

The rain slows outside, the occasional tap against the door sounding like a lost animal scratching at it to be let in. It's how I felt with Oliver before today. Before getting stuck out here with him, I craved for him to open up to me, and now that he has, it's better than I'd hoped.

To think, I cursed the universe and called her a dirty bitch. But she knew what she was doing all along.

I'm high on this day and on the man holding me in his protective embrace. I might as well have fallen from the Empire State Building and lived. That's what it felt like to be with Oliver in such a vulnerable and intimate way.

And we didn't even have sex.

My God, what would that be like?

I don't think I could survive it, but I also know it would be worth the risk—in every sense—to find out exactly what he meant when he mentioned his darker side.

"Why do you go out with…"

"Dweebs? Assholes? Weirdos?" I finish for him. "Take your pick." "Exactly." A soft laugh rumbles out of him.

"I tend to feel like the next guy could be *the one*. I always hope so, anyway, but I also…" I toy with the fabric of his T-shirt as my heart flips, and I admit, "I hate being alone."

His grip on me tightens, and he warms me from the inside out. "You don't have to be anymore."

"Are you saying what I think you're saying?" I give him a small smile.

"If you think I fancy you, then yes," he says, and from this close, I zero in on the subtle lines around the corners of his lips curving upward like dimples.

They're faint, but they're there, nonetheless, as is this attraction between us. Although there's nothing faint about the latter.

"I fancy you as well, Sir Westbrook," I say, but instead of saying it in my normal voice—or any semblance of it, for that matter—I use a terribly awful British accent as if I'm mocking him.

Oh my God.

I slap one hand over my mouth and itch to crawl into the mattress, where I can hide forever.

I should've moved to Alaska when I had the chance.

"I'm sorry," I say and start to sit upright, suddenly embarrassed to be half-naked in front of him. "I would eat bugs if I could take that back."

He holds me in place and throws his head back as laughter

bursts out of him like a light beam, and it quickly puts me at ease. "No need to eat bugs, but I appreciate the remorse," he says between fits of laughter.

"Maybe you shouldn't be so intimidating." I swat playfully at him, and he lifts his hand from my waist, his fingers barely grazing my flushed skin before he cups my cheek.

My breath hitches when he kisses me, his smiling lips slowly settling completely over mine with precision.

But he pulls back all too quickly. "How about now?" he whispers and tilts his nose against mine. "Am I still intimidating?"

All thoughts and words leave my brain, except for one thing.

More.

I want more of him.

"No, but you are sexy," I breathe, and my core weeps for more of his touch.

He narrows his eyes at me. "Flattery can be quite persuasive, and I respect the effort. But you're not going to get me into bed today."

"I'll keep that in mind when I'm actually trying to do so." I hold my finger up. "But you *are* already in bed, for the record, so I win."

"You know what I mean," he says sarcastically and sits upright. "Speaking of beds, let's get out of this one before I have you at my mercy again."

"What would be so wrong about that?" I ask around the lump of desire in my throat.

"A lot of things." He leans over, and when his lips near my ear, the hairs on my arms rise. "There would be several things wrong and filthy and very naughty about that."

Wow.

The preview was enough to blow my freaking mind. I've never said this about a guy, but I'd sell my soul to the highest bidder to experience the full Oliver show. "Something for you to look forward to." He rises to his full height and offers me his hands. "I know I will."

If his tone and smirk are any indications, he's extremely pleased with himself. Why does it make me so giddy to know he likes making me squirm?

Blowing out a frustrated but sated breath, I accept his help and get up, feeling thrillingly bad about what we just did in this strange cabin.

What I just did with my boss, no less.

Bree is going to have a field day, and oh, God—what would Katie say now?

I swipe my pants from the floor and put those on. As I balance to slide each foot in, my legs are wobblier than if I just finished an excruciating yoga session. "What did you do to me? I don't think I'll be able to walk down the hall tomorrow."

His smug grin deepens like I said his dick is the biggest I've ever seen.

And if the feel of it against my leg told me anything, it might actually be the biggest. I should feel guilty about thinking of my boss's cock, but butterflies in my lower stomach are the only things fluttering through me at the moment.

From the second I learned Oliver felt the same way I did, not even a hurricane could've deterred me from hopping into bed with him.

He hooks his arm at the elbow and holds it out for me.

"Shall we go for a walk?" "I'd love to." I loop my arm through his and practically swoon out of my body

when he rests his free hand on top of mine.

He engulfs it in his, his warm palm covering my knuckles like a blanket.

It's such a sweet gesture, and I'm salivating for him again before we even step off the porch.

I'm so caught up in him that I don't stop to check if it's still raining, but I assume he did since he doesn't seem surprised to find the clouds have cleared. For the most part, anyway.

Between all the changes in weather and our relationship, it feels like we've been stuck here for a week, but only a few hours have passed.

"I chose a camping trip because I grew tired of the city," Oliver says.

As he leads the way, he dips his head to watch where he's going as we walk the campgrounds. It's like we're in one of Ian's post-apocalyptic movies. As if we're the only two people alive.

"It can be loud and distracting, and I wanted us to get away from it, so we could enjoy each other's company and breathe fresh air."

"Is New York that much different than London?"

"Not quite." His lips twitch. "I was growing tired of London as well."

"Guess it was good timing for you to move, then." I smile.

But something dark crosses his expression right before he looks away, and my stomach sinks as I wait in silence for him to explain. "I didn't know I had a sister before last summer."

"What do you mean?" I stop and face him as he scratches the back of his head. Oliver exhibits enough emotions to span an entire spectrum.

Angry. Sad. Guilty. Regretful. And back to angry.

His jaw tightens. "My mother never told my father and me about Rebecca, so I haven't been part of her life. I'm trying to change that."

I squeeze his upper arm, and my stomach sinks further as the weight of what he said settles at the bottom of it. I try to imagine what this must be like for him, but I come up empty and can offer only one thing. "I'm so sorry."

He rocks sideways, his frown deep and contemplative. His muscled arms seem close to ripping the sleeves of his snug shirt, like they're screaming with the news of a long-lost sister.

My heart is heavy as I look at this man—a strong, capable man—in such a vulnerable state.

He's hurting.

"Want to talk about it?" I ask lightly. Oliver locks eyes with me and nods.

As we resume walking along dirt paths, he expresses how much his mother's betrayal has wounded him. How hard he's working to gain his sister's trust and be part of her and Malcolm's lives. How important family is to him, whether he's known them allnhis life or for the last few months.

He's gone from Rebecca ignoring his calls to talking with her every couple of days, either in person or via phone call.

"When I saw her a couple days ago, she even starting opening up to me about her father." He beams. "It's a subject she once avoided almost as vehemently as she does any mention of our mother, but for different reasons, from what she's said."

"I'm sure it's hard for her."

"Of course, and I'm a patient man. I'm just happy to make progress." He stares off at the lake, the twigs crunching beneath our feet.

The air smells fresh and earthy after the storm, and I'd be colder if I weren't sidled up next to Principal Hot Brit, who retains heat like he's the center of a volcano.

His voice is low and warm too, and I could listen to it for hours, especially when he's being as candid and honest as he is now.

"I'm glad she had a pleasant upbringing." He works his jaw back and forth. "Before he died four years ago, Rebecca's father was a standup role model from the sound of it. While it doesn't absolve any of the mistakes made, I'm relieved that they had a strong bond."

I grip his forearm with my other hand as we continue in comfortable silence. My heart squeezes for the time lost, but there's hope in his voice when he speaks again.

"I always wanted a sister. To take her for ice cream after school. To scare off any wankers who came sniffing around." He chuckles, and lightness slowly seeps into him— a peaceful air that lifts my own spirits. "I may not have gotten to do those for Rebecca, which kills me, but I'm fortunate to have the opportunity to be there for her and Malcolm now."

"They're lucky to have you."

Humming, I follow his lead over a log across our path, using his shoulder for balance. On the other side, I get caught in a web of fallen branches and leaves. "Shoot," I mutter and bend down to untangle the woodsy debris from my shoelaces. Once I'm free, I stand and exhale, ready to continue our enlightening walk.

"All right?" He checks me over, concern etched in each line around his skillfulmouth.

And oh, the skills.

"Great," I chirp and resume my position next to him.

I'm surprised he can be a strict administrator, a sexy man in bed, and a protective friend all in one. He's a loving brother and uncle. I mean, he moved across an entire ocean to a different continent to be with his sister.

I respect the hell out of him for that and so many things.

But as we continue walking the grounds, my nagging thoughts get the best of me. What are his flaws? He has to have some, right?

Other than curt comments about my obsession with horoscopes, he seems… perfect.

Which I most certainly am not used to.

I'm also not used to men paying so much *attention* to me and my needs as Oliver did in the cabin, which will forever be marked by us. We all but carved our initials into the wooden bedframe.

He listened to me and my body, hungry to pleasure me, and his need to do it was a big, fat, giant turn-on. The last time I had sex, it was over in under seven minutes, and he called out another woman's name at the end.

It's about time the universe rewarded me with Oliver. No matter what flaws he's hiding, I'm going to enjoy this moment of just the two of us.

We talk more while we walk, opting to discuss lighter topics. It's easy and comfortable, and we tease each other too, especially when I suggest he might enjoy meditation.

"I'd have to respectfully disagree." He smiles.

"I think it would do you some good to center yourself every now and then with a few minutes of silence." I poke him in the chest. "There's way too much brooding and tension pent up in here, and you need to let go of it all."

"But I thrive on that tension. What else would fuel me?"

He peeks at me from the corner of his eye, and it's obvious he's humoring me.

I squeeze his hand and pull myself into his embrace, where I playfully run the tip of my finger between his lean pecs. "How about tranquility? Just think—you could be fueled by a clear and focused mind," I muse.

"Make it naked meditation, and I'm sold." The edges of his lips crinkle upward. "Principal Westbrook… I didn't know you had such a dirty mind," I whisper. "You haven't seen anything yet," he mutters right before he covers my mouth with his.

He inhales as he draws my lips farther into his mouth, like he's drinking me in, and it sweeps me away.

I'm captivated by this kiss and the backdrop of the gazebo and the sky. It boasts of deep pink and yellow hues. The colors brighten the otherwise gray portions of the thick clouds, and they reflect beautifully off the water of the lake.

To think, I wasn't excited for this trip.

If we're being honest, I was actually starting to hate that I was attracted to Oliver at all, and not only because he's my boss. I didn't think he felt anything for me other than contempt.

Up until a few hours ago, I was contemplating my move to a different state, but since he revealed the truth about his feelings, I'm imagining what a future with him would look like. That's the kind of man he is—the type to settle down. I don't get the impression he's content with one-night stands, which bodes well for me, even if I am getting ahead of myself.

But it's hard to exchange such real and personal secrets with him—to share a kiss as raw as this one—and not picture how we might spend Sunday afternoons from now on.

Reading a book on the couch by a fire. A record playing in the corner.

One fuzzy blanket covering us both.

But once the sun fell, we'd turn up the heat in the bedroom, or just take to the floor…

The sound of gravel crunching under car tires echoes around us, and we turn in the direction it's coming from.

Tommy's here.

He's come to take us back to the city—to reality.

I note the second Oliver realizes it too. His body tenses, each muscle scrunching in his back and preparing for a fight-or-flight reaction.

And I dread he'll pick flight.

Especially when he drops my hand faster than if it were a scorching pan right off the stove, and my wishful thinking bursts into a cloud of smoke from a pipe dream.

"Listen, I meant what I said before. I do like you, and I desire to see where this goes." He cups the back of my head with his large hands and kisses my lips, then the tip of my nose and forehead before he drops his arms back down. "But let's keep this thing between us for a while, all right? Just until we figure it out."

Nodding in agreement, I lose myself in his bright blue eyes, clarity and confidence beaming in the aqua sea of each one.

I believe in his conviction that there's something between us. I believe in him.

FOURTEEN

Erin

"**Y**ou ate meat?"

"But you were doing so well!"

"What now?"

"It was one piece of beef jerky, and I could've died without it," I emphasize the last part and scoop up my margarita glass as the crowd buzzes with families, friends, and couples. Two kids in the corner fight over a crayon, and a few more sitting next to the opposite wall loudly complain when their parents tell them they can't have soda.

Margaritas, chips, and napkins litter our table, around which my closest friends sit. All is back to normal—except for one extremely delicious aspect, of course.

Madison, Tessa, and Bree stare back at me with blindsided expressions. I haven't yet told them the most scandalous thing

I did last weekend.

"I'm back on track, though," I reassure them. "I'm back to being same ole vegetarian Erin. Well, almost the same." I mumble the last part, but nothing gets past Bree.

"What is that supposed to mean?" She pulls on my arm, her dramatic fashion having no bounds. "Did something happen between you and British McBabe?"

Keeping what happened between Oliver and me to myself all week has been exciting. One coy glance from him makes the most boring parts of my day thrilling due to our own dirty little secret.

But it's margarita night, and we're at the place where secrets are shared.

Celebrations are had. And memories are made.

It's time to tell them.

Besides, withholding this piece of gossip from my friends would be like lying to a priest during confession.

"As a matter of fact… we hooked up," I chirp, and I get squeals of excitement with a hint of disbelief in return.

It's obvious they didn't think I'd go there, but I definitely did.

I, Erin Hayes, certified good girl, let my boss go down on me last weekend, and I have no regrets.

"What?"

"How?"

"What does this mean for you two?"

"I don't know what it means, and I wouldn't have to even think about that had you not left me stranded!" I shriek.

"I don't have a car, nor have I driven a car in nearly ten years. You know this!" Bree points at me with her half-eaten chip. "Besides, from the sound of it, I did you a favor. You should be feeding me grapes and writing me poems."

"Hardly." I roll my eyes and nudge her with my shoulder, then pick up my margarita and try to take a sip.

But I'm smiling too hard.

I've been smiling since we left the camp a few days ago, through every meal, class, and workout.

Even after-school detention has been a joy. Not because I'm glad to see the students there—just the opposite—but my inflated good mood has seemed to rub off on the kids. We haven't had too many repeat incidents with the same ones this week.

It's all because of Oliver.

"The dopey look on your face says otherwise." Bree points to me and looks to Tessa and Madison for backup, which they offer with hums and knowing grins.

"Okay!" I toss my hands up. "Oliver makes me feel… amazing." Dreamy sighs echo all around.

"I mean, at first, he made me feel crazy and ridiculous, but I had him pegged all wrong. He's as attentive and charming as he is downright hot and sexy." I fan myself. "Seriously, what he did to me in the cabin was filthy, but I felt so safe and worshiped." I shimmy in my seat and touch the back of my hand to my warm cheeks.

I'm close to grabbing an ice cube from my drink to run down my face and chest like I'm in a damn cheeseburger commercial.

"Oh my God." Madison taps my forearm. "Do you need to get a room for some *alone* time?"

"You look and sound like you're in a romance novel." Bree scoots her drink to the side, leaving a trail of salt and spilled margarita along the way. "Here's some space to work through your feelings."

"I think it's great to see you this way." Tessa bounces in

place and claps, her glasses falling to the edge of her nose. "You deserve it."

"I just can't fucking believe you three." Bree shakes her head. "How the hell is it possible for you all to get stuck with guys, and then fall for them? Although, if I had to pick any scenario, I'd pick the cabin like you and Carter." She points at Tessa.

"Yours could happen soon," Madison sings. "I recommend staying away from small spaces, though. It's not as sexy if you're stranded in a sewer or some shit."

Tessa nods. "True."

"Oh, don't worry. I already thought of the perfect plan." Bree licks her lips. "I'm going to hide out at a fire station until I'm trapped there with the hunky firefighter from June."

"What happened in June?" I ask. "I'm talking about the calendar."

"Oh," the rest of us draw out in unison, followed by a burst of laughter.

I hold my drink up and urge them to do the same. "Cheers to being stuck together!" "Hell yeah," Madison says and is the first to clink my glass with hers.

Once we swallow our sips, I lean in and whisper, "I bet sex with Oliver will be *Fifty Shades of Grey* level, but without the kinks..."

"What do you mean?" Madison quirks her brow. "That level is *all* the kinks." "Whoa!" Bree jolts forward. "I thought you slept with British McHottie." She

leaves the underlying question hanging in the air. "No, we just hooked up a little." I shrug.

"You can't hook up *a little*. That's like saying Tessa was *kind of* a virgin when she started college, which she totally was. Fondling tits and a finger bang do not qualify for losing a V-card."

Tessa snorts. "I already took that back. What else do you want from me?"

"Then what would you, oh wise one, call two orgasms in a row by mouth and fingers?" I face her and blink rapidly with more sarcasm than a parrot.

"Hooking up is what sorority girls do at a frat house, or ironically enough, at summer camp—sex," Bree shoots back. "Making love is what old married couples do in their bed after dark. Fucking is what one-night stands are for, which can— and should— be dirty, filthy, bed-breaking, earth-shattering nights. Should I go on?"

"Please, stop." Mads holds one hand out and uses the other to wipe drops of margarita off her chin. "You've said enough."

"And yet, you didn't answer my question," I say.

"Right." Bree snaps her fingers and points at me. "What you did was high school shit."

"Didn't feel that way," I mutter with a mischievous edge to my tone.

"I think it's hot when a guy is there for you and not just the other way around," Tessa comes to my defense.

"Thank you! Oliver and I have not had sex yet, but our connection was out of this world," I insist.

"How can you form such an attachment to a person whose dick you haven't seen?" Bree cries out, turning a few heads our way.

My cheeks on fire, I clamp my hand over her mouth to shush her, and across the table from us, Madison and Tessa duck their heads lower.

"All I'm saying is," Bree starts in a sarcastic whisper as she swats my hand away. "He could have a weird sex fetish that you'll probably overlook because you're already emotionally attached, and the next thing we know, you'll stop coming to margarita nights because you're in some cult, where they brainwash you into believing sexual favors are required to save your soul."

The bubble of laughter rising in my throat is too forceful to stop, and when it explodes, it's louder than Bree has ever been.

I can't help myself.

"She knows how to paint a picture, doesn't she?" Tessa asks in an amusingly rhetorical way, then sips her drink.

Madison picks up a chip and points it at Bree. "Honestly, I'm worried something similar would happen to *you*, although I'm not positive it hasn't already."

"No, my sexual favors are totally voluntary for the sake of pleasure and fun." Our adventurous friend shrugs. "Besides, I can't let my talents go to waste. I'm *very* good, whether we're doing it in a bed, against a bathroom stall at a bar, or on the beach after a Fourth of July cookout."

Madison tsks as Tessa pins her with a stare. "All we're saying is—no dark alleys on your own, and no more underground tours with strange guys who smell like shrimp."

Bree taps her chin like she really needs to think about heeding Tessa's warning, then relents, "Fair enough."

"By the way," I start. "When was the last time you went on a real date?" The three of us turn to Bree, who now taps her chin in actual contemplation.

"If the underground tour guide doesn't count, then it's been a few months." She keeps her eyes cast downward on the dewy pitcher as she fills her glass.

"*Months*?" we all repeat and simultaneously lurch forward.

"Why are you so surprised?" She furrows her eyebrows and smiles, seemingly more relaxed than if she were at a winery. "It's not like I've ever dated much to begin with. You know me—meet someone at a bar, club, or grocery store and spend the night with them before going home for a satisfying night's sleep in my own bed." She quickly sips her drink and holds a finger up. "There was the guy I met at the aquarium too. He was so hot we had a repeater at my place, for once."

I snort, and the other two shake their heads.

"It's how I've chosen to live my life, okay?" Bree spreads her arms, and I must say, I admire her confidence. "Besides, why would I want to go on an actual date? Look at how many of Erin's dates have ended in more disappointment than the final episode of *Dexter*."

My smile falters. "But I did meet someone."

"Which proves my point. You've never actually gone out with Principal Skilled Tongue, but you're totally into him. So, dates are useless sometimes."

"I hate to say it, but you make a lot of sense." Tessa rests her elbow on the table and shrugs toward the rest of us. "Carter and I didn't go out before we fell for each other."

"Same with Ian and me." Madison nods.

We all lapse into silence as the revelation sinks in like the crushed ice in the margarita pitcher.

"Did we just make a dating discovery?" Bree whispers. "I think we could sell this anti-dating secret to *Cosmopolitan* for a fortune."

We toast to our imaginary millions—well, Tessa technically has billions, but that's beside the point.

For the rest of the evening, we finish one more pitcher—

classic lime—while we discuss Tessa's bachelorette party, which kicks off tomorrow with a trip to Vegas. It's what my students might call a banger. If they were old enough to enjoy a weekend in Sin City the right way, that is.

The four of us debated skipping margaritas tonight since we'll be together all weekend, but then we agreed we wouldn't really have the chance to catch up since a few of Tessa's other friends will be joining us too.

Plus, they wanted the details of being stranded at the camp, which I was more than happy to dish.

This is the first time I've had something to gush about, since I normally only have horror stories to recount, and I was not going to pass this up.

Tonight, I had a story of hooking up—that's what I'm going with, no matter what Bree thinks—with my boss. It's more delicious than the final sip of my margarita.

At the end of the night, I grab my jacket off the back of my chair and stand with the girls as we wave goodbye to Harvey.

Bree gives him a wink, too, because old habits die hard, indeed.

As I ride in the cab toward my apartment, I still have a certain Brit on the brain, and the second I step inside my door, my phone vibrates with an incoming call.

Oliver.

Smiling, I swipe to answer, and the first thing he asks is, "Are you a Pepsi or a Coca-Cola fan?"

Humming, I settle onto my couch and pull a throw blanket over my legs, my skirt from school fanned out around me. "This is a very important question I need to ponder."

He chuckles, and I hear a ding in the background on his end. "Where are you?" I ask.

"The supermarket." After a pause, he urges, "As for my question, what do you

say?"

"I'd say Coke because there's extra carbonation and an overall better taste for the

buds."

"I beg your pardon—buds?" "Taste buds. That's all I meant."

"If I weren't at the supermarket, I'd tell you what direction my head took."

My giggle gets caught in my throat, and a sound much like gagging escapes me, instead.

"Now, back to our discussion—you presented your idea with clear facts to back it up. I'm rubbing off on you," he says, and I envision he's smirking right in the middle of the aisle next to the two-liters.

"Since I'm alone in my apartment, can I tell you what dirty direction my thoughts just went?"

"I'd absolutely love to hear it, but I fear you'd miss your bachelorette party if you did."

"How so?"

There's another short pause before he says in a low voice, "If you tell me what cheeky thoughts you're having, you'd leave me no choice but to come over and do something about it, except I'd need all weekend to show you just how chuffed I'd be."

A shiver runs down my spine, and I shake in my spot from the sexy promise in his tone.

Knowing he's in public and making these comments makes this so much hotter too. "I could skip the party. Who wants to go to Vegas on a billionaire's private jet, anyway?" I bite my bottom lip.

I'd never miss the party for my best friend, of course, especially not because I'm hornier than Bree in heat, but it doesn't stop my imagination from running freely. What this man would do to me if he were here right now…

"Sounds positively awful," Oliver says, playing along.

"Totally," I joke. "Extravagant clubs, drinks, and hot strippers—*blech*." He groans. "Don't remind me of the latter."

I tuck my foot underneath me and grin. "I'm sorry, but is Oliver Westbrook jealous of oiled-down dancers?"

"If jealousy means I'm seeing red because the aforementioned oiled-down dancers will be shaking their plonkers in your face, then… yes, I'm jealous."

"I wish I could see your face right now."

"And I wish I would've called you when I was alone in my flat," he says. "The woman buying a Sprite clearly did not appreciate our conversation before she stalked off."

I throw my head back and let my laugh loose.

"You're going to pay for making me suffer and laughing at my expense." "No, no. I'm not laughing *at* you. Just *with* you," I say in between snorts as I

struggle to clear my throat. "What will you be doing this weekend, anyway?"

"I'm attempting to cook for Rebecca and Malcolm tomorrow night, but that's all I have planned." He sighs. "I wanted this weekend to be relaxing, but I have a feeling I'll resort to cleaning the baseboards out of boredom by the end of it."

"I can have my friend Bree send you over some enlightening quizzes to get to know yourself better. Things like what *Bridgerton* character you most resemble, whether you believe Ross and Rachel were, in fact, on a break, or if your earthly age is the actual age of your soul."

There's a pause, and then I hear, "Oh, Christ." "Now, I definitely wish I was there to see your face."

"And I can't wait to see you when you return, mostly because if I reach the point of doing those kinds of quizzes, I'll need help regaining my sanity."

"Is that the only reason?" I ask half-jokingly, half-Ross-and-Rachel-*were*-on-a- break serious.

Although, I will argue until the end of time that Ross was still out of line to sleep with the girl from the copy place so soon after Rachel mentioned the break.

But I concur.

"No." Oliver's voice sobers, and all thoughts of my favorite *Friends* couple fly out the window. "The main reason is that I want to take you on a proper date."

My exhale comes out in a forceful whoosh, and I clutch my chest.

He's such a gentleman. Dwayne, the last guy to take me out, asked me to dinner via Facebook messenger. If that alone wasn't bad enough, his exact words were, "*There's a new place that's supposed to be fire. Get lit with me?*"

It should've been enough of a warning to indicate he didn't have a PhD, nor would he be my forever.

Oliver must be my reward. He's so different.

We've been sneaking around all week and pretending he didn't go down on me with the drive and intensity of a Greek god. Even though it's been difficult keeping the flirting and touching under wraps, it's been exciting.

And hot.

Being so secretly intimate with the boss is *so* much hotter than I ever thought it could be.

FIFTEEN

Oliver

I tap my thumb against my thigh as the city vibrates outside the window. Erin has been absent all weekend, and I can't stand it any longer.

I promised her a night out, and while I plan to keep my word, I need her now.

The last few days were pleasant enough. Dinner with my sister and nephew was the main highlight. They came over to my flat, and Malcolm asked several questions about my décor—and lack thereof.

He made his mum promise they'd bring me a fern the next time they visited just to liven up the place, and I appreciated his candidness, as I do his mother's.

They had plans for the rest of the weekend to visit one of her friends in Connecticut, or else I would've asked to meet them again. Not just because I was bored and did, in fact, resort to cleaning the baseboards after I watched the Atlanta Rising Football Club match at Deidra's pub. It was a close game, but unfortunately, the excitement of it didn't last long.

In any case, I wanted to see my family again because dinner at my place was one of the best nights yet. We played games, and Malcolm told me of the hot summer day he spent at Coney Island with his father before he passed.

He was animated and detailed, describing everything from the messy hot dog he ate to the exact color of the ocean that day. I was delighted to see such affection in his eyes for his father.

Rebecca must've seen how well we were getting along. While Malcolm busied himself with my collection of *Harry Potter*, which I bought specifically for his perusal, my sister told me more about her own father.

"He did his best," she said at dinner. "I had a toolbox with my name on it before I'd gotten my first tube of mascara, and I might've been the last of my friends to buy my first bra. But Dad did all right."

"He certainly did," I agreed.

And because my sister is an open book, she proceeded to tell me all about her trip to the store for her first bra. Her grandmother was occupied with a weekend-long Scrabble tournament at the senior center, so her father was the lucky bastard to accompany her.

"He ended up tossing me his credit card and asked if I could meet him at the food court once I was finished," she told me, her smile nostalgic and appreciative.

Overall, we had a whale of a time, and the only person I wanted to talk to about it was on the other side of the country.

While Erin was away, I made myself useful and re-read the school handbook for the tenth time, focusing specifically on faculty relationships. Although it's not technically against the rules, romantic involvement between staff and their superiors is heavily frowned upon since it opens the door to unfair favoritism, leniency, and other issues.

But I'm confident in my ability to maintain an objective stance when it comes to my work. I've never wavered from ethically and effectively fulfilling my duties, and I'm not going to start now—no matter how positively intoxicating the math teacher is.

As I exit the cab, a tall apartment building looms over me, stretching high in the evening sky. I pull my phone out and ring Erin.

"Have you returned home?" I ask as I climb the steps, one foot in front of the other. So simple.

Yet, I'm more wound up than if I'd just run a marathon.

"I am," Erin says, ending on a sigh and a slight *oof* as if she just plopped onto the couch.

"I suppose you might want to be alone, then." It's more of a question than a statement, and I hope to God her answer is no.

I'm pleasantly satisfied when she says, "If you recall, I hate being alone." "That's a relief."

"Why?" she asks as I raise my hand to knock on the door, a big brass *2D* staring back at me. "Sorry, hang on. There's someone at the door…"

She swings it open, her jaw dropping as if the shock itself pulled it open, and I sweep in to capture those lips, eager to taste her.

"Being without this mouth for three days has been

absolute torture," I mumble against her soft but fervent lips and kick the door closed behind me.

No need for prying eyes.

Especially considering what I'd like to do to her.

Speechless, Erin melts against me, her body falling slack and brilliantly heavy in my hold.

But she kisses me back with as much zealous desire as I'm feeling, and I scoop her up, one hand around her back and the other under her knees.

Nuzzling her neck, I walk us to her bedroom, except…

I curse under my breath and pull back. "It just occurred to me that I have no idea where I'm going, nor do I know if you even have a roommate. You've never mentioned one, but there could—"

She places her hand on my cheek and stops me, her smiling lips a breath of fresh air. "First, the door behind me is the bedroom. Second, I have no roommate. And third, *hurry*."

Bloody Christ, I love how in tune we are with each other after such a short time.

It's only been a week since the infamous calamity at the camp, a disaster which surprisingly changed my life for the better.

Placing her back on her feet, I continue kissing her in the same way I'd like to make love to this woman—tenderly yet full of passion.

I want to devour her.

She makes quick work of my pants, and the clinking belt buckle is like an alarm of warning ringing in my head.

"Wait, wait." I swallow in an attempt to tamp down my carnal urges and catch my breath. "Are you sure you want to do this? I know I showed up unannounced, and I still would like to take you out."

Her eyelids flutter, and my gaze falls back to her swollen lips. "But I'd also very much like to fuck you," I say in a gruff voice.

A visible shiver runs through the length of her body like an electric current, and she leaps back into my arms. "God, yes," she breathes and smashes her mouth to mine with more force than I'd expect from such a small person. "I've discovered dates are sometimes useless, anyway."

"What do you mean?"

She claws at me to bring us closer. "No time to explain—I need you."

We're frantic, urgently ripping at each other's clothes and scattering them along her floor in a messy trail of desire.

The first thing I notice is the dainty bow of her bra, playful and cute just like her. The small ribbon sits between two heaving breasts, and I'm mesmerized by them—and all of her.

My hand is wrapped around my loosened tie, my shirt wide open, when she gasps. "What is it?" I freeze.

"You have a... tattoo." Her eyes bulge the longer she stares at it. "Is it a good thing, or does it turn you off?" I ask hesitantly.

"Not at all." She gulps, and lust flashes across her coffee-colored eyes, bright flecks of hazel swimming in them like sparks of a fire. "I have so many questions, but like I said, there's no time."

Erin resumes plucking her clothes off in hasty fashion. "I've wanted you since the first day we met," she says in a rushed voice as we fall into bed with a bounce, her bra and panties still covering the parts I'm craving to pay special attention to.

My pants grow tight as she bites her lip, and I nearly

blackout when she reaches a tentative hand between my legs.

"Really?" I whisper, and a single word has never been this difficult to utter. "The first day?"

She nods and scoots closer, tightening her grip around my achingly aroused length.

My abs squeeze as I peer down between us where her thumb rubs my head over the fabric. What she's doing sends pulsing pleasure through my body, and she has yet to touch my naked skin.

"You are a cheeky little minx, aren't you?" I growl.

I didn't know what to expect when I came over. I just knew I wanted to see her, but this... this is beyond brilliant.

"Your tie is still hanging from your shoulders." She drops her heated gaze to my lips and grabs my balls in her palm. "I need everything *off.*"

Dear God.

This woman is surprising me at every turn. Who knew this woman, with her floral patterns and colorful personality, would have such a sinful side to her?

A woman who knows what she wants is my undoing, and I'm positive Erin Hayes will be the end of me.

I reach up to my chest, where the tie hangs loosely across my pecs. I thought I'd yanked it off when I pulled my shirt off, but evidently, I was in too much of a hurry to get my hands on her to notice.

"Why are you even wearing a tie today? Or do you always wear your school attire on the weekends?" She removes her hand from between my legs and tucks a strand of hair behind her ear.

"No, I also wear ridiculously tight T-shirts I find at summer camps," I joke between labored breaths.

"I like your ties," she whispers.

"Maybe that's why I wore it tonight." As I pull the silky material from around my neck, sliding it across my hot skin, I imagine it on Erin's.

Which gives me an idea.

"How about I make you *love* them?"

Her eyes flash with interest, and underneath it, there's unyielding trust. The way she peers up at me with her wide eyes is something out of an erotic fantasy.

I lay her wrists together over her head on a pillow, and she parts her lips, halfway distracting me as I drag the tie up along her bare waist and arms.

Her pink bra still covers her breasts, taunting me. The delicious anticipation drives me mad with lust, especially as I take in the rest of her.

Erin is petite, but not without soft, feminine curves. Her body is exquisite.

I've had The Met on my list of places to visit for a while, but drinking her in, I suddenly don't feel the pressing need to. She's a work of art herself.

"Oh," she says as understanding dawns.

I tie a knot around her wrists and lick my lips, my body's screams echoing in my head.

I'm fully aware I'm about to be inside of Erin, and the thought alone has me buzzing.

She wiggles under me and glances up to where her hands are joined. "Is this the darker side you mentioned at the cabin?" she whispers in a soft voice that's equal parts seductive and seemingly innocent.

But I know better.

There's a devilish flash of intrigue in her eyes as she waits, like she knows the answer and is thrilled about it.

I start to take my boxers off but stop when I detect a touch of relief. "What did you think it was?" I chuckle.

"I've gone out with a lot of guys who would describe anything from a Fruity Pebbles obsession to murder as dark, so this is... pretty good." She squirms, and I squeeze my thighs around her waist.

"Murder?" I quirk a brow, then hold up a hand. "Let me venture a guess—you'll explain later?"

"Preferably." She struggles in an attempt to lean up but surrenders. "I still need you," she says, a pleading air to her words, and when she runs her tongue along her bottom lip, it urges me forward.

"As you wish." I narrow my eyes and leave the games behind as I drag my legs backward, cupping her breasts and eliciting a moan from her wet lips.

I slide her panties down and deeply inhale. "So perfect," I praise, then pull her ankles through the thin material, eager and straining to make her forget any guy who came before me.

Murderer, or other.

But I practice patience, so she may experience the most pleasure possible.

Leaning over her, I tease my finger up the seam of her slick folds, and she lets out an even louder moan than before.

"Yes," she pants, squirming under my touch.

When I insert a finger into her wet and quivering heat, her eyes shoot open, and she pulls her arms down.

I tsk and move them back above her head. "Don't touch. Just feel," I say, dropping my voice a lower octave.

Her hands relax in my grasp, and I bring my fingers back down the length of her arm as I continue working her.

Erin stretches with each pump of my hand, and I ache to

bury myself there. "That's it." She wiggles. "Right… there."

As she tightens around me, I caress her stomach, then her breast, slipping my hand inside her bra and cursing myself for not removing it already.

All in good time.

Her chest rises and falls at a rapid rate, her bottom lip wedged between her teeth as she tenses.

Almost there.

"Come, Erin." I clamp my teeth around one nipple over the bra, and I can practically feel the scream that roars from her throat as her release spills over my hand and onto the bedspread.

I hum with pleasure as she again tries to bring her arms down.

Chuckling, I put them back into place. "You are trouble, aren't you?" She makes an incoherent sound, and right when her eyes are about to close again, I say, "Keep them open."

She finds me, and I take my time to lick my finger that's soaked in her. "Wow." She gulps.

"And I'm not finished with you."

I slide off the bed, and her gaze follows my every movement as I pull the last of my clothing off, my cock springing free.

I'm so fucking hard.

Erin gives me a once-over, her focus lingering between my legs, and when she gulps again, it's a lot louder this time.

"Is this what you want?" I stroke myself, running my trembling fingers up and down my turgid length as arousal swims in the air.

I'm bursting at the seams, dangerously close to being the older man she fucks who came before he was even inside her.

"Yes, finally," she sputters, nodding with enthusiasm. "Are you ready, love?"

Instead of answering with words, she scoots to the edge of the bed near me, and I meet her there, stepping between her legs and spreading them open.

With my free hand, I reach around her arched back and undo her bra, letting her breasts spill free and uninhibited—exactly the way I like her.

And exactly the way I like myself right now.

Nothing matters outside of these walls, and I'm going to take advantage of this night without worry.

My tip glistens with excitement, and I rub myself along her swollen heat, pausing at her entrance and teasing her.

Erin arches her back higher, like she's attempting to touch the ceiling with her hard nipples, and she starts to pull her arms down but stops.

I didn't have to tell her to keep her arms still this time.

"Good girl." I grind my teeth as sweat beads trail between my shoulder blades from all the energy it's taking to restrain myself and make this good for her.

To make this night unforgettable.

She swallows as she watches me roll on a condom until I finally inch inside her—*dear God in Heaven.*

My feet remain planted on the floor, and I hold her legs up on either side of me.

Once I'm halfway into her, I pull out, then plunge back in deeper, magnificently stretching her tight channel even further.

Each of my breaths is strenuous as I roll my hips, and we both adjust to this new sensation.

The tie around her wrists moves up and down as she squirms against the pillow, her fingers wiggling with arousal like she's playing an imaginary piano.

The minute I start rocking into her, we're more in tune than ever before.

"So… bloody good," I strain. "Do you feel that, Erin? How my balls tighten around you? How my cock fits so perfectly inside you?"

She nods, and her chest heaves to the rhythm of my thrusts.

"Close your eyes," I instruct, and my nostrils flare when she automatically follows my request. "Tell me what you feel, love."

"I…" She licks her lips and moans, the slapping sounds of my body against hers bouncing off the walls and driving me forward. "I feel your hot skin."

"That's right. Give me more." "Your strong hands."

I grip her tighter.

"I hear your strangled breaths."

I sink into her as deep as I can go and pause.

She gasps, and her eyes flutter open and closed. "And your… your pulsing… cock inside me."

My grin is one of victory. She's absolutely sensational.

Her toes curl and dig into my ass as if they're the only things grounding her to the planet during this earth-shattering moment.

And call me competitive, but I want to make her feel even better.

I pull out and flip her onto her stomach, heaving a yelp out of her. I climb onto the bed as well and guide her onto her knees, her ass mine for the fisting. I knead one cheek in my hand as I line up again and plunge inside her.

"Oh, yes. Shit," she cries out as I fuck her hard and fast at this new angle. "Is this how you like it, Erin?"

"Harder."

Did I hear her correctly?

I spread her cheeks with both hands, my balls squeezing and swinging at her clit with each thrust. I fear I'll explode as I rock into her at a dizzying pace, my abs clenching with my impending release.

I'll be surprised if I don't pull a muscle from driving into her like this.

She bounces in front of me, and the headboard knocks on the wall, adding a carnal bass to the music of her moans and my grunts.

Unraveled. That's what I am.

Especially when Erin meets me thrust for thrust, her stomach tight under my palm like she's about to explode too.

She urges me with her cries for release.

And the second I give it to her, my own climax hits me like a freight train, my entire body drumming from this foreign feeling of ecstasy.

I've been with women like this, just as she's been with other men before me, but nothing compares.

As black spots taint my vision, I know there is no *before this.* No past before *us.*

"Fucking hell," I groan and fall onto my side next to her, the condom full and ready to be discarded.

She turns onto her back and swipes at the hair sticking to her damp forehead. "Guess you were bored with all those magazine quizzes, after all, huh? Not as fun and fulfilling?" Her grin is coy, and her cheeks are flushed from a proper shagging.

God, it was proper, indeed.

"Not at all, but this was all that and more." I angle my head toward hers. A small smile stretches across her gorgeous face.

"Agreed."

SIXTEEN

Erin

I cover myself with the comforter, then throw it off my legs—I'm too hot. I shift onto my side, then flip onto my back again.

The bathroom sink turns off, offering me a touch of solace from the noise, but it just means I can hear the city outside louder—and my pounding, nervous heart.

For as blissfully sated as I am right now, I'm also more fidgety than I was when I first applied for my job at the school.

A job I'm risking everything for to be with Oliver. We just had sex.

Mind-blowing, insane sex. It pulled me out of my body, then put me back together again. We can't just take such a phenomenon back, and I definitely can't pretend it never happened.

I never knew it could be like this, and I already fear what this level of chemistry will do to me.

But not fearful enough to stop myself. How can I?

Oliver opens the door and steps into my bedroom. The sheer sight of him has me sitting upright like a king is walking in here.

He wears only his boxers as he stalks toward me. I peruse each lean hill and valley of his sculpted abs and the lines stretched over his round, sinewy shoulders.

A spatter of hair is dusted across his broad chest.

His taut skin is marred only by the one black tattoo, and I wanted so badly to dig my fingernails into it to mark him further.

To claim Oliver Westbrook as mine.

I'd never wanted to touch a man so badly. Maybe it was because I couldn't since my hands were tied up. Not being able to skim my fingers over him was… wow.

Tauntingly erotic.

"Never seen a man before?"

As Oliver crawls into bed with me, the frame squeaks, and the mattress dips and sways under his weight. With his powerful presence, the room is suddenly too small for the both of us.

"No," I answer honestly, and my shy smile spreads slowly as I speak from the heart. "I've never seen a man like you."

"A compliment, I presume?" He rises onto his elbow and walks a finger up my arm—the same one he had inside me, then licked like he enjoyed it more than a finger of expensive scotch.

"Definitely." I reach up, wrap my hands around the back of his neck, and pull him in for a searing kiss.

It sends an awakening flame down my body as I'm hypnotized by him. Who even am I?

I talked somewhat dirty to a man tonight. I fucked my boss.

And I let him tie me up while we did it.

I'd say Bree is rubbing off on me, but it's Oliver. He pulls out a side of me I've never known.

While I'm nervous to see the full effect of it, I'm also giddy.

He lays his head on the pillow but keeps one arm around my waist as he angles himself toward me. "It was absolute torture seeing you around school last week and not being able to touch you."

"I know what you mean." I flatten my palms over the fluffy comforter, smoothing out the wrinkles as my voice shakes through a laugh. "I ran into a kid drinking from the water fountain and splashed water on myself because I was staring at you. Couldn't help it."

He laughs, and even though I've seen and heard it before, it never gets old.

Oliver strokes my cheek, moving the strands of my hair away, and a tic in his jaw winks at me. "About this murderer…"

I bury my face in the pillow as he chuckles again and nudges me to answer the question crowding the room. "I'd rather not comment," I say, my voice muffled by the cushion.

"We can do this the easy way, or I can coax it out of you with a little magic."

"I didn't think you believed in magic." I peek at him, and he pins me with a truthful stare.

"I didn't believe in a lot of things before you." My breath catches.

Some might call me pathetic, but just like that, I'm willing to tell him every one of my secrets, from embarrassing moments to my unrestrained fears.

From my need to wash my running hoodies every Tuesday out of superstition to my morning meditative ritual.

Because when Oliver Westbrook watches me through that hooded gaze of his, my defenses happily crumble.

I tug on a loose thread as I relent and say, "I'm not positive if the guy was a murderer, but he definitely had *killer* instincts."

Curiosity lifts his brow.

I shift to get comfortable as I settle into the story. "We were walking to dinner, and he literally sniffed the air, said there was something rotten coming from the alley, and followed the smell until we reached a dead cat by the dumpster." I take a deep breath. "I was devastated about the animal, but he inspected it like he was a detective or something. When I asked if he was at one point, he said he no, but he had always been intrigued by dead things."

"Please tell me you ran away unscathed." He furrows his brow, and concern replaces his earlier fascination.

"I almost twisted my ankle trying to hurry away. I think that may have been the only time in my dating life I did not apologize for leaving them, and it was the second time I'd ever canceled before we even got to the restaurant."

"Why would you need to apologize? They're the ones who should've taken a good, hard look at themselves and apologized for making you uncomfortable," he states like it's the simplest idea in the world.

It puts me at ease.

"What happened the first time you canceled?" he asks, placing his cheek in his palm against the pillow.

He's never been to my place before this pleasantly unexpected, sexy surprise, but he already seems comfortable and satisfied to be here.

"You don't want to know about my disastrous love life," I warn with a nervous giggle.

He threads his free hand through mine between us. "If it's part of you, I want to know."

"You're going to need to stop saying things like that. Otherwise, I'm going to start believing you're too good to be true," I tease.

But I'm also very serious.

"I mean, you don't even have a flaw," I continue.

"Ha!" He throws his head back. "I have plenty of flaws. Look at this tattoo."

My jaw hangs open as I run my fingers across what he seems to think is an offensive part of him. The curvy strokes and details make the design very unique, and I already love studying it. "This is the opposite of a flaw."

He turns his questioning gaze to me.

"It definitely caught me off guard to find out someone as buttoned up as you would have one of these, and I mean it in the best way. It's hot as hell," I blurt.

But when Oliver pulls me tighter into his side and places a scorching kiss on my lips, I don't care that my tongue is looser around him than a dog running through Central Park.

He obviously likes it.

"What flaw do you actually have?" I ask, still blissfully reeling from this new kind of high.

I lean up onto my elbow for a better look at him. To see for myself if he's telling the truth once he makes this big reveal.

Because until he opens his mouth and tells me he's addicted to the smell of armpits or something of that caliber, I won't be convinced.

"I have to line my shoes up at the door the moment I step

inside my flat." I scoff. "I do the same thing. That doesn't count!"

He snaps his fingers. "I like futbol, which is a colossal flaw to most of you. The teachers, anyway, but I happen to know several Americans who enjoy the sport."

"I've never watched a game."

"Never?" If the man were capable of a squeak, the noise he makes now would be it. I nudge him, and as suspected, he doesn't budge. "We're talking about your flaws, not mine."

"All right, all right." He holds a hand up. "I can't parallel park or dance to save my life. Not with my two left feet."

I chew on the inside of my cheek and shake my head. "Seriously, who's good at parallel parking? And dancing is a skill not many average people possess, either, so try again."

"I'm beginning to think it's a bad idea to list all the things that are wrong with me." He narrows his eyes at me. "Don't want to scare you off."

"With this body?" I run my hand down his bare chest, appreciating his hard-earned muscled pecs. I'm still flabbergasted—for lack of a better term—that he also has a tattoo on this marvel he calls a body. "I think I'll keep it around a bit longer."

Oliver plucks his tongue as I grip his upper arm, my fingers covering only half of it.

"I actually find these flaws endearing, and they make me like you more." I shrug. "In that case, I have plenty more." He smiles and rubs his chin as he seemingly

thinks of another one. "I don't like seafood, and it can be annoying for some people." "Don't you eat pork rinds?" I ask, recalling our conversation on the phone last week when he told me about Deidra's pub. He'd just left there after eating a bunch of the weird and potent snack.

"Yes…"

"But seafood is where you draw the line?" I ask, more confused than surprised by his confession. "Pork rinds are pretty…"

Understanding dawns, and he gives me a tight-lipped, amused smile. "Minging? I

thought so myself at first, but they grew on me."

"I don't understand anything you're saying, starting with minging."

"Right." He scratches his chin. "Disgusting."

"I'm going to add *minging* to my vocabulary," I say. "How about you just tell me about England, instead?"

"Are you trying to distract me from my question about the wanker you left before dinner?" he asks.

"Of course. And if you keep asking, I'll have to pull out the big guns and flash you my boobs."

A dark shadow crosses his usually bright eyes, and it's obvious I've caught him right where I want him. "Tell me about the bloke," he presses, but it's weaker than before, like he's not as interested.

He just wants to provoke me.

I keep my word and yank my shirt up to my chin for a quick show of my bare breasts, the cool air of the room sweeping across my nipples, along with his hungry gaze.

"I'm sorry it had to come to this." I suppress my smile, but I'm sure it can be heard in my voice.

"I'm not." Oliver leans over and kisses me, his body halfway on top of mine, and I happily melt into the bed beneath him.

This is how we spend the next hour, talking and stealing kisses in between.

He tells me about England while he caresses my arms and gets lost in his recollection of his life there. Of the futbol matches he and his friends would get together to watch. Escaping the bustle of London by taking train rides up to Staithes with his parents. It's where he and his father would hunt for fossils along the beach, and he and his mother would explore the countryside and big gardens.

As he reminisces, I detect a twinge of homesickness, and I squeeze his hand in comfort.

Around midnight, he stands and reaches for his pants. "As much as I'd love to stay the night with you, we have to get to school early tomorrow, and I don't have any of my things. Besides, we shouldn't show up together, anyway."

"Totally." I wrap my arms around my bent knees, and a knot of dread forms in my stomach as reality knocks the wind out of me.

"I'm sorry it has to be like this," he says, sincerity infused into each evenly stressed syllable.

Nodding, I straighten my legs and stand, my body already deliciously sore from being with him. We walk together toward the door, our easy conversation transforming into palpable tension like bringing up work was a brick tossed into our glass bubble.

He puts me at ease when he places a firm kiss on my mouth, though, and after I close the door behind him, I exhale with a pleased *whoosh*.

Then I knock on my distressed wooden coffee table for good luck.

SEVENTEEN

Erin

"**R**eal talk—if I was stuck at a camp with him, we would've definitely needed to sign a statement disclosing our dirty relationship by now," Nancy gushes, and the coy gleam in her eye is brighter than the one on any cartoon villain.

This is a similar comment she made last week, but she says it as if it's the first time, probably since most of us are here now instead of the small handful who eat lunch together.

I check my watch, ready to get this meeting started and go home. It's been a long day of teacher-ing, the highlights of which consist of scolding two students who were cheating off each other during a pop quiz and spilling coffee all over my desk.

But it's over, and I survived. My reward is seeing Oliver.

It has now been two weeks since he and I were abandoned

at the camp, and the other teachers have yet to cease their gossip over the matter.

Not that there's necessarily anything to gossip about, as far as they know, but this group tends to make the smallest incident sound like a scandal.

"Nancy, my dog is less delusional than you, and he barks at trees like they're the devil," Bobbie says and rolls her eyes as she sips from her tumbler.

The snappy, pint-sized English teacher lifts the corner of her mouth in a scoff. "You're just jealous that my dating life is more exciting than your boring married one."

"Pa-ha!" Bobbie uses the back of her hand to wipe the spilled soda down her chin, but it doesn't break her snarky stride. "What dating life? The man won't even come to your book club, let alone agree to a date with you."

Katie dips her head, and I suspect it's to hide her grin—she's enjoying this almost as much as I am, and she doesn't know the half of it.

I haven't told her what's transpired between me and the new boss just yet.

Nancy starts to make an excuse for his absence from her beloved group, I'm sure, but Bobbie stops her. "You do not have a dating life with the principal. Please tell me you know this, because unless I hear it, I'll have to start a prayer circle for you."

Nancy sneers. "I'm just saying—he and I wouldn't have walked away from the camp without him knowing my bra size."

We all shake our heads, and I suppress my grin.

It's probably the hardest I've ever fought to contain my laughter.

"I don't understand what you bloody see in him," Oscar cuts in. "What does he have that I don't?"

"Charisma. Muscles. A tie." Nancy ticks each one off her finger. "To name a few." "Ties are overrated," he clips.

"You wear a tie every day," Bobbie points out.

"Aren't we *little Miss Nosy* today?" Oscar throws back at my friend.

"I think ties are, um… nice." I cough in the middle of my sentence as I feel Oliver before I lay eyes on him.

He strides into the lounge quietly, the pads of his loafers gentle but purposeful, his presence loud and commanding.

I had *his* tie wrapped around my wrists while he did filthy things to me a week ago.

We've done more of that since then too. Last night, I surprised him at his place this time, and we almost pierced a hole through his wall while he plowed me into another dimension. It was his response when I told him how much I love him in glasses.

Before I made my confession, I had his hands tied up, but it took about three minutes for him to cave. I would've objected had he not used his teeth to free himself, rendering me totally speechless as he climbed on top.

His only mission was to please me.

Flashes of our night together make my breaths come out in difficult puffs like I'm suddenly at a higher elevation.

"You okay?" Bobbie leans over. "You look a little flushed."

I swear Oliver smirks, but he turns his back to us all too quickly.

Johanna bounces in, too, with more pep than I've seen from her in all the four years I've worked here. She appears tanner too, and—is she wearing actual mascara around her eyes?

She never wears makeup.

Oliver greets us, and we quiet down as he starts the meeting, his shirt a light red that perfectly matches the fall leaves outside.

Once he covers the dreaded—my word for it—parent-teacher conferences next week, he applauds us for a "smashing" kickoff to the new school year, reiterating how fun and insightful the retreat was.

"We're just glad you were stuck there with sweet little Erin, instead of… someone else." Bobbie tips her glittery tumbler up for a slow sip as she cuts her eyes to Nancy.

My friend has some real feisty energy this morning.

Heat floods my face as Oliver coughs, avoiding eye contact as he nods to the vice principal. "Mrs. Peters would like to say something before we conclude this meeting."

As she begins telling us how much she enjoys working with us, I'm distracted by the man next to her. The déjà vu of our first faculty meeting isn't lost on me, either.

Oliver is brooding, and his eyes are tired, likely from our late-night shenanigans. He's so freaking hot.

Will he *punish* me later for not paying attention?

I hope he uses his tie again…

"I'm retiring," Johanna announces, pulling me out of my daydream—I should really stop doing that. "Lawrence and I put in an offer for a condo in Pensacola, and we're finally moving forward with our plans to retire in Florida."

There's a brief pause as the faculty and I absorb the information. We've known this moment would come, but it's been one of those things that we didn't think would really happen. Like when Oscar says he's going to get a dog, but he always makes excuses as to why the timing isn't right.

Or when Karen says she's going to ease up on her complaints over no one refilling the paper tray for the copier—that'll be the day.

But Johanna put in an offer on a house in a state very far from here. She's doing it, and she's leaving, which means…

Nancy's hand flies into the air, and at the same time, she asks, "What does this mean for your position? I know you just announced it, but there are a lot of questions."

"Of course." Johanna smiles with understanding. "I will finish out the school year, and we will search for my replacement in the meantime."

"Will you hire internally?" Karen speaks out and cuts her eyes to Oliver.

Johanna answers, "This is still in the early stages. We have not decided on the details just yet, but I assure you, we will happily and fairly consider hiring internally. If any of you are interested, please think about filling out an application."

A few of the faculty turn to the colleagues next to them, and Nancy wears a smug grin like she's already been offered the job. Oscar folds his arms across his chest, and Oliver frowns.

Why is he frowning?

It's probably because his number two is leaving, and he might be stuck with Karen or Nancy—I'm not positive who would be worse. I don't blame him, but it's still unsettling.

Maybe our late night is not the real reason he's brooding.

"No matter what happens, we will work diligently to make the transition as smooth as we have with Principal Westbrook." Johanna holds her arm out to him. "I know this is yet another change, but that's the way of life, right?"

We all smile in agreement, and I'm still stunned that she's

actually leaving after all this time of dreaming about it.

Johanna hands the proverbial mic back to our boss, and he nods to everyone. "That's all we have for now. More details are forthcoming. In the meantime, keep doing what you're doing."

He doesn't glance in my direction as he walks out of the lounge with Johanna and Rita right behind him, and the rest of us are left to speculate who we think will replace her.

"I don't know, but it definitely won't be me." Bobbie grabs her bag and tumbler, standing with a low huff. "I have a kid to get home to, so I'll leave you all to your theories."

She's the first of the faculty out the door, keys in hand, and it's not just her kid she's heading home for. From what she told Katie and me earlier, it's also her anniversary tonight, and she wants to make dinner for her son and the new babysitter before she and her husband take off.

They're celebrating at one of those fancy steakhouses that require reservations to be made weeks in advance, and while she described the eclectic menu, all I could picture was my date with Oliver.

He said he wants to take me out, and I'm giddy just at the thought, especially after this last week. We've gone out for coffee, but with our busy schedules, we just haven't set a time and day yet for the big date.

The truth is, I don't need a real date to know how I feel about him, and vice versa.

Every touch, small or firm, tells me all I need to know on that front.

"What are you daydreaming about over here?" Katie nudges me, and I realize we're the only two left in the lounge. "Are you thinking about applying for the job?"

"For vice principal?" I stand and run my damp palms over my skirt. It's now wrinkled from sitting too long, and as I smooth it out, I notice a few stray drops of coffee stained in the pink fabric. I was likely caught in the line of fire during the spill earlier. "It's not for me," I say absentmindedly.

"Why not? You'd be great at prioritizing the budget for things we actually need— specifically, SMART boards. They would change my life. *Seriously.*"

"Here's a thought," I say over my shoulder as I make my way toward the door. "Why don't you apply? Out of all the faculty, you're the one I'd trust the most in that position. I'm not just saying it because we're friends, either."

Katie scoffs, following close on my heels. "No way. I wouldn't get ten feet near that job."

"It's not a bear." I laugh as we walk down the hall, our shoes clicking and tapping along the tile.

"It might as well be." We round the corner and run into Tommy, but instead of stopping to talk and play the coy googly-eyed game she normally does, Katie barely makes eye contact at all.

I have to skip to catch up with her after she races past him, but when I reach my friend, I whisper, "What was that about?"

"Hmm? Oh, Mr. Hall?" Her voice rises to a dangerously squeaky octave as sarcasm seeps through. "We decided to part ways but keep things civil."

I place my hand on her arm and stop us next to the lockers, which are close to Oliver's office and near the front door. "What happened?"

When she exhales, more than just a breath seems to leave her. It's like a whole wall melts away, exposing her sad and vulnerable exterior. "He dumped me."

"When? And why have we not talked about this? I can't believe I just called you a friend," I tease in an attempt to diffuse the tension holding her hostage.

It doesn't seem to work, though.

"It happened last night." She slumps against a locker. "I was going to tell you this morning before class, but I'm so humiliated. I knew he wasn't ready for anyone new after his divorce, but I was stupid enough to think I could be the kind of woman to bring him out of his funk. I really didn't want anything serious, but evidently, even a fling was too much for him."

"Don't blame yourself." I rub her upper arm. "From the sound of it, this can be explained by the cheesy, but true in this case, cliché—it's not you; it's him."

She smooths her hand over her thick blonde ponytail and laughs, the quiet sound carrying down the empty hallway. "I'm sorry to complain like this to you. I know you haven't had any luck lately, either."

My response gets caught in my throat like the corner of my rug did in the vacuum last week. I make the same gurgling sound too.

Do I lie or tell her the truth about what's going on with Principal Sexy Body with a Tattoo?

Speaking of Oliver…

I smell his cologne, not because it's so strong, but because it's spicy and unique.

The earthy scent makes it seem like he's constantly smoking a cigar. In a blink, he's right beside us.

"Ladies," he greets us. "I figured you would've left already. The rest ran out of here faster than horses loose from their starting gates."

"Except for one," Katie mumbles while I suppress the

need to twirl my hair like I'm a student here and not a teacher.

A teacher who's sleeping with the principal and can't wait to do it again.

Tommy passes us and risks nearing Katie's atmosphere of rage by reaching over to fist-bump Oliver. "See you tomorrow, boss."

"I'll see you later." Katie gently squeezes my arm and takes off in the opposite direction as Tommy. She must've parked in the farthest lot on purpose since their night didn't end well.

"So…" Oliver checks over both shoulders, and even though we're alone, he still stands with a couple feet between us, his voice low. "I think we should speak about what was just announced."

"Sure. I'm happy to help however I can," I offer, keeping my tone professional in case Rita or Johanna pops around the corner.

"That's very gracious, but it's not what I'm referring to." He adjusts his tie, and my ovaries swoon.

My notions of the normally boring accessory have forever been changed. "Eri—I mean, Ms. Hayes?" Oliver stares down at me. "Does that sound good?" I lick my dry lips and swallow to wet my even drier throat. "Excuse me?"

There's a bounce in his cheek as he asks, "Can you meet me at a coffee shop in fifteen minutes? I'll text you the address."

"As long as it's not the one on Seventh and Thirteenth," I joke. "The coffee is great, but that's where my stalker waits for me."

He tilts his head. "I definitely need to hear more about that and ensure your safety."

I wave him off. "As you may have noticed, there are plenty of other amazing places to get coffee."

The pinch between his brows deepens, and after a pause, he relents.

"Are you about to tell me you have another 'flaw'?" I curl my fingers into quotations, bringing up the game we've been playing over the last week. But instead of confessing actual flaws, he still claims things like not loving peanut butter or frozen custard. To me, these mild revelations just make him more endearing in my eyes.

Besides, frozen custard is okay, but I much prefer gelato or plain ice cream myself. "Because if you tell me you hate sunshine and gray sweatpants, I'll have to seriously rethink our involvement." I tap my finger against my chin and say, "Oddly, I'd prefer the former if it's between the two."

"Why gray, in particular?" he asks, and believing it's a joke, I laugh.

Who isn't aware of the magic of gray sweatpants? Although, perhaps it's more of a shared phenomenon outside of Oliver's jurisdiction.

"We still have a lot to learn about each other," I say, leaving a hint of a question in the air. "Start with coffee?"

"Absolutely." The touch of amusement coloring his features now fades.

I thought I'd put him at ease, but it appears it's going to take more than a few jokes about stalkers and sweatpants.

As I skirt around him, I clutch my phone to my chest and impatiently anticipate his text.

I arrive at the quaint little café a few blocks from the school, grab a soy latte, and take a seat in the corner. I figure Oliver chose this instead of the one directly down the street from the school because it's less likely there will be prying eyes around here.

In any case, the shop is, as he would say, quite lovely. White and pale teal tiles line the walls behind me, and overflowing green ferns hang in each corner. The glass case of muffins larger than my fist or current appetite sit on pink plates. White doilies beneath them add to the charm, and next to muffins, slices of different-colored cakes and thick cookies are neatly arranged.

With the busy few weeks I've had, I haven't had time to bake anything for myself or my neighbor who enjoys my chocolate energy balls. The first time I took them over, Mrs. Jenkins thought they were cake pops and gave one to her granddaughter, who quickly spit it out. Once I explained that they're high in oatmeal and fiber but low in sugar and delicious taste, we had a good laugh over it.

And I won the granddaughter over when I brought her regular, yummy cake pops. Heat trickles down my arms when Oliver enters the coffee shop, and his piercing

blue eyes land on me. Over the other patrons' heads, he nods toward the counter in a questioning gesture that asks if I need anything, and I hold up my warm cup in answer.

A couple of minutes later, he has his coffee in hand and takes strides faster than the rhythm of the soft music playing overhead.

"Hi," I breathe as he slides onto the chair across from me.

He smiles, but it doesn't reach his eyes, nor does it settle my nerves. When he remains on the edge of his seat like he needs a quick escape, my inner thighs start sweating where they meet out of panic.

"Listen," he begins, shifting on the wooden chair. "I know things are complicated between us. I showed up unannounced last weekend, and the spiral it's caused has royally muddled our situation further. I want you to know that I am sorry."

Oh, God.

My heart sinks into my stomach faster than a blink.

Stunned, I sit back. "You didn't seem sorry when I left last night," I say, cringing at how weak I sound.

Oliver reaches across the table and takes my hand in his large, comforting one, confusing me further. "That's not at all how I meant it," he says, leaning over so only I can hear. "Bollocks. I'm not sorry at all for what we've done or how I feel about you."

I relax into my seat, but I'm still not sure where this conversation is going. "Then what are you apologizing for?"

He drags a hand over his tired eyes. "For making a mess of our professional relationship."

I raise a brow.

"If you want to apply for the vice principal position, I won't stop you, but obviously, we'll have to stop whatever is budding—"

"Whoa, whoa. That's what this is about?" I push forward and place my other hand on his. "I don't want the job."

"You don't?"

"I've only been working at the school for four full years, and I still have so much to learn. Although I'd like to work my way up someday, that day is not now." I ease into what I believe is a reassuring smile.

"Are you positive? I'd hate to be the one to stand in your way." He twists his lips into a guilty grimace.

"Oliver," I say gently, appreciating how torn he is over this morally gray area we've dug ourselves into. But ending things between us is not the answer. "You're very sweet to be so considerate, but I don't want the job."

He blows out a long breath and gives me a real grin. "Then would you like to accompany me to dinner tomorrow night?"

His request, along with the glowing expression of hope he gives me, makes my heart flutter. What started off as a rocky conversation has turned into a special moment— a proposal for a date. He's asking me in person like a true gentleman too.

No Facebook Messenger or sleazy Instagram DM.

On a relieved exhale, I say, "I thought you'd never ask."

EIGHTEEN

Oliver

"You look beautiful." I kiss Erin on her blushing cheek.

"Thank you. Bree said I had to wear this dress tonight, and if you'd met her, you'd know she's just not the kind of person you disagree with."

"I can see why you wouldn't—it's a fantastic choice." I drink her in, appreciating the way the dress falls over her narrow hips with ease, and I'm practically salivating by the time my admiring gaze reaches the black pumps on her feet. The heels add a few inches to her height, but the top of her head still only reaches my neck.

My throat bobs as I attempt a slow swallow and tamp

down my caveman instincts to haul her into the bedroom. There are no words to describe what she does to me, but simply put, Erin makes me happy.

And very bloody hard.

"Shall we?" I rasp and offer her my arm.

Erin finishes putting her coat on, covering up the beautiful dress much to my dismay, then accepts my arm. Using her free hand to smooth down my wool coat, she says, "You look pretty great yourself."

As we exit her apartment building and walk to the restaurant for our very first real date—meeting for coffee hasn't counted—her wicked heels click along the sidewalk to the beat of the city.

The chatter of people crowding patios while they enjoy the last bit of sun before it sets. Scattered fire pits and heaters roaring to life. Plentiful honks and construction workers shouting instructions over the beeping of their machinery.

And right in the heart of it all, this gorgeous young woman and I chat about our day, her friends and their margarita night tradition, and how marvelous things are with my sister.

Not to jinx anything—as Erin would say—but things in my life are going rather splendidly.

I thought we'd hit a snag when Johanna gave me her notice. I believed Erin might want the job, which would bring our heated nights to a devastating halt in order to avoid any conflict of interest and other minging possibilities. But I trust her to tell me the truth about her wants and desires in her career as she does in the bedroom.

Since the beginning, she's told me exactly how she feels, and it's no different with this.

At the elegant French bistro, we check in our coats at the door, and I lead her

toward the hostess stand as she skips to keep up with my long strides, the patter of her heels quickening.

"Welcome. What is the name on the reservation?" the woman with her hair tied back asks in a polite and chipper tone.

"Westbrook."

"Right this way." As she leads us toward a corner table, one I requested over the phone, we pass white-washed brick walls and vast open windows that stretch from the floor to the ceiling, beyond which is a brilliant view of twinkling skyscrapers. The bar is dimly lit with shades of deep red cast over it, as is the rest of the intimate and romantic space. To add, the vintage sofas delicately placed to one side bring together the ambiance of the room and are rather delightful.

"You made a reservation?" Erin asks, eyeing me as I pull the chair out for her. "And you're so well mannered?"

"Of course, but none of this is hardly so impressive." I search her stunned expression, the logic behind it lost on me. "What?"

"I had to ask my Ouija board to pick a restaurant for a recent date. Anything was better than letting him take me to TGI Friday's for half-priced appetizers and nothing else." She snorts, then covers her mouth as she sits. "Sorry."

I smirk. "Again, you're not the one who should be apologizing."

Once she settles in, I round the table and take my own seat. "One of these days, I'm going to need to find all these pathetic blokes who didn't treat you well and teach them a lesson about being a gentleman."

"That would be advantageous for their future wives, but I'm afraid they wouldn't take out their AirPods or stop playing their video games long enough to listen." She shrugs, and her hair falls forward as she picks up the menu.

Her lips slightly move as she takes in each dish, and she sways in her seat to the piano music.

How could anyone take their eyes off this woman?

I haven't been able to stop myself from studying every inch of her since I picked her up.

Not only is she stunning, but she's also witty, intelligent, and refreshing.

Their loss; my gain.

Once we order, I clasp my hands together on the table between us and ask, "Speaking of other blokes as we were, how was Vegas?"

"Smooth," she teases. "How long have you been holding that one in?"

"You've been back for eight days, so…" I pretend to count on my fingers. "Eight days."

"Do you really want to talk about male dancers on our very first date?" "So, you did go to a strip show, then?" I say, careful to speak low.

The edges of her lips twitch with smug amusement, and I instantly regret asking the question. I don't even want to know the answer, especially since her cheeky expression makes me think she enjoyed it.

"You're right." I wave my hand. "We should talk about something else." She pauses, and it makes me squirm even more.

What is wrong with me? I never fucking squirm.

The volume of the piano seems to rise, the keys played with increased passion and fervor. At any other time, I'd appreciate it, but right now, my blood boils more and more with each deafening note.

Why isn't she responding?

Finally, she shakes her head and says, "Seeing your jealous face in person is definitely more worthwhile than hearing it over the phone."

"I'm not jealous," I insist and adjust my tie. It suddenly feels too tight. "Simply curious."

"Well, if you *were* jealous, I'd tell you how… sexy I find it." She idly toys with the stem of the water glass, and when she locks eyes with me, she slowly licks her lips in a way that makes me question everything I once knew to be true.

"I'm absolutely jealous," I mutter and fight with Herculean strength to keep my growl out of my admission.

Her grin is wide and victorious as she picks up her water for a sip, and I'm instantly so hot I could dump the glass over my head.

"Your wine," the server announces, thankfully pulling me out of this temptress's seductive mind games.

But it is certainly not over.

We will address this again when we're in private, and it will be nothing short of magnificent.

He presents a red for me and a white for her, and once we're alone again, we clink our glasses in a toast. "Cheers," I say.

I revel in my sip of Pinot Noir, the berry flavor and earthy tones a smashing combination. With the faint spicy taste on my lips, I peer at Erin, who does the same with her own wine, turning it over on her tongue with enthusiasm.

The air of the night swirls with possibilities like the wine in our glasses, and I've never felt as carefree as I am right now.

It's ironic since this is the most serious rule I've ever broken.

But it doesn't matter. Not right now when Erin and I are

having such a lovely time. "Did you say you have a Ouija board?" I ask, recalling what she'd said about a previous date.

"Yes, and before you give me one of your lectures, I'm aware it's a silly game." She narrows her gaze at me.

I tsk. "I was just going to ask to see it sometime." "Only if you behave."

"But where's the fun in that?" I tease over the rim of my glass, and again, my trousers grow tighter. If this weren't such a classy place, I'd sneak my hand under the table, find her leg, and snake my palm up between her thighs.

I'm not brazen or disrespectful like the other guys she's gone out with, and although I pride myself on that, how am I supposed to get through our meal with thoughts like this?

I'm absolutely charmed by this woman.

"I can see where this is going, so how about we discuss something else?" she offers with a twinkle in her eye.

"Tell me more about your friends," I suggest, suppressing a frustrated groan.

Over the course of our dinner, we talk with ease. The words flow between us like the ones in a Hemingway novel, smooth and insightful.

Raw and sincere.

Yesterday, Erin mentioned that she and I have much to learn about the other—and we do—but we also know each other rather well.

Our connection is so strong already that reading each other is second nature. I never thought it was possible, but she's definitely showing me that inexplicable phenomena exist.

One of the main miracles she's showing me is that I can be… fun.

Erin makes me want to let loose and do things I wouldn't normally partake in. By the time we finish our meal, my stomach is pleasantly full. Yet, I'm feeling lighter than I have in months.

And randy.

But there's one more thing we need to do before I give into temptation.

I place my hand on Erin's lower back and lead us toward the front of the restaurant for our coats. While I help hers over her shoulders, she peeks over at me. "My place, or yours?"

"You read my mind, but…" I lick my lips, mentally running through a spreadsheet of timelines for the evening. "I sort of made plans."

"With another woman on the same night?" She whirls around.

"No!" I slip my arm inside her coat and wrap it around her waist, uncaring that people might see us. No one we work with is here to witness how intimately I touch her, so I continue holding her as I say, "I thought I'd already convinced you that I'm not a wanker like the others you've dated, but it appears I'll have to work harder."

She buries her face in her hands and leans against my chest, groaning. "I'm so sorry."

The hostess's stare on us grows heavy and uncomfortable, so I lead Erin outside for more privacy.

On the sidewalk, she tightens her coat around her, and I steel myself against the evening chill. "I'm not seeing anyone else." I hold her gaze.

"I'm not, either."

"I bought us tickets for a show," I explain, and when she looks up at me with so many questions in those eyes, I smile. "I can't move to New York City and never experience a Broadway show."

"That's fair," she whispers.

"I will admit, though—and you're more than welcome to consider this yet another flaw." I inch toward her and take her petite hand in mine. "I dislike musicals, but I appreciate live theater. I researched a delightful play about a boy and his dog, and I thought we might enjoy it."

She eases into my embrace. "Perfect."

I tuck a strand of her hair behind her ear, and emotion clogs my throat. "Yes, you are."

"I don't think I've ever wanted to sucker punch another person before."

"I was close to doing it myself!" Erin clings to me, her fingers curled into my sleeve.

"He was so loud, he made the blaring train near my flat sound like a sweet lullaby." I shake my head. "How disrespectful. I mean, who debates football matches during a live show? Especially one so profound and moving."

It was a beautiful play, indeed, and the actors were spectacular and talented. The only thing that ruined this evening was the obnoxious jabbering of the wanker behind us right after intermission. Fortunately for our sakes, he was warned, then asked to leave after he refused to shut his trap.

"I only hope the next time he interrupts such a thing— and he does seem like the type to be a repeat offender—that someone steals his phone and tosses it into the river," I assert.

She throws her head back and laughs, her breath a small puff painted like a cloud across the evening sky.

"I'm serious."

"I am too. I'm just surprised." She rubs her small hand up and down my arm. "I've never seen you so unraveled like this."

"Yes, you have." I steer us to the edge of the sidewalk to hail a taxi. At least this is one task that's similar to London. "You, love, have seen me in my most unraveled state over the last week," I whisper and kiss her lips, lingering in the moment of bliss as I drink her in.

"I could take you meditating with me," she whispers, but she sounds far away, as if that's not at all what she's thinking. "It would help you with some of your... pent-up tension."

"Or I could do something *else* with you," I say in her ear, my voice trailing off, and she shivers next to me. "What would you think about that?"

"I think we should... hurry."

I wave down the first taxi I see and guide her inside, then slide in next to her, my body buzzing and aching to have her bare beneath me again.

To hear the sexy little noises she makes and the strangled cry of my name ripping from her throat as she writhes with pleasure.

My touch does that to her, and each time she climaxes, I feel the dire urge to beat on my chest like an animal.

The ride to my place is long and torturous. Everything is a bright blur out the window, since all I can seem to focus on is Erin.

When we reach the front of my building, I place my hand on the small of her back again, heat radiating from the spot where our connection meets.

My lips are on hers the moment we reach my floor, the winding stairs and air of seduction having left us rather breathless.

We stumble inside my flat, and I'm instantly grateful that the décor and furniture are so scarce. Had I filled this place with such things, they'd all be broken as Erin and I stagger through it in the dark.

The ever-present smell of coffee wafts over us as we pass the kitchen. In the sitting room, I trip over the rug and bounce onto the couch, bringing Erin down on top of me.

My chuckle against her mouth gets caught in my throat, promptly cut off just like my oxygen supply.

Erin leans up, reaches behind her back with excellent flexibility, and slides her zipper down, the sound of which makes my cock rise to attention.

As more of her chest is exposed, she snaps her eyes to mine and playfully rubs her panty-covered heat over the tent in my pants. My guttural growl cuts through the silence as her lips part, and her head falls back, her bare breasts spilling out of the stretchy fabric of her dress.

A defined line runs proudly between the visible part of her toned abs before it disappears into the bunched material around her waist. Her stomach rises and falls, hiding that line with each salacious pant of desire.

She's aroused and aching for my touch.

It's the most erotic display I've ever witnessed.

I reach out for two handfuls of her perfect tits and rub my thumb over each hardened nipple.

Groaning with impatient lust, I lean forward to take one between my teeth, but she backs away, tsking. "You're up."

I peer between us and say, "I certainly am."

She rolls her eyes and throws a leg onto the floor, sliding off me. "I mean, it's your turn."

Sitting up, I reach for the top button of my shirt, but

again, she stops me. "Strip for me," she whispers.

I freeze with my fingers and thumbs in place on my shirt. "I beg your pardon?" "The last guys who danced for me were Vegas strippers, so if that's the last image you want me to have, then fine. I just thought you'd want your chance to remedy that," she says.

The little siren knows how to drive me crazy, and she's now goading me. "Is that so?" I rub my chin, hopelessly falling under her spell.

"You told me to let you know what I want, and this is what I want." "Then you shall have it."

This daring, tantalizing game between us further provokes me, and my heated adrenaline fuels my every move to do something I never in a million years would consider doing, let alone actually go through with.

But here I am, playing music through my Bluetooth speaker and kicking my shoes off, one at a time, to the beat of the sensuous song while Erin settles between the couch cushions.

Her dress is still wrapped around her waist as she claps and sways to my striptease.

When I'm shirtless, I drop my pants, along with my boxers, and she freezes with her jaw dropped.

Standing naked in front of her in the middle of my sitting room, I narrow my gaze, put both hands behind my head, and move my hips in a motion I can only describe as gyrating.

I've already admitted to her that I'm a terrible dancer, but this moment is about so much more. It's about being ourselves—for each other.

Besides, I can't be embarrassed or insecure about my moves when Erin watches me with such fascination, as if she's itching to touch me.

What she does is touch her breasts, and my cock strains with need.

She's fucking incredible, as she kneads and plucks her own nipples, her eyes dazed with pure heat.

I take back my earlier thought. *This* is definitely the most erotic display I've ever witnessed.

As the song decrescendos to a softer and softer volume, I sink my teeth into my bottom lip, imagining her lip instead, and I slow my movements to mirror how I'd like to move inside her—with ease.

Feverish precision.

Burning desire.

I'm on fire from the intense way she watches me. She doesn't stop fondling her breasts as I slip onto the floor on my knees in front of her.

This woman deserves to be bowed down to.

Rising in front of me, she drops her dress down to her ankles, revealing a scant white thong. It hardly covers anything, much to my delight.

Erin steps closer until my head settles between her thighs, and my fingers immediately sink into the flesh of her arse, vigorously plying and massaging it until I'm sure I'll leave an imprint.

Her sweet scent fills my senses as I lose myself in her, nipping and sucking the fabric covering her pussy.

Gasping, she bends at the waist, grips my hair, and tilts my head up to kiss me, her mouth fused to mine as if she's never letting go.

And I drown in her, hoping to God she doesn't.

As she straightens back up, I dip my fingers into her panties and tug until they freely float down to her ankles. Without wasting another second to fully take them off her, I bury my face between her legs again, pressing my nose to the tight bundle of nerves above her clit.

My tongue works swiftly to the heady melody of her pants of approval.

Her legs tremble around my head, and I blink as she cuts me off by shoving me toward the couch. With my back against it, she grabs protection from my wallet and covers me with it herself while my eyes bug out of my head.

"Come here," I whisper hoarsely, and she eases onto both knees, straddling me with determination.

As soon as I'm nestled inside her, I take her fast and hard, her bouncing form clumsy and beautiful.

"Oh! Yes!" Erin cries out as she slides on and off me in a marvelous frenzy.

I grip her hips to hold her steady while I continue hammering into her from my spot on the floor, completely unhinged and relentless until the sensation becomes too much for either of us.

"Oliver!" She slams against me as her walls clench around my throbbing shaft.

Her petite hands roam through my hair and onto my shoulders as I surge forward with my own release. I catch her right before she hits the coffee table, and I grunt, my body pulsing with all the pleasure she's elicited.

This woman is every fantasy wrapped into one, and I hold onto her with an unyielding grip for as long as possible.

NINETEEN

Erin

I click the button to turn on the blender, and the room fills with an awful grinding sound as the blades crush the fruit and mix it with my organic protein powder and yogurt. Twirling around in the teachers' lounge, I sing to myself and grab an empty cup for my smoothie. I keep the fridge stocked with the necessary ingredients for mornings like this one when I'm running behind.

Oscar enjoys the occasional fruit out of the stash too. I'd argue, but I think it's the only way he eats from this healthy food group. If he's not munching on one of my apples or celery stalks, he's devouring a bag of Doritos, so I happily share.

I sip on the fruity mixture as I move over to the table to enjoy a few minutes with my thoughts before I go to my classroom. Since I didn't sleep until after midnight, I skipped hot yoga this morning, and instead of making a smoothie at home, I enjoyed extra time beneath my warm covers.

I still had remnants of Oliver on me.

His masculine smell, expert touch, and spicy taste still covered me, and I basked in it like I did my first time swimming in the ocean.

Simply exhilarating.

I've just sat down when my phone lights up with a new text in the group chat I share with the girls. We've been using it a lot more lately since Madison is mostly in LA, and she insisted we keep her updated on all the gossip.

With the time difference, we sometimes get a delayed response from her, but it works.

Tessa: How was the big date?

Me: It's big all right...

Bree: WHO ARE YOU?

I giggle as I receive another text from Bree.

Bree: The Erin I know never makes dirty jokes without a margarita in her!

Me: You've never known me to be in a happy and healthy relationship ;) There's a pause before I get a new message.

Tessa: And no one at work suspects anything?

Me: Not as far as we know.

Bree: How many times have you done it in the teachers' lounge? If you say less than five, I'll be disappointed. Don't disappoint me...

I glance around the room, noting the perfect sex spots, then shake my head and type out my reply. It's not one she'll like, but there's still plenty of good news to share.

Me: He's only ever squeezed my ass in the teachers' lounge, actually.

Bree: I'm devastated.

Tessa: I think it's smart. Anyone could walk in and catch you!

Me: Thank you for your voice of reason.

Me: Bree can learn a thing or two.

Bree: You could learn a few things from ME.

She sends a GIF of a woman winking suggestively, and I almost spit my smoothie out.

Me: Oliver has already taught me new things, including how sexy ties can be...

Me: Did I mention he also did a striptease for me after our date? Naked Heat style!

Bree: WTF

Tessa: Oh my God!!

Me: I'll fill you in during margaritas tomorrow night :)

Tessa: Okay, but are you bringing him to the wedding in 10 days?

Tessa: Oh. My. God. 10 DAYS. This is not a drill!

Bree: Did you just crack a molar? I feel like I just heard it from my office down the hall.

Me: Please check on her, Bree. We can't have a toothless Tessa showing up to her own wedding.

Tessa: I'M OKAY, I'M OKAY...

Bree: You're still screaming.

Tessa: I just dropped my glasses and bumped my head on my desk when I went to pick them up.

Me: Ouch!

Tessa: Back to Erin and Principal Love. Is he your wedding date, or what??

I chew on my bottom lip and lap up the tangy flavor of strawberries there, but the sweet and refreshing taste does little to distract me from the overwhelming stress flooding my body.

Me: I haven't asked him.

Bree: Are you going to?

Me: No. Maybe. I don't know!

Me: It's probably not a good idea.

Tessa: Only one way to find out.

Mads: What are you all babbling about so early this morning!?

Bree: Oh look who decided to finally join us.

She then sends a GIF of Robert Downey Jr. rolling his eyes—it's one of Bree's favorites to send.

We message back and forth for a bit, and it's mostly Bree complaining about her outfit choice for the day. Apparently, her pants keep riding up her ass anytime she moves.

We end the long string of texts with all three of them urging me to ask Oliver to be my date for Tessa's wedding.

I'm definitely not hating the idea of showing up with a man like Oliver next to me.

He'd look so good in a tailored suit, and we'd have a lot of fun—during the event *and*

afterward.

He'd make every other lousy time I've had at a wedding feel like distant memories. For once, I'd be able to look back on one of these things and smile. It's even better now since this special day is one of my best friend's.

"What are you smiling about?" Katie saunters in, wiggling her finger at me. I've barely glanced up when she gasps. "Did you go on a date that actually ended well?"

"Yes," I breathe, then realize what I've done. "No! I mean, no, of course not." Katie sits across from me, cautious and confused.

"I'm just smiling because I found a new recipe for gluten-free lemon poppyseed muffins. It sounds good, and I have most of the ingredients at home already. Don't you just love when that happens? When the universe brings everything together, and you finally start to think it doesn't hate you, after all?" I pause my rambling to inhale and hope it calms my sudden nerves.

"Are we still talking about… muffins?" The confusion in her furrowed brows deepens.

And sweat trickles down the valley of my breasts.

Good thing I'm wearing a light-colored sweater, which can hide it for me. Isn't that the point of sweaters? It's in the name.

Oh, God. At this rate, I'm totally going to spill my secret.

"Yes," I assert. "Muffins. I'll bring some this Friday for parent-teacher conferences, so you can see—rather, *taste*—for yourself."

I grab my half-drunk smoothie and bolt out of there. Since when did the teachers' lounge turn into a sauna?

As soon as I sit behind my desk, the bell rings, and across the hall, I catch Katie's gaze and wave as she enters her own classroom.

I hate lying to my friend, but what can I do?

The gossip around here travels faster than it takes the

Keurig to brew their coffee. I don't believe Katie would out Oliver and me, but these walls have eyes and ears in their cracked paint.

Students filter inside, talking and nudging each other. They're probably sharing gossip of their own. I did the same with my friends in high school, although I didn't have as much of a grasp on the consequences of it.

Then again, our secrets included silly things like what questions we all struggled with on the last test, or what we were wearing to the next dance.

Not which teacher was screwing the principal.

The second bell rings, and I round my desk to address the class. "Good morning," I sing in a voice far more sure of itself than it was with Katie a moment ago. "Please pull out your homework, get with a partner, and check each other's work. We'll go over the answers as a class afterward."

Sheets of paper crinkle as the class retrieves them from their backpacks, and the scraping and squeaking of desks fills the room as they shuffle to get close to one another. The perfect music of their laughs and chatter fills the room for yet another day of magic.

It's all I need to focus on them and not the hole Oliver and I keep digging ourselves into deeper and deeper.

But the relief only lasts until lunch.

As soon as the bell rings, I'm back to where I started, because I have thirty minutes to stew with my thoughts until I'm on lunch duty.

I have to tell Katie, but I should talk to Oliver first. I can't divulge our relationship without his knowledge. It's his secret too, after all.

But am I ready? I've told Tessa, Bree, and Madison, but

they're outside my school faculty circle. Oliver and I don't see them every day when we go to work.

We'd see Katie—what if it gets too stressful for us all to maintain the ruse?

In the lounge, I dig into the fridge and busy myself with my Mediterranean-style bowl of quinoa topped with yellow and red tomatoes, cucumbers, chickpeas, and tahini sauce. It's a tried-and-true meal I put together myself—one that tastes amazing and makes enough for several servings.

I've eaten this nearly every day the last couple of weeks since I haven't had much time to prep my meals between Tessa's wedding activities and Oliver.

Which brings me back to my earlier question—to invite Oliver or not to invite him.

There's no harm, right? It's not like I'd be asking him to marry *me*. Just to sit in the crowd of guests while two people I love vow to spend their lives together forever, then maybe dance to the "Electric Slide" at the reception.

I take a bite of tomato and quinoa, the flavor bursting on my tongue, then wipe the drop of sauce from the corner of my mouth as Karen and Nancy enter, talking in hushed tones. As they near, they get louder, and I catch the end of their conversation without even trying to eavesdrop.

"I wish we didn't have to wait until after Christmas break to find out who they're going to pick. That seems extreme, especially since the obvious choice is between the two of us," Nancy says with a shrug, her know-it-all attitude reflected in her raised brows.

Karen nods and purses her lips—I don't think I've ever seen the woman smile.

But I will say, she knows her subject well. We may not

agree on teaching styles or what constitutes as proper criteria to deserve detention, but she's damn good at science.

"Oh, we didn't see you there, Erin." Nancy turns to me and clutches her chest like I popped out of a closet with a Halloween mask on.

I plaster on a smile and greet them.

"We were just discussing the vice principal position," Nancy explains as she sits across from me. "I don't suppose you're going to apply."

She says it as more of a statement than a question. It's laced with a brush-off as if to imply that it would be silly for me to throw my hat into the ring.

And it grates on my nerves.

"Why do you say it like that?" I ask, pushing my bowl away and folding my arms on the table in front of me.

"Well," Karen chimes in, hovering over me. "I think Nancy means you're not exactly the most effective leader of us all. There's nothing wrong with that. You make great… baked goods."

From the sound of it, she does *not* like my baked goods.

"We each have our own skills," Nancy offers. "This position just wouldn't suit you."

Are they seriously complimenting a skill that has nothing to do with the subject I teach?

We've never been super friendly, but Nancy, Karen, and I have always been polite. Their tone now is so dismissive, and I curl my fists where they rest under my shoulders.

"I could be vice principal," I say firmly, my blood on fire. "I wouldn't rely on scare tactics and flirting to get it, either." My glare bounces between them. "I'd get the job because I am, in fact, qualified, and I'd be good at it too."

They wear matching stunned expressions.

As I stand, I pin my heated stare on Karen and clip, "And my baked goods are fucking phenomenal."

I swipe my bowl from the table and dump it into the trash can on my way out of the room, my appetite no longer as strong as it was when I first walked in.

Adrenaline courses through me like I jumped out of an airplane.

My stress level was already high because of my predicament with Oliver, and their offhanded insults only made it worse.

I'm not normally one for confrontation, especially with the people I work with, but enough is enough.

I may respect them each for their knowledge of their respective subjects, but as leaders of this school? I wouldn't bet on either one.

If Karen's not giving students detention over forgotten pencils, she's complaining about the squeaky doors on lockers or the smell of feet in the gym. And if Nancy isn't strutting down the hall in her low-cut dresses, she's five minutes late to class because she was fixing her lipstick.

Neither one of them would have a clue how to be a good vice principal, and I send a wish out into the cosmos that someone else is picked.

I march toward the cafeteria, round the corner, and bump into a hard chest. One covered in a lavender shirt and gray tie.

The combination of colors works well to reflect the balance of warmth and sleek fashion.

"Hi," I say on an exhale and stare into Oliver's bright blue eyes.

"Are you all right?" He grips my shoulders to steady me on my wobbly knees.

This crazy energy will probably still be coursing through

me until the end of the day. Add lust for my boss to the mix, and I'm a complex ball of emotions.

"I'm fine." I shift out of his grasp and brush the loose hair away from my damp neck. "I'm sorry I bumped into you. Just a little flustered."

"Anything I can do?" he asks in a low voice and checks around, seemingly to ensure we don't attract an audience.

I give him a small smile. "No, but I appreciate the offer."

"How about another offer?" He squints at me with hesitation. "Have lunch with my sister, Malcolm, and me this Saturday before the dance."

Instantly, my rattled nerves quiet, and my heart soars. "Really?"

Oliver eases into his grin like he does his stance, gracefully leaning one shoulder on the locker next to us.

And I have my answer.

He's very serious with his question, and clearly, he likes me a lot.

Rebecca and Malcolm are so important to him, and the fact that he wants me to meet them is a huge step forward for us—more like a huge leap into another dimension.

"I'd love to," I say, without a doubt that I'm ready for this leap.

"I'll call you with the details," he says, putting more emphasis on the last part of "details" due to his accent, and it's endearing.

I nod and reach out to grab his arm but stop myself when a few students walk by. "Sounds good," I whisper, my mood lifted into the clouds I'm suddenly walking on.

As I move toward the cafeteria, there's an extra sway in my hips. And I feel his gaze on me the entire way.

TWENTY

Oliver

"I was beginning to wonder when I'd ever get muffins from you again." I reach over to snatch a divinely glazed concoction.

Only Erin can make a gluten-free muffin so brilliant I'd eat it off the floor. Just as my fingertips brush the top of one, she smacks my hand away.

"What on earth was that for?" I skid to a halt on the sidewalk near Bryant Park. "These are for your sister and Malcolm," she chides. "Besides, I didn't think you liked these."

"What gave you that idea?"

"You didn't eat the ones I brought to your office the first week of school." She worries her bottom lip between her teeth.

I use my thumb to pull it free, then place a gentle kiss

there, whispering against her mouth, "I devoured every last crumb."

Her eyes flash with appreciation, but my compliment is not enough to win me a muffin. She still smacks me away.

"You mean I don't actually get to eat one?" I clutch my chest, only partially exaggerating my wounded feelings.

"Not until they try one first." She walks ahead and holds the containers out in front of her trim waist, the skirt of her green dress swaying with each victorious step.

"They don't even know how many were in there to start with," I grumble. "You always have to get the last word in, don't you?" She rolls her eyes.

I'm about to open my mouth to do just that, but we arrive at the edge of the park, where we agreed to meet my sister and Malcolm. We were going to have lunch at a place near my flat, but then we changed course after we realized what a lovely day it is outside.

Malcolm doesn't say no to a warm Saturday at the end of September. Evidently, they're as rare as snow in Florida, as my sister said while we were deciding on a new plan.

I've only been to this particular park once before, when I first arrived in the city. I'd gone exploring and somehow ended up here, then bought a coffee from the walk-up window and enjoyed the sunshine—which I love, despite Erin's guess earlier this week that I don't.

And after learning why exactly she loves gray sweatpants, I decided I love them too and bought a pair.

She definitely *appreciated* the photo I sent her when I tried them on by sending me one of her in the bathtub. The suds covered up the good parts, but she promised me the real thing this weekend.

I wrap my arm around Erin's waist, enjoying the ability to openly show my affection instead of being stifled by the walls of the school. As I search for my sister among the scattered groups, Erin melts into me with a contented sigh.

Past a couple of teens with skateboards tucked under their arms, I recognize Rebecca's face, which has become so familiar to me that I don't remember a time when I didn't know it.

She finds me about the same moment and waves while Malcolm runs circles around her, holding what appears to be a toy car in the air like it's flying.

"There," I say to Erin and steer us in the right direction.

"So, um," she stutters and balances the two containers in one hand to use the other to swipe hair out of her eyes. "I probably should've asked you before, but what exactly have you told Rebecca about what I am to you?"

"Everything."

"*Everything?*" she repeats with a squeak, jerking out of my embrace.

"Not the dirty details or that you make a glorious mess when you come, obviously." I smirk. "I was just honest with her about my relationship with you."

"Oh."

Ahead, Malcolm leads Rebecca on a zigzagging detour, so I take the opportunity to stop Erin and clear the air.

Gripping her shoulders, I say in a tone as firm as my hold on her, "My absence in my sister's and nephew's lives is because of my mother's lies. I can't be yet another liar to Rebecca and little Malcolm, so I told her the truth. She knows I'm seeing you outside of the school, and while that might seem deceitful in itself, it's only temporary. We're not hurting anyone, and there's no need to create drama or discomfort before we know where this is going."

Her eyes dart all over my face, and her expression is no more readable than it was before I'd started my attempt at an explanation.

"I probably should've discussed this with you before, and I apologize." I scratch the back of my head, instantly flooded with guilt.

But she settles my concern when she stands on her tiptoes, grabs the back of my neck, and presses her lips to mine, the containers crushed between us.

"Thank you." She leans her forehead to mine and eases against me.

"Okay, lovebirds. You're now in the presence of a child, so let's watch the PDA."

We pull back to find Rebecca and Malcolm, his eyes playfully covered by his mum's hand. She wears a knowing grin, and my cheeks heat.

Dear God, I think I'm fucking blushing, but instead of being embarrassed, I feel… wistful. Isn't this the sort of thing siblings do? Embarrass themselves in front of each other when it comes to dating?

This moment almost feels like a rite of passage, and even though it's me who's bearing the effects of humiliation, I revel in it, nonetheless.

"What's your name?" Malcolm asks, directing his question to the beautiful woman next to me.

"This is my friend, Erin," I say.

"You have a friend who's a girl, or is she your girlfriend? There's a big difference." He raises his eyebrows.

I chuckle under my breath as Rebecca shakes her head at

him. "I guess you might call her my girlfriend." I eye Erin, and a blush of her own colors her cheeks in the brightest shade of red.

"I have a girlfriend too," Malcolm announces, and Rebecca's snorts turn into gasps. "Wait, what?" She bends down to match his height. "When did this happen? Why didn't I know about this? Who is she?"

"Mom," he draws out. "It's no big deal. She's just a girl in my class who likes anime like I do, so we read it at lunch and stuff."

Rebecca sighs, and it's obvious she's relieved. The way her exhale rushes out of her sounds as if she feared they were making out in a dark alley after school or something.

He's a good kid, but I suspect she'll have her hands full when he gets older, especially if he's anything like I was in my teenage years. I was young and lived carefree like my mates, for the most part.

Of course, I wasn't all that reckless, but I definitely wasn't such a stickler for the rules back then as I usually am now—Erin not included.

After I introduce the two women, Erin offers them the muffins for our picnic, and Malcolm's gift sways in my hand in a bag.

"Can I have one, Mom?" Malcolm asks.

"Just one. We have sandwiches, and I don't want you to spoil your appetite."

Before Erin has the chance to explain that the top muffins are gluten-free and sugarless, Malcolm grabs one and sinks his teeth into it like I've seen videos of crocodiles do to their prey.

His face twists in disdain. "This isn't a muffin," he says around the mouthful.

Erin reaches out, her eyes wide and panicked. "I'm so

sorry! Those are the ones for the adults to try, but these…"
She uncovers the special ones she baked specifically for him
and holds them out. "These are for you. Chocolate chip mini
muffins."

Malcolm inspects them but doesn't accept.

"I promise, they're the good ones," Erin insists, her voice
thick with uncertainty. "It's the real stuff."

The kid finally reaches out to grab one, and this time, he
takes a slow, wary bite. Once he has enough proof that it is,
indeed, the good stuff, his eyes light up. "So good!"

Erin dips into an adorable curtsy and thanks him for the
compliment, then leans into my shoulder, muttering, "Phew."

"No matter what you think, it wouldn't kill you to try a
new food," Rebecca tells him, ruffling his hair.

I hold up the white bag. "My turn."

The moment I present him with the toy airplane and
walkie-talkies that Erin helped me pick out—after we nixed
the tie—Malcolm's mouth hangs open in awe.

"What did I say about gifts?" my sister hisses, covering
one side of her mouth as if it'll keep Malcolm from hearing
it. He's standing merely three feet away.

Then again, he is engrossed in the gifts.

"You said I couldn't bring him anything to the first dinner
we had," I argue. "You didn't restrict the foreseeable future."

She tsks, but there's no hiding the amused curl of her lip.
"Uncle Ollie, can we play?" Malcolm pleads.

"Of course."

"He calls you Ollie?" Erin whispers, clutching her chest.

"It's the very cool nickname my favorite nephew gave
me," I say, following behind him.

"I'm your *only* nephew!" he calls out with a laugh.

"Keep your eyes on him at all times, please," Rebecca yells out.

We each take a walkie-talkie, then cross the park to opposite sides, a large white tent between us, and we pretend to be on a mission.

"We're spies," he says, his voice crackling through my unit, and his eyes flash with excitement while he obviously gets lost in his imagination. "We're spying on Mom and Erin, and we need to steal lunch away to feed our two dogs."

"Smashing." I bend down and try to get into character. "What are our dogs' called?"

"Billie Goat and Thunder," he asserts as if he's already given this extensive thought.

"Billie Goat, the dog, huh?" I lift a brow.

Across the way, he nods, his eyes darting around the park. "Ready?" "Ten-four."

While we play, Erin and Rebecca sit at one of the small tables along one side of the park near the café. They laugh and eat the muffins like old mates, and my chest squeezes.

It's not that I was worried they wouldn't get along, but it's marvelous to actually witness them together. My worlds are colliding, and it's overwhelming me with gratitude.

I have no inkling of what I did to deserve this, but I couldn't be more blissfully happy about it.

At one point, Rebecca calls us over to eat the sandwiches she packed—ones she admitted Evie picked up this morning while my sister completed her hospital shift.

Before we walk over, Malcolm gives me a hug. "Thanks, Uncle Ollie."

I pat his back, and by the time we reach the ladies, I'm a big pile of bloody mush. "You two worked up a sweat,"

Rebecca observes, then asks Malcolm, "Did you behave?"

"Yep." He nods and points to the muffins. "Can I have another as my reward?" "You've got your hands full with this one," I tease my sister, who sticks her tongue out at me and suggests Malcolm wait for his second treat until after he's had his sandwich.

As Rebecca passes them out, I lean over to Erin. "What were you two going on about?" I whisper.

"A little of this. A little of that." She shrugs coyly and laughs with my sister.

"We should be more worried about you two behaving," I say to the table and give Malcolm a fist bump.

"Take smaller bites," Rebecca advises him. "The muffin isn't going anywhere. Take your time eating the sandwich before you choke."

Malcolm chuckles a high-pitched sound, sinking into his seat as if he needed his mum's reassurance that we wouldn't eat his baked goods.

As he slowly chews, we discuss his school and whether he'd like to play futbol next year.

"I want to be like Uncle Ollie," Malcolm announces, then tears off another bite.

Erin clings to my arm like it's the sweetest thing she's ever heard, and it might just be for me as well.

"Like me?" I ask and place my hand over my heart, the button of my shirt digging into my palm. "What a compliment."

He makes me smile when he shrugs it off as if it's not an enormous deal—*kids*.

Everything is so simply and ordinary, except for their games and toys.

"We'll kick about and prepare you for the team, so you knock everyone's socks off next year," I promise.

The kid continues eating his toasted ham and cheese, eyeing the muffins harder than if they were the finish line at a marathon.

The appetite on him is astonishing.

"Erin was telling me about the homecoming dance tonight," Rebecca says. "What time do you need to head out to help decorate?"

"We'll probably need to go here soon, actually." Erin slumps next to me. "I have to change and get over there before Karen sends me to detention for being five minutes late."

"She's one of *those*, huh?" Rebecca shakes her head and sips from a coffee cup. "One of what?" Malcolm chimes in.

"Just a nice lady," Rebecca says and throws an arm over his shoulders for a squeeze.

"Totally," Erin adds for good measure.

I kiss the side of her head and let my lips linger there, the smell of her shampoo infiltrating my senses. "Thank you," I whisper.

And when I pull back, the tender smile gracing her lips says more than any words.

She knows exactly what I mean. I'm ecstatic over her joining us, and more than that, I'm pleased she's getting on so well with my family.

I figured as much. After all, Erin could charm anyone from Father Christmas to The Queen's Guard outside Buckingham Palace.

She's extraordinary that way, and she makes me want to be better too. Before we leave, Malcolm insists Erin sees "something awesome."

"Can I see this awesome thing?" I ask, halfway stepping

toward them, but I stop from going any farther when he holds his hand up.

"This is just for Erin," he says firmly.

He takes a shrugging Erin by the hand and leads her toward a flower bed along the sidewalk, leaving me alone with Rebecca. We both watch after them as they politely sidestep a woman pushing a stroller. The pair comes to a stop by a rose bush and bend down. A man jogging with a well-tempered husky by his side crosses in front of them, and the rest of the park's visitors carry on with their activities around us.

This might be a normal Saturday for them, but to me, it's turning out to be one for the history books. I can't help the grin spreading until my mouth is sore.

"I've never seen you so happy," she muses, nudging me with her shoulder. "It's nice."

I dip my head, teetering on my heels.

"Much better than your grumpy, kick-all-the-puppies attitude." "I'd never kick a puppy."

"You would if it peed on your precious shoes." She snorts. "A couple weeks ago in the park, I thought you were going to have an aneurism when the black lab brought its muddy paws toward you."

"Even so, I'd still never kick it. Maybe just shoo it away like a fly, but I'd never inflict harm upon it." I laugh.

"But with Erin next to you, you'd probably scoop the thing up and let it get your entire shirt muddy without batting an eye."

"I assume that's a good thing." I peek over, squinting in the sunlight. I forgot my sunglasses in my haste to arrive here on time after kissing Erin got out of hand. She spent the night with me, and for the first time in months, I didn't want to get out of bed.

Rebecca sighs, and her expression falters. "It is, but I just don't want to see you in trouble with your career. I can tell this thing between you two is real, but it's not like you to blatantly disregard your morals. I mean, you wouldn't even take more than one napkin from the food truck a couple weeks ago because it was wasteful. Now, you're dating someone who works for you and risking what you've worked so hard for."

I flinch as the gravity of her words weighs me down.

"I don't think there's any reason you can't sign a waiver or something in order to stop hiding. Just…" She grips my arm and turns me to face her. "Just be smart."

I grind my teeth like I'm chewing on her advice, which goes down as painfully as shards of glass might.

During the drive to Erin's place, I mull over my conversation with Rebecca. She's right. Erin and I aren't simply a fling anymore.

I already knew that.

It's why I wanted her to meet my sister and nephew in the first place.

But I'm simply having a difficult time making my indiscretions public. Disclosing our relationship to my superiors would be the smartest thing to do, but it would also involve publicly announcing to the rest of the staff that I'm involved with a teacher.

I've worked hard to establish boundaries. To show them I have integrity. To earn the faculty's respect and trust. This might wreck all that and disrupt the flow of our workplace.

The daily stress from backlash might be too insurmountable to overcome, and then what? Will Erin realize none of it is worth the trouble?

Will she come to believe *I'm* not worth it?

Later in the afternoon as I'm about to leave for the dance, all I keep thinking is that I'm willing to take the risk. I believe in what we have enough for the both of us.

TWENTY-ONE

Erin

"Hi, Ms. Hayes!" A few students greet me as I walk into what's normally the gym.

Tonight, we've transformed it into a garden party.

I gasp as I take in their sparkling dresses and the guys' button-up shirts. "You all look amazing," I gush. "Have fun tonight!"

Katie sashays up to me. "Speaking of amazing…" She follows her appraisal of me with a low whistle.

Blushing, I smooth my hands over my high-waisted silk skirt and look down at my tucked-in, fitted cream blouse. "It's nothing that special."

"Yeah, right. My advice would be to cover yourself by the time Principal Westbrook sees you, or you'll end up with a smudge on your record," she teases.

And little does she know—he's exactly the guy I want to impress tonight. Since lunch with his sister and her son earlier, I've been floating.

Oliver looked more relaxed than the Hudson during a calm morning, and it was a sight to take in all its own.

"You two hardly ever bicker anymore, but I see the way he looks at you. He'd like to do a lot more than argue over herbal remedies." She wiggles her eyebrows as Karen approaches us.

For the first time in my life, I'm happy to see this woman. Because of her interruption, I don't have to comment—aka *lie*—to my friend about the principal's affection for me.

She points around the space as she divides orders, starting with Katie. "Can you make sure we have enough snacks out? The same group of kids has been standing by the cookies since they got here, so make sure they haven't eaten them all."

She then turns to me, and I have to suppress an eye roll. She's already acting like vice principal, but based on what Bobbie told me yesterday, they haven't even started going through applications yet. "And can you take the wet floor sign back to the storage room? We had a spill earlier. I already took care of the difficult task, so can you manage the easy task of putting the sign back up? As chaperones, we have to share the work."

"Of course," I mumble, and as I take off in the direction of her pointer finger, I again send out my hopes and wishes to the universe that she doesn't get the job.

I can't put up with her condescension from a higher, holier-than-thou level.

As Katie shuffles toward the table of snacks and punch, I meander through the middle of the dance floor. It's still early, and there are only a few small groups of students here as of right now, so no one's dancing just yet.

When I was in high school myself, my friends and I would be late to arrive, and it wasn't because we were fashionably late. It was because they had to wait on me to get my hair *just* perfect and my eyeliner *just* thick enough.

I still take pride in doing my hair and makeup, especially since I met Madison, who gave me life-changing tips to quicken my primping routine, but it used to matter a lot more, as everything did back then.

Being a teenager is such a difficult time, which is why I do my best to pay attention to each student and help whenever I can. It's why I'm the first to volunteer for things like this Homecoming dance—to ensure they have a good time with their classmates outside of school.

To make memories.

"Do you need any help?" the deep but squeaky voice of a sixteen-year-old sounds from behind me.

With the sign folded, I hoist it under my arm and find Brandon from third period with his arms out, ready to take the sign from me. "I'm fine, but thank you so much. Go enjoy yourself. Tonight is all about having fun. No work for you."

"Thanks, Ms. Hayes."

Smiling, I shake the hair out of my eyes as I walk toward the custodial closet in the hall, passing the photo corner on the way.

The makeshift gazebo stands a few feet taller than me. The tulle is bunched at the top of thin poles to form a point, and twinkling lights cascade from there. We created a path leading up to it with green felt and white construction paper cut out to resemble stepping stones. Alongside it, we used two rolls of reflecting paper to create the illusion of a river, on top of which is a boat we borrowed from the theater department.

They used it in the play last spring, and it works perfectly for the students to sit inside for a photo.

It wasn't easy to agree on the theme, but we picked one for the books. I greet more students as I continue walking past the tables.

But I stop in my tracks when I feel him.

Oliver.

He stands on the other side of the dance floor, his piercing eyes glued on me.

A rush of air leaves my lungs and sends a thrill through my body, especially as an onslaught of memories from the last time we were together race through my mind.

His grip, kisses, nips—it was all so possessive. Seductive. All-consuming.

Being with him—engulfed in every way—is addictive.

I tighten my grip on the sign under my arm and ground myself in reality. We're in public.

At school.

With too many prying eyes to count.

Clearing my throat, I hold my head high and walk forward, but my gaze still wanders back to him. We continue our stare down until Johanna pulls him away.

"Whoa!" Katie appears out of nowhere, and I accidentally step on her foot. "Ouch!"

"I'm so sorry," I say, nearly panting.

I'm so flustered and shocked that I forget the sign is still in my grasp, and I drop it on her other foot. I cover my face, which muffles my voice when I say, "Oh my God."

She grinds her front teeth together like she's biting on a cloth, and her deranged grimace belongs to the likes of Pennywise.

"Are you okay? Let me grab you some ice," I offer, my nerves skittish. "What happened?" Oliver joins us, his arms out and ready to assist. "I'm fine. It's no big deal," Katie says, but it's not convincing.

I scoop the sign up and out of the way as more students file inside. Then Oliver and I help Katie to an empty chair at a table along the edge of the dance floor.

"It's just that I stubbed my toe on my dresser this morning, so it was already bruised and sore," she explains with a wince.

I run my hands through my hair. "I'm so sorry."

She waves me off as Oliver places ice wrapped in damp napkins on her foot. "It's not your fault."

"But it is. I wasn't watching where I was going."

"You did seem to be in a daze. What were you thinking about so hard?"

My gaze involuntarily flashes to Oliver, who stands to his full height next to me. "Nothing. I was just… I was trying to…"

"Were you thinking about one of the mothers from the parent-teacher conferences yesterday?" Oliver swoops in to save me. "I told you not to worry about it. I'll take care of it."

"Right. Yes. The prickly helicopter mother." I scratch my head and force a smile. "She's been weighing on me."

"I have it under control." He nods, oddly calm about this vague lie we're improvising.

"You didn't tell me about her." Katie grabs my forearm from where she sits. "Everything okay?"

"Yes. It is now because Ol—Principal Westbrook is going to take care of it." I shrug like it's no big deal, but I'm two seconds from sweating through my shirt. "If you're okay for a second, I'm going to take the sign back to the closet before it hurts anyone else."

"Don't worry about me." She smiles, and the reassurance in it eases my guilt as I brush past Oliver.

"Meet me in the health classroom in three minutes," he whispers.

His words are like his caresses along my cheek—hot, promising, and thrilling.

With a tingle spearing through my core, I move toward the closet, forcing my feet to walk at an easy pace instead of running.

I slip into the closet where I set the sign against the wall, and before I rush to the classroom to meet Oliver, I check the main room again for Katie. She's removing the ice and wiggling her foot around while she smiles at one of the other teachers.

I'll definitely bring her cookies on Monday for my blip.

It was Oliver's fault, anyway. He's the one who distracted me with his brooding eyes and his impeccable attire. He wears the aqua shirt he's paired with the navy suit like the devil himself picked it out with the intention of enticing me to sin tonight.

And sin, I will.

But first, I check for any lurkers, but the hallway is empty. Everyone is in the main room getting the dance off the ground. The music is louder, and they've dimmed the lights.

We're in the clear.

I duck into the PE room, positive no one sees me.

Once inside, I mutter under my breath, "I can only hope Oliver is about to school me in *physical education*."

I squeeze my eyes closed and let out an exhale, glad no one heard that. Am I really doing this—sex at the school? Bree would be so thrilled.

After a couple minutes of pacing and studying posters of diagrams of the body, Oliver enters, locks the door behind him, and pulls the shade down.

"Is Katie okay?" I ask, twiddling my thumbs in front of me.

"She's up and about again," he says, putting me at ease, but my senses quickly heighten when his eyes darken.

Need pools between my legs, rendering me frozen in place, especially as I take a moment to drink him in without witnesses or other teachers in danger of me hurting them.

The pants of his suit are wrapped snugly around his legs like I'm dying to be, and each quad thickens with every step he takes.

"Come here," he rasps and scoops me up to sit on the edge of the counter in the back of the room.

I gasp as my skirt fans around me, and the whoosh of air from the movement cools the heat between my legs in the most delicious fashion.

Oliver slips between my open thighs and smashes his lips to mine in a searing kiss that works me into a frenzy.

I squeeze my legs around him and tug his bottom lip between my teeth, which earns me a feral groan.

He tightens his hold on my hair to a nearly painful level, and I moan into his mouth from the pleasure of the sting.

"You look beautiful," he whispers, then plunges his tongue back inside my mouth with unleashed intensity.

I have seen him unraveled, but it's different tonight.

Oliver is raging with a chaotic need for me, and it drives me to the brink of insanity.

While we kiss, I unbuckle the belt at his waist and drop his pants to rest haphazardly on his hips, his impressive length springing free and bobbing to the tune of our labored breaths.

Lifting to the side, I slide my panties down and scoot to the edge until I feel the glistening tip of him at my dripping, quivering entrance.

"I have an implant," I whisper, panting and arching toward him. Begging for him to fill me and give me what I need—*him*.

"I'm tested regularly." He cups my cheeks between both hands and urges me to look him in the eyes. "Are you sure about this?"

I quickly nod and lean forward until I almost fall.

Oliver catches me and thrusts inside me, his cock bare and unyielding as he pumps into me with ease. It's not long before we fill the room with the smell of lust and sex.

I bite my lip to keep from screaming and alerting anyone outside of what we're doing.

He wraps his strong hands in my hair again and tugs my head back.

My mouth falls open as my face tilts toward the ceiling, my eyes squeezed closed as his hot breaths come out in quick pants against the column of my throat.

Oliver places wet kisses there as he rocks his hips into me, and the sweet friction against my walls is almost too much to bear.

"Almost there, love," he grinds out, the bulging veins in his reddening neck screaming like I need to.

I want to cry out his name so badly, but I use every muscle—ones I didn't even know I had—to refrain. I feel like I did the time he tied my hands above my head, and I couldn't touch him.

This restriction is just as delicious. I never knew I'd enjoy it this much.

I bite my lip again until I'm close to drawing blood as he drives into me faster and harder. Clinging to him, I come with a silent cry, and he quickly follows, warming me from the inside out.

I'm definitely sweating through my shirt by the time Oliver leans back, his jacket halfway down his back.

I must've pulled at it while he was giving me a proper fuck, as he would say. It's the only way to describe it, that's for sure.

The high from it keeps me in a daze for a few long seconds, and it's hard to collect myself.

"I don't want to keep this a secret anymore," he says.

At least, it's what I *think* he says. Did I hear him correctly, or did my ethereal orgasm damage my hearing?

He grips the back of my neck and levels me with his gaze. "I know it's only been a few weeks, but I'm serious. I want to tell the board, the superintendent, the rest of the faculty—everyone. I don't want to hide how I feel about you."

I gulp and let the weight of what he's saying settle inside my chest.

"What do you think? You're never this quiet, and I can't tell if it's a good thing." He chuckles, but it's nervous.

It makes me smile. "Let's do it."

He brings my face forward and meets me in the middle for another kiss. "It's settled then," he says, his lips brushing against mine. "On Monday, we'll walk into the school and tell the world—together."

My heart races as I kiss him again, flying high off him and this night.

I've never had so much fun at a high school dance before.

"I'll come over tonight, and we can talk, all right?" He searches my expression, and again, I'm speechless.

He wants this as much as I do.

My tongue is tied up with all the things I'd like to say. To tell him I've never been happier with a guy. That I think I love him.

But it's too soon, right? Too crazy and unlike me. While his request to share our relationship with everyone is a decent indicator of how significant his feelings for me are, I can't stand the thought of scaring him away by coming on too strong.

We're taking it one step at a time, starting with escaping this classroom undetected.

I manage to nod, and he promises to call me after the dance. With another heated kiss, we agree I'll walk out of here first, and he'll follow after a few minutes.

"I'd hate to raise questions before we have the chance to come clean on Monday." He squeezes my hands.

With imprints of Oliver still on my body and heart, I slip into the dark and empty hallway and close the door with a soft click. He waits on the other side while I run my fingers through my hair in an attempt to tame it.

I should go to the bathroom first.

I enter the nearest one, and as I straighten my clothes and fix my smudged lipstick, my heart thunders in my head.

We're doing this.

We're going to tell everyone on Monday.

Shit. Just. Got. Real.

My wide grin makes it difficult to fix the pink lipstick smeared in the corner of my mouth.

I need to tell Katie. She should hear it from me before the gossip mill broadcasts it.

The other teachers will surely embellish the reality too

with their own assumptions, as they tend to do. My friend needs to have the real story from me, as does Bobbie. I owe them as much.

They've been lifesavers during my time here, and I need to be upfront.

Resolute, I leave the bathroom dazed and happy.

When I enter the main part of the gym again, students jump and dance to a fast- paced song, and multi-colored lights dart in every direction. Some girls sit at one table, laughing, while others crowd around the snacks and punch. There's a small line leading up to the photo corner as well, but I can't locate Katie anywhere.

Operation: Come Clean is cut short, though, when Oliver re-enters the gym. Nancy is on his heels, and the tight frown on his face makes my stomach sink.

His hair is smoothed down, and his suit is in place and neater than ever. In fact, there's no sign that he just had sex at all.

I lurch in his direction but stop myself when he meets my gaze. There's a warning in his eyes.

I place a hand over my chest and try to calm my heart rate, but it's no use. Panic races through my veins with a sole mission of ruining a perfect evening.

Something's wrong.

TWENTY-TWO

Oliver

Something was wrong, but I've never felt more right.

I spent the last two nights in Erin's bed, absorbing all the sexy noises she makes each time we're together.

The ones that prove she's not as innocent as she looks.

Those stolen moments even settled my nerves, especially when she told me, "This is the happiest I've ever been."

The confession came out after round two sometime at four this morning, and it completely consumed me. I feel the same, which is why I'd gladly take the professional consequences that might come our way after our big reveal.

It's not so simple, though.

I'm back at work this morning, far from Erin's bed and all its filthy memories.

Here, I serve as her boss, and it's the day we agreed

to disclose our relationship. To make it a real, breathing thing.

It felt like a brilliant idea when I first brought it up, but now that the time has come, my throat is tight. So much has happened since I first uttered the notion.

Erin and I were caught in the health room—at least, I believe we were.

Nancy saw me coming out of the classroom soon after Erin left. The nosy English teacher gave me a compliment on my suit, which was nothing out of the ordinary. What was dreadful, however, was the way she eyed me suspiciously as she stated, "I sure hope the vice principal position goes to someone who's deserving and isn't being unfairly favored due to… personal connections."

Nancy clearly put two and two together of my relationship with Erin. We wouldn't have raised suspicions had I not suggested our secret rendezvous to begin with. I shouldn't have asked her to meet me in there for a quick tryst.

But I got greedy. Careless. And it was in direct violation of my promise to keep things professional.

We are not off to an ideal start by having sex on school property during a school event.

It was fun, but it was so unlike me. Now that I'm sitting in my chair—the proverbial chair at the head of the table—shame overcomes me.

To make matters worse, I ran into Karen right after the brief but damning conversation with Nancy.

"She thinks she'd make a good vice principal, but I'm not convinced. Did I tell you she cursed at me?" Karen rambled toward the end of the dance on Saturday night. "That's beside the point, though. I asked her to do one thing—to put the wet floor sign away— and she couldn't even do that right. She disappeared for the rest of the night. *Figures.*"

I push back from my desk and curse under my breath as the muffled ringing of the phone sounds from Rita's desk. Placing a hand on my hip, I stare out my window at the rain coming down.

Fall is officially upon us, and instead of feeling hopeful of a new season, I dread what the future looks like.

Truthfully, those aren't the only things that have my stomach in knots. No, if those were the only problems, I'd easily solve them.

But alas, there's the issue of what I noticed before I left Erin's flat this morning. With coffee dancing through my veins, I grabbed my coat to leave but stopped when I laid eyes on a blank vice principal application with a yellow Post-it stuck to the front that read *Fill out,* followed by an obscene number of exclamation points.

The question for an explanation was on the tip of my tongue, but she kissed me with such intensity, she wiped the urge right off.

It didn't mean anything, anyway. She told me she wasn't applying, so there's no need to stew.

Except that's what I'm doing. I'm pacing my office, the muscles in my back anxiously ticking away like fingers on a typewriter.

I believe Erin—at least, I want to. She told me she's not applying, and it didn't come up all weekend, either.

Why does the knot in my stomach keep growing, then?

I jolt at the knock on my door and turn to find Rita tiptoeing inside. "Yes?" I ask. "Bill called. He says he'll be in to speak with you later this morning," she answers, placing her hands behind her back, then clasping her fingers together in front of her.

She's shifty—nervous and hesitant with a hint in her expression that I'm not going to like the answer to my next question.

"Why does he want to see me today?" I ask, anyway.

"He wasn't specific but said he wanted to discuss a sensitive matter with you." She grimaces. "He sounded serious."

I grip the back of my chair until my knuckles turn white the same way they do when I pick up a fifty-pound dumbbell at the gym. "Thank you, Rita."

She hesitates at the door, then scurries back to her desk and leaves me alone with my confusing thoughts.

Did Nancy tell our superintendent what happened at the dance between Erin and me?

It's the only explanation, isn't it? Unless he wants to discuss the budget, but that

meeting isn't scheduled for another week.

He's here to scold me about the dangers of becoming romantic with a teacher, and I'm not prepared. I was going to tell him, anyway, but it would've been on my own terms and conditions. I'd have control of the situation, but now all I have is a pile of burning rubbish laid out in front of me.

Rebecca was right.

I swore I would be smart, but I was tempted with Erin. I took from her when I should've done what's best for her—I should've left her alone.

Now, both our careers could be jeopardized.

Unsurprisingly, I'm sure the reason for our demise is none other than Nancy. I should've known something was up when she didn't aggressively flirt with me or grope my arm the moment I stepped onto school premises.

Then there's the comment she made the night of the dance. It nags at me.

I grow more and more restless with warring thoughts, neither side emerging victorious without the proper information, until Bill finally strolls into my office a couple hours later.

Silently and without greeting, the short, plump man steps inside, closes the door, and remains standing on the other side of my desk, hands clasped in front of him. From my seated position, we're almost the same height, but instead of that relaxing me, I'm more tense than before.

The man brings with him an air of disappointment, and it crowds my office. "How's the golf game lately?" I ask cautiously and sway in my chair, my nerves shot to Hell.

He eases a fraction, as he does every time his favorite sport is mentioned. "It's been a little rough, especially since I tweaked my shoulder last week. Nothing serious, but it's caused a nasty hook in my drive."

"That's tough," I say, unable to offer much more since I don't know much about the game myself. As I tap a pen against a notepad, I study him closely for any indication of what he might say but come up empty.

There's nothing I can do at this point to regain the upper hand, anyway. It's out of my hands.

"This conversation is tough too, but I have to ask." He finally takes a seat and flattens the tie down the middle of his chest. "There's a rumor…"

"Yes?"

As he leans back in his chair, Bill sighs. "There's a rumor

that you're *involved* with the math teacher—Ms. Hayes."

I drop the pen, and my blood freezes.

"I hate to ask this because I know what a stand-up guy you are, but I have to investigate this particular allegation. It's in the best interest of our school, and we need to deal with it before the board steps in. You understand, right?"

I cringe at his word choice.

Allegation seems so criminal, and what I have with Erin is nothing of the sort. Just the opposite—it's pure and lovely.

"Listen, Bill, I can explain." I fold my hands on the desk as he speaks over me.

"I wouldn't need to ask, if she weren't applying for Mrs. Peters's job, but since she is—"

"What do you mean? Ms. Hayes is not an applicant."

He shifts in his chair, seemingly more uncomfortable than I am. "That's not what

Mrs. Peters said when we spoke yesterday. She said Ms. Hayes had all but turned it in and that she'd be a great candidate."

My head spins.

This can't be right. The Erin I know wouldn't lie to me about something so significant. Bill and Johanna must have made a mistake.

There's a knock on the door, and we both turn toward it.

"Oh, I asked Ms. Hayes to join us." He stands and makes his way to the door.

I remain perfectly still, besides my rapid blinking, which brings Erin in and out of focus so fast I don't recognize her right away.

What is happening?

"Good morning, Ms. Hayes." Bill holds his arm out for

her to enter, and the first things I see clear as day are her black ankle boots.

The thick heel adds only an inch to her height, but she seems taller and more confident than the last time I saw her.

At her apartment, where we kissed goodbye after a night of lovemaking.

I had my hands on her bare body less than six hours ago, but everything feels different now.

She smiles at me, and it appears genuine.

It does nothing to curb the unease weighing me down, though.

I want to believe her. To insist that I haven't been deceived, but other people around this school seem to know more about her plans than I do.

Has she been so easily lying to me all this time? And if so, what else has she kept hidden from me?

"Glad you could join us," Bill says as they both take a seat across from me. "Good morning," I say through my tight-lipped smile.

"I'll cut right to it." Bill holds his hands up. "Is there anything romantic between you two?"

She visibly tenses with her mouth open as if she's having trouble getting air into her lungs.

I feel the same.

There's still the irritatingly persistent part of my mind that gives me doubt. It's the part repeatedly asking, "What if she *does* want to be considered for the position?"

I'd ruin the possibility for her if I told the truth. "No," I blurt.

They both snap their heads in my direction.

Bollocks.

What have I done?

"I mean… We're not…" I struggle with my words harder than Nancy's students reading Shakespeare last week during my observation of her class.

I fidget with the collar of my rigid shirt and rise from my seat to resume the role I was brought here to uphold—a leader.

One who selflessly defends his faculty.

Right now, it's not about me or us. This is about Erin.

And I have to be noble and wary enough to set my feelings aside. "The rumor you heard is just that. Ms. Hayes and I have become good

acquaintances since my arrival, as she's been a tremendous help with my transition, but we only have an *appropriate* working relationship," I emphasize, fighting hard not to steal a glance at her.

But I can feel the hole she's burning in my chest from the heated anger rolling off her.

"Is this the case, Ms. Hayes?" Bill asks.

"Yes," she clips faster than a natural reflex, but if Bill detects any hostility in her one-word answer, he doesn't show it.

Instead, he throws his hands up as if this is a party. "What a relief!"

I sit back in my seat, and Erin and I wait in silence while Bill celebrates on his own.

"I told the other teach—I mean, the *source*—that there are many explanations as to why you two might have been in the health room during the homecoming dance, but she insisted there was something going on."

Nancy.

It was her, after all.

"Among the many concerns I'd have if it were true, is that this would obviously complicate things since we're filling the vice principal position, and we need to remain objective and fair. A relationship would've given conflict of interest a whole new meaning."

"I'm sorry, but what does that have to do with me?" Erin shifts in her chair to angle her body toward him.

"You're an applicant, right? I understood as much, anyway. I haven't seen any paperwork myself, but we haven't begun the process just yet," he explains, and I sit on the edge of my seat in anticipation of Erin's response.

Something to get us to the bottom of this web of rumors. "I'm not applying for the job," she states.

"Oh. In that case—"

"But you told Ms. Hubanks and Nancy you are," I cut in. "Then there's the matter of the application at your—on your desk." I clear my throat and nervously adjust the lapels of my jacket, thankful I caught myself before I gave Bill the truth—that I saw it at her apartment after I did exquisitely sinful things to her.

Erin turns to me with only confusion etched across her marvelous face, her mouth clamped shut.

"If I may," Bill starts. "I just want to reiterate that it's a relief we don't have to worry about a romantic involvement during the interviewing process. Many questions would've been raised regarding the ethical nature of the relationship. Whether anyone was taken advantage of. But I won't get into it since there's nothing going on. You've made my day a lot easier." Bill claps and stands, his shoulders far more relaxed than when he first entered. "I'll see you next week,

Westbrook." I barely register him referring to me by my last name as if we're partners out on the golf course. Like he didn't just toss a grenade into my life.

Instead, my gut churns as Erin follows him out.

"Er—Ms. Hayes, a moment?" I call out to her, but she continues out the door with Bill and shuts it behind her.

She figuratively slams it in my face.

Their muffled chatter drifts through the thin walls, and I remain seated, my elbows on the desk and my chin resting on my hands.

I'm frozen, except for the ball of dread settling at the bottom of my stomach. What did I just do?

TWENTY-THREE

Erin

That *cowardly asshole.*

Before I left Oliver's office, I heard him call my name but pretended not to. I can't speak to him right now, not in the current state I'm in.

Plus, we're at school, and he's my boss, and I can't talk to him the way I really want to until we're alone.

But I don't fucking want to be alone with him because he's a frightened douchebag who lied to me about disclosing our relationship. We had the perfect opportunity to do so, but he took the easy way out.

I trusted Oliver, and he took that trust, crumpled it in his strong grip like a piece of paper, and threw it into a trash can as my students do in a stupid game of basketball.

I can't believe this.

As soon as I enter my classroom, I'm dangerously close to locking myself inside. I need time to think. To clear the mess in my head. To dull the pain in my chest... But several rows of wide eyes stare back at me and my slumped body against the door.

Right. My job.

My students.

They're depending on me, and I cannot afford a meltdown. I can address my disorienting thoughts later. "Hi, class," I manage.

I get a few murmurs in response. They could've yelled, and I wouldn't have comprehended it, though.

Still rattled, I sit behind my desk and blink at the papers in front of me until the numbers and shapes come into focus. "What are we doing..."

I slide my pointer finger down the piece of paper to find any clue as to what lesson we're on today. As soon as my brain clicks into action, I announce, "Pythagorean theorem," but it's more for myself.

On the board behind me, I draw a triangle, but I press the chalk so hard it breaks in half. I blow out a frustrated breath, and the hair on my face is swept away.

As we blaze through the lesson, I break two more pieces of chalk and blow out several more frustrated breaths until the bell rings, signaling the end of class.

If I could even call it that. This period was a disaster.

Alone, I slump into my chair and squeeze my eyes closed, drained and weary. Thank God, it's time for lunch, and I'm not on duty for another thirty minutes. Plenty of time to get my head on straight.

Except it doesn't work, nor do I have any better luck

focusing for the rest of the day. All I can think about is Oliver. Any second I get to myself before the final bell rings, I replay every moment he and I spent together as if I'm trying to convince myself it wasn't a dream.

But maybe parts of our relationship were.

Did we even have a relationship? Sure, he was the last person I texted after sending my goodnight messages to the girls, as I have for more than a year. Oliver was also the man I was most comfortable with. I felt safe with him.

Where did we go wrong? More importantly, what did I miss? Because I clearly wasn't paying attention. The meeting this morning and his blatant disregard for our connection slapped me in the face with such a surprising force, I need a freaking ice pack.

At the end of the day, I'm defeated. I've exhausted the synapses in my brain to find answers. Yet, I've come up with nothing.

"Hey." A high-pitched whisper sounds at the door, and Katie tiptoes inside. "What happened today? I heard Bill was here to meet with Principal Westbrook about some rumor."

I sit upright from my slouched position. "Do you know what rumor?" "Um…" She bites her lip. "It's about you and the new boss, actually." "Oh my God." I bury my face in my hands.

Can this day get any worse? As if the meeting with Bill wasn't bad enough, now the entire faculty will know my shame.

"I told them it's not true." Her small feet in low block heels tick across the tiled floor, and she stops at my desk like she's done many times before when we've traded gossip.

But this gossip is about me.

It's about the terrible thing I've done.

I deserve what Oliver did to me, don't I? I shouldn't have dated him in the first place, and my horoscope did warn me to end the month with caution.

Did I listen? *Nope.*

"It's not true, right? I know I tease you about the way he looks at you and how red your cheeks get when he's around, but it's all in good fun. I mean, it would be crazy if there's anything going on." She giggles, but it's hesitant.

And I feel her curious stare on me like I would a blistering spotlight. I groan and drop my hands to the desk with a thud. "It is true."

"What?" she whisper-screams, and the way her eyes widen would probably be more suitable after hearing a murder confession. "You and Principal Westbrook? How? When? *What?*" She keeps sputtering for a few more seconds, further confusing me with missing syllables and words, until she freezes. "Is that why you've been acting so weird lately? More skittish than usual, anyway."

"Since when have I ever been skittish?" I scoff. "Makes me sound like a starved mouse or something."

"Don't change the subject."

Frowning, I grab my purse from the bottom drawer of my desk and loop my arm through the strap. "I know I just dropped a big bomb on you—bigger than when Nancy showed up with a nose job last fall—and I'll explain everything. Just not now."

And more sputtering.

"I'm sorry, but I need to go. I can't..." Standing, I glance around the shaded room, and more doom settles over me. "I can't be here right now."

As I pass her, she grabs my arm. "Please call me if you need anything."

I give her what I hope is a reassuring and thankful smile, since that's all I can manage at the moment, and I trudge out of the school with a heavy heart.

Oliver's waiting for me. On the stoop.

At my apartment.

Oh, the nerve...

"What're you doing here?" I snap as I approach and rush past him up the steps to my door.

"You ran out of the school earlier before we had a chance to talk, and I think we should."

I try to close the door on him, but Oliver reaches out to stop me. "I thought we said plenty this morning."

He narrows his gaze, and I scoff.

Spinning on my heel, I march up to my apartment, and his hurried steps follow. For once, they're not perfectly calculated. They're rushed and uneven.

Maybe this is yet another way to unravel him.

I just wish it was for a better—and sexier—occasion.

As soon as I'm inside my place, I go straight to my refrigerator for a glass of water "I'm sorry, all right? I was blindsided, and I lied because I thought it was for the best," he says from behind me.

I whirl around toward him, the water sloshing from side to side in the glass in my grasp. "It was for the best because I'm Oliver Westbrook, and I know everything," I mock in his British accent, and I'm immediately embarrassed for not thinking that through.

But I'm too frustrated and hurt to think hard enough for a mature argument.

It doesn't help that he looks so put together and handsome. He doesn't appear crushed at all, and it stings.

Add that to the painful list of heartbreak he's ticked off one by one today. "Now you're just being petty." He places both hands on his hips.

I squeeze my eyes closed and drink my water, letting it slide down my dry throat, which cools me. All the while, he remains silent, and when I open my eyes again, he watches me with hurt marring his distinct features.

"Why didn't you tell me the truth about the vice principal position?" he asks. I blink. "What truth?"

"That you wanted to apply," he states firmly. "If you would've just been honest with me, we could've ended things before they became so complicated."

"Complicated? That's how you'd describe us?"

"You know what I mean." He tilts his head in such a condescending way that it only fuels me further.

"I don't know what you mean, actually. None of this makes sense!" I set the glass down and grab both sides of my head as if my brain is going to explode. "I don't want the vice principal position. I was never planning on applying, and that hasn't changed."

"There are four people who told me differently."

Never mind—my head isn't going to explode, but my heart might.

"You trusted them over me?" I whisper, dropping my hands to my sides.

"No." He lunges forward, but I hold my finger up to stop him from coming any closer.

It's already hard to breathe, and Oliver invading my space with his all-consuming power wouldn't help.

"I didn't believe them. But when I saw the application here"—he points to the now- empty coffee table—"I was confused. I couldn't get the nagging idea that you'd at least consider the position if it weren't for me, and I can't be the one to stand in your way from dreaming big."

"I was," I mutter, getting lost in his eyes as I let my meaning sink in.

I was dreaming big with him and not settling for the creeps I've been dating lately.

And more than that—I was happy with Oliver.

"I threw the application away." He freezes the moment the sentence leaves my mouth. "Katie had snuck it in my purse the last time I saw her."

He still doesn't move or speak as I pause to take another drink. I need strength and hydration.

I freaking need Oliver, but I can't run into his arms.

"I wish you would've told me all this. Instead, you blindsided me." I fold my arms across my chest, protecting myself from the sudden chill between us. "You had no right to make the decision for me. To lie to Bill without talking to me first."

He's crestfallen.

Every wise and charming line around his eyes and mouth is frowning.

"You're absolutely right." He rubs both hands over his guilt-ridden eyes and down the stubble covering his cheeks. "I'm so sorry, Erin. I made a snap decision for the both of us, and it was unfair. I should've handled the meeting with Bill differently, but I got scared that I might be holding you back. In the moment, I truly thought I was doing the right thing."

I gulp, and my earlier resentment backs down. What he says makes sense, after all.

If I were in his position, I'd probably do the same, wouldn't I?

Leaning my hip against the edge of the counter, I say, "I would not have applied for the position had Principal Garth still been around instead of you because I'm not qualified, nor am I prepared, for such a leadership role. The biggest responsibilities I've had outside of my actual classroom are decorating for dances, stocking the fridge with fruits and vegetables so that Oscar eats something other than chips, and volunteering to help Bobbie with book fairs. Sure, I'm involved with theater and their plays. I assist with the Christmas fundraiser every winter, but I'm not in charge of anything. Not yet." I pause to take a deep breath, and he finally raises his head. "I am in charge of my life, though, and I don't like when others make decisions for me."

"Nor should they, and I certainly don't want to do that to you ever again. Next time, I will excuse myself from the meeting and divert the discussion until you and I get on the same page."

I hold his stare as the sounds of the city gradually replace the ringing in my ears.

He's sincere, and it's hard not to let more of my rage go. "So, you want there to be a next time?"

He lets out a long breath and runs a hand through the buzzed side of his hair. "I want a thousand next times with you."

A soft laugh rumbles through me, but it catches in my throat. "What I mean is… we're going to tell Bill, right? But together this time."

He steps forward and threads his fingers through my hair, then cups my cheek. "Yes, but I would like to wait."

"What do you mean?" I whisper, on the verge of losing myself to his touch. To agreeing with anything he says, even if it's a dare to jump off the George Washington Bridge.

"We just claimed there's nothing going on between us. We can't call Bill tomorrow and go back on our word. We'd look absurd. But in the meantime, we can pick up where we left off this weekend." He strokes my cheek with his thumb as he leans in, leaving the dirty suggestion hanging in the air.

It's how we are.

We're intense. In sync. And in love.

I thought I was falling in love with him, anyway. Today has shown me a new side to us, and I'm having trouble grappling with what I've seen and experienced.

"I don't want to wait, Oliver." I place my hand on his chest and push him back. "People around the school are already talking about us. I can't keep lying if it comes up again."

"Again?"

"Katie told me the rumor of us has already gotten around to the other faculty. I'm not applying for Johanna's job, so what's the harm in confirming it at this point?" I flash my hopeful gaze up to meet his, but I'm not content with what's reflected in them.

"I don't think it's a good idea. Not yet." He steps away. "It would be better timing to wait until the position is filled, and the dust has settled."

I twist my lips as I let the message between the lines hit me like a bag of bricks. "You're having second thoughts about us."

"No. I've been very clear about how I feel when it comes to you."

"You like me, but not enough to subject yourself to looking *absurd*," I say sarcastically, tossing his own word back at him. "You are more worried about your reputation than us, and that's always been the case. It's why you wanted to hold off on disclosing our relationship to begin with, and Bill coming in today was your out. It was perfect."

"We were so new. It didn't make sense to make such a fuss so soon."

I laugh, but there's no humor in it. "Point made—we were just a fuss. Well, here's a suggestion to make sure I never ruin your life with complications and fusses: get out."

"You can't seriously believe I'm in the wrong for wanting to wait." He scoffs, and the implication that I'm so unreasonable strikes yet another nerve.

"I can, and I do." I match his offensive stance with one of my own.

"Fine," he mumbles, but it's reluctant. The veins in his neck scream in protest as he reaches the doorknob, where he pauses.

And I hold my breath.

Will he drop his stubborn defenses and agree I'm right?

After a few tense seconds that stretch beyond the logic of time, he releases a sigh and keeps his back to me.

His coat is far too thick to show the muscled back underneath. His sinewy forearms. The tattoo down the side of his rib cage.

There's not a hint of any of it, and I know this is how I'll have to see him from now on.

Guarded.

I could stop him. All it would take is a simple "yes." One quick word would turn this whole dumpster fire around, if I could just agree to wait.

But that's not the only problem.

How long would we wait? Would he keep finding reasons to hold off? Worse—what's the real reason he doesn't want to take us to the next level?

I can't help the trail of insecure thoughts flooding my mind and paralyzing me as Oliver leaves me alone in my quiet living room.

The worst fear that slams into me is wondering if I'm not worth the temporary public scrutiny and discomfort.

I've lowered my standards plenty of times in the past, making excuses for every jerk who treated me with little to no respect. Assholes who didn't appreciate and prioritize me.

I thought Oliver would be different when the time came to stand up for me, but instead of rising to the occasion, he cowered and took what meaningful future I thought we could have with him.

TWENTY-FOUR

Oliver

"Look who it is." Deidra holds her arms out, a white cloth over her shoulder. "Haven't seen you around these parts in a while."

I give her a tight-lipped smile and squeeze between two barstools, resting my elbows on the counter. "What have I missed?" I try to play along.

It has been a while, indeed, and if I couldn't discern it was true from memory alone, I'd know by how strong the smell is. I'd gotten used to it during my first few weeks in New York, but after having spent so much time at work and with Erin, I haven't popped in to see Deidra.

"I got new curtains for the window there." She points behind the bar, where a small window is covered by a red-and-white checkered fabric. It's similar to those I might find at a pizza shop.

"Smashing." I've never been the enthusiastic type, but this response is abysmal, even for me.

"What's eating you?" The guy sitting at the bar with an empty beer glass stares at me.

Before I can muster a vague response, Deidra swipes his glass. "Not your concern.

Now bugger off, Gary," she scolds as a mother might a child.

It's obvious they've known each other for a while, and at a second glance, I recognize him as one of the regulars.

"What can I get you to drink, dear?" she asks me.

"The usual, please." As she gets to work, I add, "Can I also have a white wine? My sister will be joining me this evening."

"Your sister?" She sets a chilled glass in front of me and wipes her hands on the rag. "I didn't know you had one here in the States. Did you move here together?"

"It's a long story for another time, Deidra." I tilt my head apologetically. "Fair enough. White wine coming right up."

I grab the drinks and find a vacant booth along the wall, working my jaw back and forth, not having been reminded of why I'm here in the first place in a long time.

I've been distracted—and pleasantly so.

My life was going rather swimmingly up until this week.

It's been difficult to focus since the debacle. I've seen Erin exactly three times in the teachers' lounge, each of which we skirted around each other like boss and employee.

As it should be.

But it was dreadful. I despised every moment, and I loathe the fact that I won't be touching her silky skin again.

Nor will I hear the sexy sounds from her perfect mouth or wrap her slim legs around me.

It's been torture for days, especially since I overheard Erin speaking with Katie about her friend Tessa's wedding today. She gushed over meeting new people and dancing the night away as if she weren't heartbroken at all.

Erin went so far as to tease the possibility of meeting a new guy.

I was instantly overcome with an envy so fierce I almost cleared the lounge to beg Erin to take me to the wedding—to take me back.

I want to be with her, but I also don't believe it's the right time for us to shout it from the rooftops. Not yet. How can she disagree so vehemently about that?

I'm being logical for once since I met her. All I've done since I succumbed to temptation is make everything go pear-shaped because I haven't been thinking clearly.

Now that I am, I'm still being punished for it and paying with my sanity. "Knock, knock." Rebecca appears next to me.

"Hi." I raise my eyebrows and drink from my chilled glass.

As she slides into the booth across from me, she shakes her head. "That's not how you answer the door."

"I beg your pardon?"

"Have you ever heard of a knock, knock joke?"

"Oh. Yes. Of course." I run the tip of my finger down the dew clouding the glass. "Who's there?" I play along, but I'd much prefer sticking my head under the beer tap behind the bar.

"A broody Brit sitting in a booth."

I finally face her head-on and notice she's glaring at me. "You're not funny."

"I save the funny ones for Malcolm. He used to like them anytime he was sad or happy—the occasion didn't matter.

He'd laugh whether it was a knock, knock joke to announce the arrival of the Tooth Fairy or just that it was lunchtime." Her smile is wistful, and as she figuratively waltzes down memory lane, it eases the tension between my shoulder blades.

The same tension that's been there all week like a jagged knife. Each step forward feels like my guilt reaches inside and twists.

"What happened with Erin?" she asks tentatively.

I rub my cold finger along my chin. "Who said anything happened?"

Rebecca waves her hand around my face. "I've gotten to know you pretty well, and I could picture this exact expression when we talked on the phone."

I drink more of my beer in an attempt to stall, which I never do.

What's worse—I squirm in my seat, and if there were a mirror in front of me, I couldn't bear to look at it.

"It's very confusing," I mutter, meaning it more for myself. "What is?" Rebecca scoots her wine to the side and leans forward.

After one more generous sip of beer, I give her the details of what transpired with Erin this week. It all comes out in a rushed breath, like the waterfall of beer from the tap as Deidra pours more drinks. I've been holding all this in for days, and I've been dying to share it with someone I trust, like my sister.

More patrons occupy the barstools around Deidra, and someone turns the volume on the telly higher as they get lost in the match, sloshing their beer around without care. A stain from the spill settles into the carpet while Deidra grabs a rag and warns the guy— another regular—to behave, or she'll cut him off. The door to the kitchen swings open several times, and the smell of fried foods hovers over us while I talk Rebecca's ears off.

And her attention never wavers from me.

At the end of my spiel, our drinks are still half-full since we talked more than drank, and I clasp my fingers together. "What do you think?"

Rebecca takes the third sip she's had since she sat down, then shifts in her seat. "What do *you* think?"

I blink, and the muscles in my shoulders bunch up like they're trying to form a wall.

"Do you think Erin was right?" she presses.

"She was, but I was also right. Wasn't I?"

She gives me a sympathetic smile. "A couple weeks ago, Malcolm was upset about his snack. I only had oatmeal raisin cookies for him instead of chocolate chip, so he picked a fight with me the entire drive home from school. When I asked what was really bothering him, he confessed that one of his friends is moving to Florida."

"Is he all right?"

"He's going to miss him, but once he admitted what the real problem was, we were able to talk through it. It's going to be tough, but he feels better now."

I relax into my seat but immediately tense again, the leather of the booth quietly squeaking as I continue squirming.

Why am I so nervous? I'm damn right in this, and Rebecca will see it too by the time we leave here, I'm sure of it.

"I don't actually think either one of you is right. I think you and Erin are using this grand reveal—to tell Bill, or not to tell him—to mask the bigger issues."

The sudden cheer from the guy at the bar jolts us as if to say *Bingo!*

"It's work," I insist. "It's smart to wait for a more opportune time to tell Bill now that we've already assured him we're not together. What would we look like if we go back on our word so swiftly?"

"Is that what you're worried about? Or is it the fact that you'd be officially together, and making it too real scares you?" Smirking, she leans back and folds both arms over her chest, clearly pleased with herself.

I grind my teeth.

"What's her name?" Her victorious grin slowly fades the longer we stare at each other, and the bar's atmosphere dulls.

"Erin..."

Rebecca rolls her eyes. "The girl who broke your heart and made you so insecure about relationships—what is *her* name?"

Memories of my ex's golden hair blowing in the wind instantly slam into me.

"I don't—" I start to deflect, but she holds her hand up to stop me. "Fine. Julie." She chews on her cheek, then says, "You've never mentioned her before."

"You never talk about Malcolm's father, either."

She plucks her tongue and sits forward again, meeting me halfway over the table. "Fair enough. I'll share if you do."

"Deal."

We shake on it for good fun, and she points to me. "You first."

I take a big drink, drawing more than the fizzy citrusy taste—I'm hoping for courage too.

The only time I've recently mentioned her name was at the camp when Erin asked if I'd ever been in love. I don't talk about my ex for many reasons, but it's mostly because I'd convinced myself I was over the manner in which we separated. As I reveal more of my life with Rebecca, my overwhelming emotions bubble to the surface and start making me believe otherwise.

"My relationship with Julie was pleasant… at first." I lick my lips, glancing down at my twiddling thumbs. My stomach swirls with unease, and I've never felt as small as I do now, bearing my soul. But I need to do this. The urge to open up is too great to ignore. "She grew to resent me for being myself. My mundane, boring self. What if Erin does the same? I mean, what happens when the novelty of a taboo relationship wears off? How long before she realizes I'm not really the guy who gets randy in a school classroom on a whim?"

"Oh, God." She nearly spits her sip of wine back into her glass.

"Too much information?" I quirk a brow. "Consider us even for the story of you vomiting in your bed and not burning it."

"Malcolm is the one who told you about my nightmare. And yes"—she holds a finger up—"I'm very aware that he should not have known it to begin with, but in my defense, he doesn't know it was from the one time I went out drinking with co-workers." I chuckle, but it doesn't last long.

"It sounds like you're afraid what you and Erin have is fleeting," she states. "Does it feel like that, though?"

"Not at all," I answer without hesitation. "I get a rush every time I'm with her. A feeling in my chest that blossoms so beautifully and tells me it's forever. It's very unlike what I felt with Julie. When she ended things, I didn't flinch. I merely closed myself off to new relationships because I thought it would be for the best. I didn't care for the way I felt. Like I, in

my purest form, wasn't enough for someone. But with Erin…
I don't know. I felt fulfilled."

"There's your answer."

I blink away the fog rolling over my eyes. Every feeling I
gave voice to is true, but there's so much more to the story.

"It's not so simple." I scowl. "Erin played a big role in the
decision to be apart. It wasn't just me who walked away."

"Maybe you didn't leave her a choice," she argues. "I hate
to break this news to you, Ollie, but you, dear brother, have
serious control and trust issues. You don't like when you don't
get to do things your way."

My glower deepens. "That's not true."

"From what I've learned about you the last few months
and based on what you've said of your argument with Erin,
it's my professional opinion that my assessment is correct."

"What professional opinion? You're a nurse."

"Trash or rubbish—all the same." She nods as if she's
made a rational point. Yet, she's only confused me further.

"I'm not controlling," I argue. "And I am capable of trust.
I trust you, don't I? Enough to invite you down here, even
though I knew you'd possibly ridicule me."

"I'm only trying to help." She holds her hands up, palms
out while the glass of wine next to her warms.

I scoff, but it's weak.

The fact of the matter is that she is trying to help, but I'm
simply too exasperated to hear it.

"Think about why you're even here," Rebecca urges. "You
didn't have to leave your life in London, but you did by your
decision. You left on your own terms too, but not before you
secured a leadership position where your literal job is to boss
people around and hold their very future in your hands."

"That's not exactly what I do…"

"It's the gist." She places a loving hand over mine. "Now it's time to let your heart lead the way instead of your head, and you don't know how. So, you fight it."

My chest squeezes, trying its damndest to keep her words out, but it's getting harder to maintain the wall around my heart.

"Blech." She waves her hands in front of her face as she might if she'd eaten a mushroom—her most hated food. "That was so cheesy, even to my own ears, but you get my point. It's a very valid one too."

My soft laugh comes out a bit easier, and I'm instantly grateful she came when I called her.

This is the kind of bond I've been working hard to build. This right here is what I was missing in London—a family.

The sense of community.

I was part of one back in England, but it wasn't as closeknit as it was years ago.

Not since my mates and I took different paths lately. While we still ring each other every now and then, it's not the same.

But here in New York, I have found a circle of friends again with a group of people who make me feel at home. It's not only Rebecca and Malcolm, but the faculty as well.

Tommy, especially, has surprisingly worked his way into my personal life, no matter what I did to keep him out. Peculiarly enough, I don't despise it.

Just the opposite.

Beyond him, I had Erin, a woman who encouraged me to live wildly. Even though it was wrong, it felt right to be with her. More right than anything else I've done in my life.

I can't let my past derail me and ruin the good and pure

thing I had with Erin. I can't let the catty teachers come between us, either.

They already have their suspicions, anyway. They're going to say what they will, whether Erin and I get back together or not. It's just not reason enough to continue on without at least trying to win her back.

"Bloody hell." I shake my head.

"What?" Rebecca freezes with her glass halfway to her mouth. "You might have a valid point, indeed."

She does a mini-curtsey in her seat.

"Your turn to be in the hot seat, little sister." I wag my finger at her, then quickly sober—the ending to her story is not to be teased about. "Tell me about Malcolm's father," I plead, my tone more grave than before.

She toys with the stem of her glass, and underneath the table, the tip of her shoe taps nervously against my shin. "We met in college, and I can honestly say, it was love at first sight."

The idea makes me smile.

Before I moved here, I didn't believe in such things. They felt more like the rubbish sold in fairytales. After being with Erin, though, I know them to be true.

She did change me.

And now it's my turn to change her mind about us.

TWENTY-FIVE

Erin

"**W**hat are we toasting tonight?" I plaster a smile on my face like I have for the last week and a half and hold my margarita up to the center of the table. But the two girls don't follow.

"What?" I blink and set my glass down, the liquid inside swaying from side to side. Tightening my grip around the stem, I steady it, but it doesn't work in time. A few drops slide down the side and onto a napkin.

"I thought I was the only one who spilled." Bree snorts and shifts in her chair to angle her body toward me.

Madison rests her elbows on the table, and next to her, the chair is empty where Tessa should be sitting if she weren't on her honeymoon in Greece with her amazing new husband— now there's a guy who goes after what he wants and doesn't care who knows it.

Mumbling incoherently, I bunch up the damp napkin and replace it with a dry one, then wipe my glass dry too.

Anything to distract them, and myself, from what they're about to say.

Having known Madison and Bree for over two years, I sense they're going to go all intervention on me, but I just don't know what they'll say.

I continue playing with the napkin as I say, "Before you say anything—"

"How are we doing tonight, ladies?" Harvey slides into the conversation at the most perfect time, and I could kiss him for the interruption.

But I won't, of course.

It would be inappropriate, given he has Micah, and I'm heartbroken over another guy.

Rebounds have never been my thing, anyway, since I believe a broken heart can't be mended by more testosterone, unlike Bree's philosophy to fuck every chink in her armor glued shut by any means—and guy—necessary.

As the girls give him upbeat answers, I grumble a response that doesn't make sense even to my own ears.

Harvey nudges me. "You had a positive dating report for me a few weeks ago.

Don't tell me things changed."

"Oh, but they did." I sigh, then shake myself out of it with quick positive affirmations.

I'm smart. Bendy.

And I have the best of friends.

I smile, but it's more Wicked Witch of the West than the easygoing girl next door that's usually my MO.

As I take a gulp of the tangy drink to wash down my feelings, Harvey glances at the other two, his eyebrows raised in search of answers.

When they shake their heads, he backs away. "I'll check on you in a bit and make sure this one is smiling for real by the end of the night." He points to me and winks good-naturedly, but it doesn't help ease the bitterness that's been eating at me for days.

No number of positive reminders has helped, either, as they normally do. The practice has helped me since my parents' divorce, and it's gotten me through the pitfalls of adulthood.

It's what has made even paying bills and taxes enjoyable, but the only positive things I can seem to come up with these days are that New York and yoga still exist.

And while I'm grateful for my favorite city and form of exercise, those facts won't keep my bed warm at night and give me the happily ever after I crave.

"Is it scary how well we communicate without words?" Madison muses out loud. "No." Bree shakes her finger back and forth in the air. "It's just good friendship.

Harvey's practically one of us now."

That does make me smile just a touch, but I'm right back to frowning faster than a star shoots across the sky.

If only all my wishes on those marvelous miracles had come true, then I wouldn't be in this mess—with my *boss.*

That's all Principal Westbrook is to me now.

Madison clears her throat as more of a signal than a necessity from too many chips or something, and Bree sits up straighter. "We need to talk."

"Yes." I clap and ignore the stickiness on my palms from

the margarita. "How about Tessa's wedding, huh? The rooftop was beautiful and so perfect for her, don't you two think?" I gush.

"It was," Bree draws out. "She looked like a damn princess walking down the aisle with the New York City backdrop, all those flowers, and the freaking violin. Tessa deserves all the media attention she received like the star she was, and if—"

Madison clears her throat again and nods curtly in my direction. "While I completely agree…" she starts and leans forward to take my hand in hers. "We need to talk about you, babe."

"No. Please, let's not—"

"Oh, but we must." Bree rubs her palms together like she's devising an evil plan, but I quickly realize she's just trying to get the salt off her fingers. Small white specks land on the dark table like snow, but I don't get the chance to admire the resemblance. Bree switches gears from beaming over one friend to pitying another—me. "When I came over last night, you had a puzzle halfway put together on your kitchen table."

I search her stern expression. "And?"

"You never do puzzles," Madison chimes in.

"I needed a new hobby to keep me busy now that Oliver and I aren't… you know." I shrug and tear at the corner of a napkin.

"Puzzles, though?" Bree lifts a brow, and the disgust is more evident in her tone than her grimace. "It's not even a sexy version of puzzles. Just downright boring."

I scoff. "How do you make a puzzle sexy?"

"Easy." She waves her hands in front of her as she talks. "First of all, a man is involved. And not one on the TV, of course."

"I know that," I clip, rolling my eyes, but I'm still going to keep the TV turned on to my favorite show.

"Just wanted to make sure." Bree wipes her forehead with exaggeration in a gesture that reads *Phew*, as if she really needed to hear me say out loud that McDreamy isn't real.

I've been watching a lot of *Grey's Anatomy* lately, but I'm not delusional—geez. "So, when you and your guy are putting a puzzle together, for every piece you add to the whole, the other person removes a piece of their clothing. Sexy puzzling." She shrugs and takes a sip of her margarita.

Madison throws her head back and laughs, and I can't help but giggle myself. "You are the only person who could make that hot." Madison shakes her head, the

hint of a smile still on her lips. "That's a real talent right there." "I should teach a MasterClass," Bree jokes.

"Oliver taught me a lot. I tried so many new things with him," I add absentmindedly, and the second it leaves my mouth, I clamp it shut.

Both of my friends raise their eyebrows. "I mean…" I lick my dry lips and freeze.

"Oh, we know what you mean," Mads says slyly.

"I still can't believe you two did it in the health room—kudos, by the way. I didn't think you had it in you."

"I didn't. Not until Oliver. But this is what happens when you fall too fast, right?

You get clobbered." I sigh and give in to the talk they insisted on when we sat down. We've already discussed the highlights, especially since I had to report back that

Oliver was not going to be my date to Tessa's wedding, but because of said happy occasion, I haven't told them the details.

I did, however, unload the sordid tale onto Katie, since she was practically foaming at the mouth for the scoop. Gossip is like catnip to her and everyone else I work with.

Plus, I couldn't keep the negative feelings inside any longer. I knew I had to divulge them to a friend before I attended Tessa's wedding wearing a deep-set frown as my date. I would've ruined the day and had the pictures for proof. It wouldn't have been fair to her or Carter.

"He just made me feel so alive and adventurous and… sexy." I fight the shiver that usually comes knocking when I think about all the times Oliver and I were intimate.

Because that's what we were.

It wasn't just fucking in the back of a classroom. We were honest and open with each other, even though we weren't with the rest of the world.

Until our last conversation, anyway.

"When he and I were stranded at the camp, it felt like we were the only two people in the world, and it's how I felt whenever we were together after that," I say while they remain glued to me. "Oliver seemed different, but of course, I'd believe as much. I've been gullible since the second grade when my teacher said hiccups made us grow. I was convinced of its truth well into middle school."

"Maybe he—"

"And you know what Principal Asshole said to me at school yesterday?" I ask, cutting Madison off. "He complimented my pink polka-dot sweater right after he asked to speak in private. I refused, naturally."

"Why?" Madison eyes me hesitantly. "What do you mean?"

"I'll answer this," Bree chimes in and raises her hand. "I don't get why you're not together anymore. It sounds like he was just trying to be professional, and while I might not always condone prioritizing a job over a meaningful relationship, it does sound like he was trying to do the right thing."

I gape. "That's not what it was! He wouldn't even tell me the real reason until I forced it out of him. He wasn't serious about me, because if he was, it wouldn't have been so easy for him to dismiss us at the first sign of an obstacle. I've been astronomically duped. The worst duping in all my dating fumbles put together." I dig the heel of my palm into my eye. "I knew he had a flaw, and it turns out to be extreme insecurity. He's a coward."

"Since you mentioned it…" Madison cringes. "Were you just waiting for a flaw of his to present itself?"

"No." I scoff. "I wasn't rooting for him to have a flaw, especially not one that involves hiding our relationship like he's ashamed of it. Sure, I did think he was too good to be true, but I never… I mean, I'm not happy it…"

My rambling slows, but my heart rate picks up its pace.

Oh, God. Was I waiting for the other shoe to drop this whole time? And the second it did, I accepted it and ran away, didn't I? It's why I accused him of making plans with someone else during our first date.

Why I constantly asked for his flaw.

I wanted to know what I was dealing with before I let myself completely fall for him.

"I think you have your answer," Bree suggests.

After a pause, I wave my hands. "No. Nope. No. That's not what this is about, because even if I was wrongfully nitpicky, it doesn't change the fact that he blindsided me with Bill—twice. It's not fair of him to make every decision for me as if I'm so incapable of taking care of myself."

"No, it isn't fair," they agree.

"He should've believed you instead of Bill or the rumors from teachers who have proved time and again that they're not the most reliable," Madison adds.

"Thank you." I throw my hands up in the air, then drink from my margarita. "But..." She winces, and I freeze. "Be honest—if you weren't having sex with your

boss, would you have at least considered applying for vice principal? It sounds like you automatically disregarded it, but what if your situation had been different?"

"I wouldn't have applied. You two know I'm not much of a leader at the moment. I still have a lot of work to do on myself and professional development workshops to complete. You should see my calendar. If we were three years down the line, I'd be applying, for sure, but not now," I emphasize, again rambling like I took five shots of Red Bull instead of finishing a single margarita.

"Sure, but we all know what happens to the best-laid plans, babe." Madison rubs the top of my hand as if she's rubbing the words into me.

And it's true. Plans rarely work out.

I spent all summer carefully laying out my lesson plans for the year, but already, I've had to adjust a few classes since every student learns differently.

I planned on having a stress-free year, not romantically involving myself with the new principal.

And I most certainly didn't expect Johanna to retire and create an uproar among the faculty as they fight for her job like animals in the wild—which is what they're doing.

Karen and Nancy have given each other the stink eye every time I've been in the same room with them, and it's as uncomfortable as it is odd. Although they weren't exactly friends to start with, they'd usually gravitate toward each other in some weird alliance.

This job opening has torn them apart, though, as it has Oliver and me. It has brought out sides to us we did not expect.

"All I'm saying is, you don't know what you would've done, and I do believe he was trying to be respectful of your wants." Madison lifts a shoulder, adding, "I think the same is true now. He's still protecting you and your reputation by letting this vice principal drama die down before creating more unnecessary chaos."

I bite my lip as I strangely agree with my insightful friend. It's hard not to appreciate her perspective, but it's hard to wrap my head around it all.

"I'm still mad at myself for not having you approve of Oliver before I got involved," I tell Bree, half-jokingly but also very seriously.

She laughs into her refilled glass. "You've never needed me to approve of your dates, Erin."

"I did. Need I remind you of the guy who had an actual bedtime of exactly nine seventeen every night for fear the world would end, otherwise? I had the naive audacity to argue it was adorably quirky!" I bury my face in my hands.

"That was concerning," Bree relents. "But listen." She pulls my hands down and turns me to face her. "You're a good judge of character, but your confidence in your instincts was shaken after repeated disappointments. Until Oliver."

I gulp.

"You didn't ask me to vet him because you already knew he was, in fact, different.

He was an adult with his own savings account and not a creep who hid his money in a dumpster and kept wondering why it went missing every Friday, which oddly enough coincided with the trash pick-up schedule," she states sarcastically, and across the table, Madison snorts, quickly slapping her hand over her mouth. "The point is, you asked me to check the others out beforehand because you knew, deep inside, that they weren't *the one*."

"She's right," Madison chimes in. "And it seems to me that you and Oliver left a lot of things unsaid."

"I'd agree to talk to him." Bree pats my shoulder. "You have to figure out what his deal is because there's obviously more at play here than the web of rumors you two got tangled up in."

"This relationship is about you two and no one else. Don't let others come between you." From across the table, Madison gives me a reassuring smile.

They're making a lot of sense, and my chest swells with the possibility that there's still hope for Oliver and me.

Maybe I rushed into breaking things off with him because he wasn't the only one who was scared. We were both seeking out ways to destroy what we had, and I need to figure out why.

The only way to do so is to face him.

I worry my bottom lip between my teeth. "What if we just make things worse by talking? I could find out he wasn't trying to be professional at all. I could learn the hard, ugly truth that he just doesn't think I'm worth it."

"If that's the case, we'll go *Charmed* on his ass and perform a Wiccan spell to give him a micropenis," Bree answers, and Madison and I join her in a burst of laughter. "But I'm confident it won't come to that. Because, honey, you're totally worth it."

We clink to that, and I thank them.

I can always count on these two—and Tessa—to cheer me up, no matter what, but they were also right about Oliver.

The last time we spoke, I was still reeling. I was too hurt by the sudden switch in his behavior to think straight enough to say what I needed. To get down to the heart of our problems.

I'm just not sure I'm ready for what's sure to be the confrontation of the century for me.

TWENTY-SIX

Oliver

"**D**ude, you should've known—" Tommy and Oscar freeze midconversation as they roll into the teachers' lounge.

I would have given them the benefit of the doubt that it wasn't because of me, but judging by their wide-eyed, guilty stares, I'd say I'm definitely the reason they stop short.

"Cheers." I hold up my hot cup of coffee and start to make my exit with as much pride and dignity as I can manage, but I'm afraid it's too late for that.

The men have been avoiding me since the rampant rumors became a fixture in this school like the lights across the ceiling.

Rita described Oscar, in particular, as a "frenemy," which was the first time I'd ever heard the term. My talkative secretary had to explain, and although I did not confirm the idea outright, I internally agreed it's what he is.

I can't figure out why he has anything against me, but far more confusing is Tommy's distance. We don't have the same candid conversations we used to, and although I would've been thrilled for this space two months ago, it's a fucking punch to the gut now.

"Haven't seen you at the gym lately," Tommy says, and it stops me in my tracks. "Oh, I've been…" I shift from one foot to the other. "I've just been a little busy, is all."

"I'll say," Oscar mutters between a cough as I've seen a few students do when they're teasing each other.

"Dude," Tommy mumbles and gives him a warning glare.

I smooth my fingers over my tie to keep them busy as anger bubbles inside me. This is what I was afraid of, after all. I was concerned I'd lose the faculty's respect,

and that's what's happened. Before word got out about Erin and me, Oscar would've never had the audacity to make a jab at me like this.

Perhaps his piss-poor attitude is the reason we never became better friends.

"That's cool. Life gets in the way of those gains all the time," Tommy offers sympathetically. "When I was going through my divorce, I missed a lot of leg days."

I give him a tight-lipped smile, appreciating his effort.

"We'll be going." Tommy tugs on Oscar's arm as the sour lad mutters something about getting boss coffee later.

"A word of advice, gentlemen?" I peer down at them. "Don't believe everything you hear. I wouldn't want you to embarrass yourself when all is said and done."

Grumbling, Oscar exits the lounge, and Tommy gives me

a fist bump, insisting on clinging to the ridiculous form of greeting.

But it eases the tension in my shoulders, nonetheless. It's a good sign that he hasn't completely written me off as Oscar appears to have.

I'm not even certain why I said what I did. In this case, what they've heard *is* true, but I don't want Erin to think everyone is gossiping about her.

It wouldn't be fair.

As for the way they act toward me, I'll deal with it if their behavior worsens and interferes with our work.

I lick coffee drops from my bottom lip, savoring the soothingly bitter taste as I stalk down the hall. On the way to my office, I'm so close to passing Erin's room just for a glimpse of her. The evaluation I did of her class two days ago was excruciating.

While I sat in the corner with a notepad and a pen in my lap, she taught her lesson seemingly undeterred by my presence. Erin made the students laugh, and she answered their questions with confidence and precision. She was gentle but firm in assisting them as well.

It was a fascinating sight to behold.

It's why I felt so compelled to ask her to speak with me in private. If a couple of students hadn't been within earshot, I suspect she would've told me to fuck off. Instead, she politely decline—through gritted teeth, but still.

I'm riled up by the time I reach my office, outside of which Rita paces by her desk.

It's clear she wants to talk to me, and I welcome the distraction. "What's going on, Rita?" I ask, then take a sip of my drink.

"Oh! There you are." She presses her palms together in a

pleading manner. "I'm sorry to ask this, but would it be okay if I leave a little early? Maybe now? The last class is almost finished, and I want to get ahead of the traffic."

"Is everything all right?"

She nods, followed by a soft, reassuring laugh. "Everything's fine. I just need to pick up my mother on the way to my daughter's piano recital this evening."

"How wonderful," I beam, and I mean it. This is the first time today that my scowl isn't beating out my other expressions in frequency.

"My mom baked a cake for her and everything. Isn't that just the sweetest thing you've ever heard?" Rita claps, her enthusiasm infectious.

I chuckle as I agree with her. "Go on. Get out of here, and enjoy your night." "Thank you so much." She grabs her jacket and purse, sliding them both onto her arm, then waves. "See you Monday!"

Once she's out of sight, I enter the reprieve of my own office and sit behind my desk, eager to finish up the evaluation paperwork.

But something stops me.

Rita was so thrilled for her daughter's recital, as she should be, but what makes me freeze is the thought of the girl's grandmother being so involved as well. It's such a beautiful sentiment, but my gut churns.

My mother hasn't even met her own grandson. I sent a picture of Malcolm to her, but she never responded. I haven't a clue if she opened it, or if she deleted it right away.

I don't know if she'll ever free herself from the prison of the past. If she'll drop her defenses, apologize for her wrongdoing, and make amends.

At this rate, my mother won't be attending any future activities for Malcolm. No sporting events, birthdays, or holidays.

And I can't shake this surge of unresolved resentment slicing through my chest.

When we last spoke, Rebecca was correct about a lot of things, especially about me, but what she failed to mention was my mother.

Our mother.

Rebecca has a perfectly reasonable excuse not to want to talk about her, but it doesn't mean the woman hasn't played an extraordinary role in who I am and who I've become over the last few months.

The bell rings, and it jolts me into action.

I need to ring her. It's the only way I'll put this ache to rest.

As the boisterous music of the end of yet another Friday commences, I haphazardly stuff the remaining paperwork on my desk into my shoulder bag. The noises from the hallway echo more loudly from the lockers slamming shut and students rushing outside.

Prepared to follow their lead, I throw my overcoat on and flee my office with only one goal in mind.

But the second I pass the cramped waiting area where Rita's desk sits, a bright purple sweater stops me. Erin stands in the doorway, her timid eyes scanning the room as she tiptoes inside.

"Erin," I whisper with disbelief.

"Hi." She shifts, reaching up to tuck a strand of hair behind her ear.

I glance over her shoulder into the hall, which is now

empty except for a few custodians wheeling large trash bins with the occasional squeak. There are no other teachers in sight, and I take the opportunity to rake my gaze over Erin.

She's radiant in her vivid top, her hair loosely cascading over her shoulders. It's been too long since I last kissed her decadent lips.

The air is sucked from my lungs, thankful she came to me and isn't running along with the rest of the school, already celebrating the weekend.

But I'm not sure who or what to thank for this visit. Perhaps she merely needs something work-related.

Grimacing, I ask, "Is this about your evaluation? Because I'm still—"

"No." She purses her lips. "I am curious, but I'm not here to ask about that." "Is it too late to accept your request to speak privately about us?"

"Yes." I shake my head. "I mean, no. I'd love to talk, but I am just on my way out to deal with something."

"Oh, okay. I just, um, thought we should clear a few things up."

"I whole-heartedly agree, but I need to—" I stop when Tommy appears behind her.

He takes one look at Erin and backs away, practically tripping over his untied shoelace in the process.

I hold my hand up to stop him while Erin steps aside to get a better look at the interruption.

"I didn't mean to cut you two off." He scrunches his nose up like he smells something awful. "I just wanted to apologize for what happened earlier in the lounge."

"You're fine. Everything is fine, but I need to go." I continue out the door, leaving them both behind.

I'm a fucking wreck.

My head spins as I rush home, the entire walk a blur.

A soft mist drizzles from above as storm clouds hover over the city by the time I reach my flat. Once inside, I march toward the fridge for a lager.

The heavier rainfall coming down, along with the rest of the noise outside my window, becomes static. It muffles further as I pick up my phone and set it back down.

And repeat.

I take a long pull of my fizzy drink, then swipe the phone from the counter. And I ring the one person I've been avoiding for the last several weeks.

My mum forgoes a greeting and says, "I'm surprised to hear from you."

"And I'm surprised you answered. Isn't it late for you?"

"It's hard to sleep these days," she says rather faintly. "I didn't expect you to ring, but I'm delighted you did."

"You're my mother. I needed space, not permanent silence. I'd never stop speaking to you altogether." I squeeze my eyes closed and sigh.

"Good to know. So, what is it, dear?" she asks, and her concern echoes through my speaker. "I might be hundreds of miles away and can't see your face, but I know when something's wrong. What's happened?"

"A while back, you claimed I didn't know the entire story. You told me there's more to the past with Rebecca and that I shouldn't take a stance without all the details." I grip the edge of the counter and dip my head, bracing myself. "What did you mean?"

She pauses, and for a moment, I don't expect her to respond.

"Mum?"

"I'm still here, darling. The truth is, it's all very complicated."

"That's not an explanation."

There's clinking on her end as if she has her own drink in hand. "I went to New York for space after your father and I separated, and I stayed with a dear friend. I had a whale of a time, Oliver, but I never dreamed of staying. New York wasn't home for me, and I missed you terribly."

Bollocks.

She's actually telling me the story.

When I asked, I didn't believe she would, but she's doing it. Am I prepared for what she has to say?

I grab a stool and lower myself onto it as if I'm steadying myself on one of those large blue yoga balls I've seen around the gym.

"I was just over four months pregnant when your father and I agreed I'd return to London to reconcile. I didn't know what to do. I had to go, but my heart broke at just the thought of separating Rebecca's father from her." A gulp drifts through the speaker, and I tense. "So, I waited until I gave birth, after which I made the difficult decision to leave her in his care. When I discussed my intentions with Silas, he'd only agree to it if I promised to disappear entirely."

Her voice cracks at the end, and I clench my jaw as tightly as I ball my hands into

fists.

"I didn't want to agree to his terms, but it was the simplest way out, my love," she

states, and it's hard to believe what I'm hearing.

Is she serious right now?

"Why didn't you fight harder?" I whisper, unable to fathom leaving a child behind. "Darling, emotions were extremely high, and understandably, Silas was hurt. After

all, I was choosing to come back to you and your father. He didn't mean to be petty, but—"

"This isn't about him, Mother. It's about you." I let out a quick huff and try to wrap my head around the picture she's just painted.

How could she let Rebecca go just like that? Why not work out a way to be part of her life? London is a quick flight away, and she and my father didn't lack in wealth, that's for sure.

There were so many things she could've done differently. So many endings that would've been better than this one. They could've reached an outcome that wouldn't have hurt the people involved as much as it has now.

Rebecca has turned out well and fine. As a matter of fact, I'm more wounded on her behalf than she is, but my mother's "simplest way out" had consequences beyond herself.

"How could you be such a coward?" I ask her as much as I do myself. After a pause, she surprises me when she says, "Aren't we all?"

I sink farther onto the stool on a heavy exhale.

My mother gave up control with such nauseating indifference, as I did with Julie.

My ex wanted to end things, and I didn't fight back because I wanted the same.

I should've told her the truth, though. I should've been strong enough to admit I was dating her for the wrong reasons. That I was only doing what I believed was expected of me by continuing our relationship.

I took my own simplest way out and let Julie break it off with me.

It's how I've treated most of my relationships. I resign the second I face too many complications.

Given the revelations I've encountered lately, there's nothing left for me to say to my mother other than, "I suppose you're right."

TWENTY-SEVEN

As I make my way through the hall, I adjust the round green hat with "leaves" sticking out to the sides and bump into a locker. A few students linger with their textbooks in hand and continue toward the stairs when they hear me. Offering a small wave, I skirt around them and smack into another locker against the opposite wall.

The pot I'm wearing around my waist has been a nuisance all day, but the students seemed to enjoy my plant Halloween costume. It's the one they voted on, after all, during a fun poll I've made somewhat of a tradition every October.

Broccoli was going to be an option, but I would've been too creeped out if it was chosen, given how obsessed Barry—a past disaster date—was with vegetables and how often he compared me to different ones.

Instead, I went with a plant.

It's a safe option but not exactly practical when I'm walking down the hall, evidently. For the first time, it seems narrow, but it's just me.

I'm off balance.

And I'm dangerously close to becoming the crazy plant lady with all my free time. Just in the last week, I've bought two succulents for a centerpiece on my breakfast table, a snake plant, whose name I wasn't crazy about but wanted to avoid judging it by its classification, and an areca palm. The latter needs more attention than the others, but it acts as a natural air humidifier—I figured it would be the best to have around.

God, I've learned so much about plants between finishing my puzzle. I hate to say it, but I think I'm headed down a bad path.

I return to my classroom, granola bar in hand, and find Katie on the edge of my desk. She's dressed in all black, a cute headband with tiger ears nestled in her blonde hair, and my nosy friend is snooping through the papers stacked to the side.

"Are you trying to cheat on next week's exam, or are you looking for something in particular?" I snort.

She shoots up. "Where have you been?"

"In the lounge, getting my afternoon granola bar." I shrug and brush past her. "I didn't feel like making my own last night—and yes, it does make six nights in a row."

"Must be tough eating out of the vending machines like the rest of us mere mortals," Katie teases.

I tilt my head and exaggerate a smile. "I love our chats."

As I tear into my bar, she hops off the desk and holds her hand out for me. "I never did tell you about Tommy."

"No, you didn't. When I asked to have coffee to talk about it, you said you couldn't because you were looking into buying a goat to do yoga on your own." I hold a finger up. "You also took up yoga instead of drinking ten cups of coffee every day, and I'm proud of you."

"Don't be—it hasn't lasted. I never bought a goat, either. I was temporarily out of my head." She waves her hand. "Can I tell you about my latest heartbreak on the way to the gym?"

"Why the gym?" I say between crunching bites.

"The new banner, silly. Remember? I told you at lunch that I want to show it to you."

"What banner is it?" I take slow steps toward her as I swallow the toasted snack, which scratches the roof of my mouth and throat. Why do I eat this stuff? "If Karen approved it, then I see no reason to have any part of it."

Katie obviously picks up on my sarcasm and rolls her eyes, then loops one arm through mine as she leads the way.

And I follow, if only because it's better than stewing in my classroom as I did yesterday. After Oliver darted off when I asked to speak to him, I spent thirty minutes pacing my classroom the second the final bell rang.

He said he'd love to talk, but the moment Tommy appeared, Oliver sprinted away like the presence of another teacher spooked him. We were standing a good couple feet apart too, so there was no need to panic. It's not like Tommy caught us mid-kiss.

Yesterday only proved he's still not ready.

I don't know how I'm going to finish the school year alongside him. No matter how hard I try to avoid him, Oliver is inevitable.

The worst part of it all is that I freaking miss him.

Seeing him yesterday only made me miss him more for some sick reason.

"I built the whole thing up in my head, after all," Katie cuts through my thoughts. "The fling with Tommy?" I ask.

She nods and practically skips down the hall, her arm still holding mine. "I was lonely, and he's hot—a complete cliché. But at the end of the day, he called me *dude* one too many times. No amount of hotness is worth such an insult."

I giggle into my palm.

"He's a good guy, but we're better off as friends." She shrugs, and she seems to genuinely mean it.

It's far more convincing than when Bree claims she's better off without chips, but then I find her sneaking them into my apartment for movie night. Of course, it could also be because she doesn't like the kale chips I bake, but that's beside the point.

"I'm happy for you, Katie." I pat her hand, and I'm just as genuine about it too. "I'm happy for me too," she jokes. "I am still lonely, though, but my students' big

art projects are due next week. Those and the low-key show I'm organizing will keep me entertained until Christmas, after which I'll be right back here."

"You never know—you might be the lucky recipient of a holiday miracle this year." "Sure," she draws out. "And right after I meet Prince Charming, I'll learn to fly."

We both laugh, but I cut it off short. "Seriously, you never know, but in the meantime while you search for your man, let me know if you need any help with the art show."

"Will do."

As we near the gym, she picks up the pace like a kid racing toward a ride at Disney World. "You're going to love this."

"The banner?" I blink. "You never told me what it's for."

"It's a surprise," she chirps. "One you've been wanting for a while, but you're too hurt to see it yourself. This is your nudge."

"Are we still talking about the banner?" I try to wiggle out of her grasp, the hairs on my arms sticking up as I catch a whiff of the odd vibe between us.

But Katie doesn't loosen her hold on me and drags me along like an actual tiger might its cubs.

"What the hell is going on?" I ask.

Remaining quiet, she yanks the door to the gym open with unusual force and pulls me inside. She's clearly been doing a lot more yoga than she let on before. I'm inclined to believe Tommy showed her around a weight room too.

I whirl around to repeat my question, officially confused and convinced there's no banner— why did I even fall for that? —but Katie slams the door shut, a loud thunder echoing across the tall ceiling of the gym.

"What the hell?" I repeat and lunge after her, but I don't reach it in time.

Click.

My friend—she used to be, anyway—locks the freaking door. "Katie!" I screech.

"It's for your own good, I promise," she calls out from her side, and her face appears through the slim window on the door as I bang on it. "I won't apologize for this, but I am sorry I didn't make you change before I kidnapped you."

Through the window, Katie's smug grin transforms into an apologetic frown, but I barely register it, focusing instead on what *this* is that she could be apologizing for.

And then I hear it. His voice.

Deep, strong, and confident.

It's the kind of voice that commands a business meeting, as well as a woman's fantasies, and I don't have to turn around to know Oliver is here.

"…still don't know of what service I can be with this banner," I hear from the other side of the basketball court—down the hall where the health room is. "Are you sure we shouldn't nominate Tommy for such a task?"

"No, he won't know what to do."

Is that…

I spin around and catch a glimpse of Bobbie before she repeats what Katie just did with me. The sneaky librarian tosses Oliver inside and locks the door behind him as well.

"What on earth has gotten into you?" Oliver still hasn't noticed me as I stand across the room in disbelief, and he stalks toward the door. Knocking on it, he asserts, "Let me out this instant."

"This is for your own good, sir," Bobbie calls out, again as Katie did. How long did it take them to coordinate this little stunt?

Shaking my head, I turn toward the locked door and find Katie is still standing on the other side of it, her head cocked at a painful angle as she tries to get a look at Oliver.

"Let me out!" I hiss and beat on the door again, the thuds mixing with Oliver's.

I already know he's noticed me before I even glance backward, because my skin tingles with the laser beam of his heated gaze.

If I could see him, I bet I'd find surprise in his eyes as well, but it doesn't matter.

I'm going to get my traitorous friend to let me out before we can get into another screaming match.

"Katie! Open this door, or I'll tell the whole world you were on a TV show, where you played a character named Katie Bee Bumble."

As I suspected it would, this gets her attention.

"You wouldn't!" She stares back at me through wide eyes, her protest muffled through the barrier.

"Oh, I would." I dig into the felt fabric of my clunky costume and feel around until I realize I'm wearing leggings with no pockets.

Which means I left my phone and any contact to the outside in my classroom. "I swear I'll do it… the second… I find…" I keep digging around just in case I

forgot a secret compartment or something.

It's possible, but it's difficult to think right now.

My head is an absolute mess, so I let my hands figure it out. No such luck.

As my frantic search comes to an end, Bobbie appears in the window, smooshing Katie's face to the side.

"Don't you dare open the door!" she commands and shoves Katie the rest of the way out of view.

"This was not a good idea," Katie says. "She's going to tell everyone my middle name."

Bobbie gasps and turns her attention back to me. "If you tell on her, I'll just have to reveal to Karen who scratched her beloved purse last year."

"That was an accident," I say in my defense and splay both hands on either side of the window.

"Ladies, there's no reason—" Oliver's cut off by the door creaking open.

Bobbie and Katie tiptoe inside, careful not to open the only hindrance to my freedom the entire way. I still lunge after them in a feeble attempt at an escape, but they lock arms and stop me from passing.

"Whoa, whoa." Bobbie holds her other hand out. "Listen, mostly everyone is gone, and this is the farthest space from the other classrooms. Tommy is the only one we were worried about, but he's long gone. Of course, he didn't leave without giving us the key for the mythical banner we needed to stash here, but that's irrelevant. This is your chance to work your shit out."

Oliver clears his throat.

"Sorry—I mean, *crap*," Bobbie offers with a shrug. "No disrespect, sir, but don't think of us as your staff right now. Think of us as concerned citizens doing their good deed for the day."

"Exactly," Katie jumps in. "I saw you two yesterday afternoon. You have unresolved feelings for each other, and we can't let you ignore them any longer."

"How much did you tell them?" Oliver asks and enters my periphery.

I pin my glare on him, then redirect it onto Katie. "I only told *one* of them a few parts of the story."

"I told Bobbie the basics because I needed a wingwoman to get you both in here." She shrinks back, her body halfway out the door. "Erin only told me the important details, which rest assured, included nothing intimate like tattoos or—" She clamps her mouth shut, and my own falls open in horror.

"Christ," Oliver mutters and places both hands on his hips.

"You're going to pay for that and this," I warn as I attempt to get past them again, but Bobbie steps between Katie and me.

"Who cares what we know? Believe me, the rumors flying around this place are far worse than the reality." She starts to laugh but immediately stops herself. "Now talk to each other and clear up whatever mess you've gotten yourselves into. I don't have all evening. I'm meeting my family at a diner for our monthly breakfast for dinner *pancake- palooza.*"

Nearing my boiling point—and suddenly craving pancakes—I purse my lips and face Oliver. "Why are you not helping me get out of here?"

"Because they're right." He shrugs, easing into an apologetic stance.

His shoulders fall forward like he has a heavy backpack strapped to them, and his eyes hold nothing but desperation.

As the lock of the door echoes again, I dive headfirst into the realization that I will suffocate in here from the sheer devastation of having to be this close to such a specimen.

I square my shoulders, drawing strength from the recesses of my heart, and clip, "You refused to talk to me yesterday, and now, I don't want to talk to you, either."

"Perfect. Sitting here in silence works wonderfully for me." I detect a bounce in his cheek as he paces along one side of the bleachers.

"You could make them let us out. You're their boss," I point out, and I'm dangerously close to stomping my foot.

"Right now, they're not my staff, remember?" he shoots back, then goes in for the kill. "Is this not considered talking?"

I purse my lips into a razor-thin line, my overwhelming frustration reaching for the stars.

So, I remain quiet—for several minutes.

During the tense silence, Principal Cranky Brit sits on the bleacher, and right when I'm about to ask him how he can be so calm, he repeatedly taps his foot to an uneven rhythm.

He's rattled.

And my frail heart squeezes. I have to talk to him.

We need to clear the air or else neither of us can move forward.

I know as much, but it's not easy to look into his beautiful blue eyes and take another rejection.

Hurt from the possibility floods me, pulling the words out of me as I snap, "Fine. Let's talk. Where do we begin? You seem to call the shots, so please, you have the floor."

"I'm so glad we're going to be mature about this." He huffs and stands to his full height. "If I'm not the one to begin, you'd insist I sit on this side of the bleachers while you take that one." Using his thick forefingers, he points to opposite sides of the gym. It's similar to the suggestion I made when I divided the camp when we were stranded.

Somewhere underneath the red layer of anger covering my vision, I remember what that finger did to me in the cabin. What we did the last time we were in this gym together.

It was one of the last times we were open and intimate. My face falls, and his does the same.

"I'm sorry," he says.

I wrap my arms around as much of my midsection as I can with this obnoxious costume. "The only thing you're sorry for is *our affair*, isn't it?"

"Not at all, and you know it."

"If that were true, you wouldn't have insisted we keep hiding."

"It was the best thing to do, but it's not the only thing I

want to clarify right now." I toss my hands up and spin in place. "You always want to be right and in control, and you think—"

"I'm just trying to show you—"

"—you know everything. If you would listen to someone else for a change—"

"—I had a point because you blame me for how things ended, but I'm not the only

one at fault, although I am sorry for my part in it."

We finally stop talking over each other and blink. My chest heaves as my heart beats against the walls of it, threatening to leap out onto my sleeve.

I've always worn it there, haven't I?

"For which part are you sorry?" I ask, my voice losing some of its previous edge.

Oliver rubs his thumb and pointer finger along his chin as his eyes dart between mine. "For starters, I'm sorry about yesterday. I had to ring my mother."

"Oh?" I whisper, tensing all over.

"She and I had an enlightening conversation, and it helped me realize a few things." "Like what?"

"I don't want to be a coward like her." He shrugs, resigned to his admission. "I'm also sorry for my behavior when we first met. For lashing out at you over this job opening and using it to avoid what I'm truly scared of."

My heart flip-flops. "What're you scared of, Oliver?"

"You." He lets out a soft laugh, but there's no humor in it. "I'm scared of losing control, and I have when it's come to you. I've never jeopardized my own career and reputation, let alone anyone else's, especially someone whom I care a great deal for. But the truth is, I haven't been myself in a while. Since long before I ever decided to move here. In fact, I forgot who I was entirely… until you. You rattled my soul awake, Erin.

My bored, dying soul. You gave me a new, more purposeful life."

I gulp and find myself inching closer as if each word is pulling me by a string, and my feet move of their own accord.

I'm entranced by him and his vulnerability. It's hard not to be, not when he speaks with such raw truth.

His voice echoes, too, in this empty gym, making him seem more robust with every detail.

"And I'm scared I won't live up to be the man you deserve, and you deserve the best, love. More than murderers and bloody winemakers." His exhale turns into a chuckle.

I let out a shaky laugh of my own as I reach him, and my breath hitches when he squeezes my hands in his, holding them between us.

I've ached for this contact over the last several lonely nights.

"But I'm not a coward," he asserts, and it feels like it's more to himself than to me. "You terrify me, but I don't want to be without you. I can't stop thinking about you. I can't stop missing you. And I don't want to. I'm just so sorry for—" I stand on my tiptoes and fuse my mouth to his.

He doesn't immediately kiss me back, but I don't back off. Instead, I thread my fingers through his hair and kiss him harder. Because this man makes me feel the same.

Oliver makes me feel loved and special, and there's been a void in my chest ever since we parted—one he fills with each second of our kiss.

When he slips his tongue between my open lips, I moan and grip his hair tighter. "I've missed you too."

He tries to pull me closer, but my silly costume keeps me from melting against him.

Suddenly, I wish Katie and Bobbie would've locked us in my apartment or somewhere more private.

Especially when we hear muffled cheers sounding from outside the door.

"Oh my God," I mutter and tug my bottom lip out from between his teeth, then bury my face in his chest.

His arm grazes my face as he lifts it, and I tilt my head up to find him waving.

Cheeks flaming, I pull out of his embrace and chance a glimpse at the nosiest teachers, and even better friends. I wave to them too, and they smile as they continue cheering.

"You can go now," I call out to them sarcastically.

Oliver pulls me by my arms back into him and places a sweet kiss on my temple. "Also, you're the most adorable plant I've ever had the pleasure of making out with."

I let my head fall to his shoulder, and my cheeks grow hotter. "Did I mention I'm going to kill Katie and Bobbie? Because I totally am."

Smiling, he dips his head to kiss my lips again, and as our laughter subsides, the lump in my throat reappears.

I rub my hands up and down his arms as I manage, "Before today, I thought you were a coward, but the more I think about it, I was wrong. You were just trying to protect me and both our jobs. You had a very valid point—we would've looked like idiots had we told Bill we lied to him. I don't know where that leaves us now, but I want to figure it out together."

"I want the same." He nods, and a gust of air leaves him.

"You're selfless and considerate, and that's what makes you so different from anyone I've known. I'm sorry I kept trying to find something wrong with you. I was being unfair because I was scared too. My feelings for you have been so strong since the first day we met, and it seemed too unreal that I could have more than anything I've ever wanted." I take a deep breath as I toy with the hair at the back of his neck. "I'm sorry I sabotaged what we had."

"Interestingly enough, I have thoughts regarding how you could make it up to me." He places a chaste kiss on my lips and smirks. "Something you might call a win-win."

"Really?" I quirk a brow and lean in for the big reveal. As he whispers his idea, my cheeks heat further.

"A compromise, huh? You're more like the Wright brothers, after all, giving up control like this." I wiggle in his embrace, my grin coy as I recall one of the first conversations we ever had.

It was one of the first encounters that made me fall for him.

"Your grandfather was certainly an intelligent man, and I wish I'd had the opportunity to meet him," Oliver says.

"Me too. He would've loved you." I smooth my palms down his chest over his crisp shirt. He's so proper and gentlemanly—the kind of man who's worthy of taking home to meet the family. "I guess my parents will just have to do."

He peers down at me with surprise and wonder swirling in his vibrant eyes. "You want me to meet your parents?"

"Oh, um, well…" I twist out of his hold, my back sweating with panic. Why did I say that? We only just made up, and I skipped ten levels ahead because of my stupid mouth.

Why can't I, for once, think before I speak?

"It's something to think about down the line, like when we get engaged," I babble, talking with my hands and waving them around as I might if I were an actual plant being attacked by bees.

And did I seriously tell him we're going to get engaged?

Oh. My. God.

I look and sound insane.

He's going to regret patching things up with me. Oliver is totally going to make up an excuse, tell me he was kidding about wanting to be with me, and run in the opposite direction.

I'd deserve his dismissal too. I've just taken a perfectly sweet moment and turned up the crazy factor by a million.

"Erin," he starts as I bite my lip—my big, traitorous lip.

Here it comes...

He wraps his arm around my waist and scoops me back against his warm body, bringing my thumping heart with us. "Erin, I don't want you to be afraid of planning our future together. I know we have a lot of logistics to figure out, but there's one thing I don't need time to sort."

I deeply inhale and hold it, fearing if I released this breath, it'll erase this entire afternoon.

"I love you."

My lips part, and my exhale takes every hesitation in my body with it. "I love you," he repeats with a smile.

"I love you too, Oliver," I whisper against his mouth and squeeze my arms around his neck, finally grounded and tethered to something real.

Oliver is my center.

As we kiss in the middle of the basketball court, I know that now more than ever, and I'm determined to keep it this way.

TWENTY-EIGHT

Oliver

"**D**oes it feel good?" Erin says through an exhale.

It's sexy, and the fact that she's naked just makes me hard and tense—the opposite of what we're after.

Shifting on the round cushion, or a *zafu* as she called it, I grimace and whisper, "Brilliant."

"Let's begin."

"We haven't begun yet?" I ask, and I'm only half kidding. She snorts and closes her eyes, but I can't stop staring at her.

With the light filtering through her bedroom window behind her, she looks like a sexy angel—which isn't far off at all.

Her breasts are free, and her mouthwatering nipples are hard beads pointed right at me. I swear I can hear their pleas for my attention.

To make matters more painfully arousing, her glistening heat is also bare, and I have the perfect view of it as she sits with her legs open and crossed.

My hard cock is exposed as well.

I was elated to kiss and make up, so to speak, yesterday afternoon, but when I shared with her my idea of naked meditation, I didn't know what I was getting myself into. I should've known I wouldn't last. I was simply trying to give her a chance to show me what I'm missing out on.

"Clear your mind, and breathe," she says, her voice fading as she exhales.

And although the room quiets, my head fills with endless thoughts of what I'd like to do to Erin.

Plunge myself inside her.

Make her come all over this cushion.

Anything to make up for the time we lost while we were apart.

I try to do as she instructs since she's evidently very committed to seeing this activity through. Otherwise, my balls will turn blue.

I'm not sure how long we sit in meditative silence like this when Erin finally shifts onto her knees and crawls over to me.

Her sweet perfume fills my senses before she comes into view, and I grind my teeth together again.

"Please tell me we're finished," I beg in a hoarse voice.

She leans her hands on my knees and sways those perfect hips from side to side, the curve of her ass teasing me. "And what would we do if we were finished?"

I narrow my gaze and lower my voice to a daring whisper. "I'd roll you over, use the flexibility you've acquired from all your yoga to spread those beautiful thighs, and run my tongue between them." I graze my nose along her jawline and inhale my fill. "I'd feast on what's mine."

She shudders against me, a feminine whimper escaping her sinful lips, and that's all it takes for me to make good on my promise.

Done with meditating or not, nothing could've stopped me from leaning her back, pushing her legs open, and burying my face between them.

It seems like we've spent years apart instead of a mere couple of weeks, and she tastes sweeter than I remember.

She's also soaked, and it drives me far madder than I've ever been.

It's not long before she shatters into a sensational explosion of pleasure, her ecstasy coating my tongue and dripping down my chin.

She comes hard, and her body continues writhing as I pull her on top of me, desperate for Erin to ride me.

Uninhibited and wild. I want it all with her.

"Oh!" She gasps, falling forward until the ends of her hair tickle my chest. Panting, she gazes deep into my eyes and rolls her hips, aching for me as well.

My tip teases her wet entrance as we continue watching each other. It's a silent conversation.

Trust passes from her eyes to mine, and I nod in response, fulfilled in an indescribable way.

Because even before she sinks onto my naked cock, I know we're honest and bared to each other.

Connected from the first time we met. Part of each other like a limb.

And nothing's going to change that.

Our heavy breaths are in sync like our rapid heartbeats, and as she moves faster, her thighs rubbing relentlessly against my own, my body tightens.

"That's it, love." I lick my lips and thrust my fingers into her hair, pull her down, then cover her mouth with mine.

She moans, and it vibrates between us, bouncing in waves down my body.

My hips rise of their own accord, seeking hers with every drive upward, and the slapping of our slick skin grows louder.

"Oh… God…" she stammers, and I swallow those words as I revel in her shaking body.

Her stomach clenches, and she squeezes her legs around me, her impending climax

begging to be unleashed.

She comes a second time, sweat trickling between the valley of her breasts like her climax dripping down my pulsing length.

And the last of my restraint snaps.

I throw her over and onto her back, careful to cradle her head with one hand, and I grip myself with the other, stroking until my release spills onto her stomach.

With heavy breaths, I lean over her, a randy grin tugging at my lips. "Let's meditate every day, shall we?"

Her eyelids flutter open and closed in the most glorious way—she's satisfied with me in every sense. "Absolutely."

As I assist her to her feet, a smile teases her own lips, and I can't help but kiss them.

I savor them as I do her.

And I look forward to many Saturday mornings spent like this. To hours of exploring each other and trying new things.

To making her happy.

I'll do whatever it takes to show this woman how truly special she is.

"Shower?" She peeks over her shoulder, her brown eyes a lighter hazel than usual.

They're more playful too, and it's easy to lose myself in them.

But I'm not too lust crazed to miss the meaning of her one-word question. "Definitely," I say.

Holding a finger up, she spins to face me. "I'm being serious, though. We need to shower and get ready for trick-or-treating with Malcolm and some of the kids from the Boys & Girls Club. We have a big night ahead of us."

"Can't I stay here and hand out toothbrushes instead?" I tease—but I'm also very serious.

I'm convinced Halloween has to be responsible for at least thirty percent of the obesity rate in children in the world. I, for one, can't be part of it.

Nevermind the fact that I'm not a fan of wearing an obnoxious costume. "You are such a Scrooge."

"Wrong holiday, love." I kiss the back of her hand and wink.

Groaning, she jumps into my arms and kisses my lips. "You're coming to the Halloween festivities, and you'll wear a smile. In addition to a costume, that is."

I grimace. "Costumes are so…"

"Fun? I agree," she says and places another quick kiss on my lips. "Do you even know how to have fun?"

I smirk. "I'd call what we just did, fun."

She rolls her eyes and takes my hand in hers to lead me toward the bathroom. "You know what I mean!"

"I used to read Charles Dickens for my pleasure during breaks from helping my father with taxes."

"How wild," she deadpans.

"Oh, for wild fun, I read Tolstoy at my uncle's cottage when we'd visit in the summer."

She turns the shower on, and the small bathroom fills with the sound of rushing water. Over it, she says, "You totally proved me wrong. That *is* fun."

I grab her waist and dig my fingers into her sides for a tickle, and Erin erupts into a fit of laughter.

Of course, I'm only teasing.

I wouldn't miss a night of tradition with my nephew, even if I have to dress up as Harry Potter—a costume Malcolm found hilariously fitting.

Rebecca and Erin agreed.

On top of that, I wouldn't want to miss this night with Erin.

The woman has completely stolen my heart, and I wouldn't dare squash the chance to create more special memories with her.

After we rinse off, I make my way to her kitchen to brew another pot of coffee while she goes through her multistep routine of under-eye creams and lotions.

The machine kicks on with a faint gurgling noise, and the room soon fills with the smell of fresh brew. The plants decorating her apartment are extra lively and green—she has more than I remember. I study them and run my fingers over the leaves of a few unfamiliar plants. Are they new?

In any case, Erin certainly has a green thumb. I can't even take care of a cactus. She and I complement each other well, that's for certain.

And it's what keeps things interesting.

Also interesting is what I find when I sit on her couch.

The Ouija board she mentioned during our first official date.

Oh, the cheeky fun we could have with this…

"What do you think?" Erin appears in the doorway of her bedroom and does a twirl, showing off her costume.

She wears a pink birthday cone on top of her head and a tutu over black leggings with a matching pink shirt covered in black lines and letters.

A crayon. "Lovely." I grin.

But her face falls. "I didn't have time, or I would've gotten a Jane Austen outfit."

She crosses the sitting room and bounces onto the cushion next to me on the couch. "Next year."

I gape.

She never ceases to amaze me—and turn me on.

"I'd be positively chuffed with such a decision." I kiss her lips, cupping her cheek and pulling her in for a heated show of just how much I'd love to see her in an eighteenth-century gown like one of my beloved English novelists. "It's official— Halloween is my new favorite holiday."

Her giggle is faint as she regains her composure. After a kiss like that, I don't blame her.

My own words are weak as well.

Perhaps it's also because of what I need to say to her.

Erin glances at the coffee table next to us, and her eyes widen. "What are you doing with this?"

I follow her finger she points toward the Ouija board and chuckle. "I was going to ask you the same."

"It's just for fun." She reaches out to grab it, but I stop her.

"Let's try it out," I suggest, but she doesn't immediately let go or give in. "I'm serious," I insist.

Finally, she relents and scoots closer to me, the floral scent of her shampoo strong in her damp hair.

It's heavenly.

"How do we start?" I whisper, and she guides my hand over the heart-shaped pointer on the board and keeps her hand there as we move it from letter to letter.

My chest swells as the confession races to the tip of my tongue—the tip of the pointer, actually.

Because I take over and move the small object from letter to letter as I spell out, *I love you.*

She's heard it before, but my plans for this morning involve more urgency to show her just how much.

The hat on her head tilts downward as I take both of her cheeks in my hands. "I love you, Erin."

The edges of her shaky smile disappear into my palms as she says, "I love you too."

I kiss her again, a sense of peace washing over me.

"I want to disclose our relationship to the school Monday morning," I assert between kisses.

She pulls back and searches my eyes. "I mean it."

She rests one shoulder against the back of the couch, her expression unreadable as her body remains still.

I angle my body the rest of the way to face her as well. "I want to move forward with you, and if we don't say anything, I'm afraid we cannot do that. But I'm ready. For real this time."

She whispers something akin to "Okay," but this is not the time for guessing games. "Pardon?"

Erin leans back up, and her knee brushes mine. "Okay," she confirms.

Letting out a long breath, I slip my hand behind her neck and pull her mouth back to mine.

I don't know what awaits us or what Bill and the board will say, but since Erin will not be applying for the position directly under me, there shouldn't be an issue.

It's the other faculty who will give us grief. Aside from Bobbie and Katie, that is.

I imagine the others won't be as delighted as our two friends, and I'd hate for them to use their distaste to make Erin's life harder. Then again, the other teachers have already been whispering and snickering about us, as it is. At least if we come clean, their gossip will be true.

These are the thoughts that consume me as I finish getting dressed, the striped scarf settled evenly around my neck and the black garment flowing to my ankles like a graduation gown.

"You haven't said a word since you mentioned disclosing our relationship." Erin appears next to me in the mirror and smooths my sleeves down. "Are you sure it's what you want?"

I turn to face her, boring my gaze into hers as I try to be reassuring and fight my instincts to protect her against every unpleasant thing in the world. "I'm simply worried the other faculty will resent you," I confess.

"That's all? Hell, I'll deal with them." She smiles, and it's warm and understanding, which puts me at ease. "Besides, most of them are unbearable as it is. What's one more item to add to the list?"

I chuckle and place kisses across her knuckles.

"It won't be easy, but we're in this together. We'll take it one day at a time, and if any issues arise, we'll come to each other first. We'll be honest."

"Agreed," I rasp, and I let go of my fears as best I can.

It'll take time to let them all go—it's not as easy as flipping a light switch—but she's right. We'll do this together, and whatever happens will be worth it.

Nothing can change this bond between us.

For the first time, I finally feel like the usually jumbled pieces of my life have fallen into place.

EPILOGUE

Erin

One year later…

I step out into the main part of the cabin, running my nervous hands over the lace of my dress, and squeals mixed with cheers erupt.

I'm certain my friends have awakened even the Loch Ness Monster with their shrieks of approval.

"How do I look?" I ask, but it's more of a rhetorical question.

It makes them giggle and swarm me like loving bees to a flower.

My friends all start to hug me, waving their arms to the sides and reaching forward, but they stop themselves, thankfully.

I've already teared up twice and smudged my mascara, so they're obviously afraid of messing something up a third time.

Not that it would matter.

Nothing could ruin this day for me, especially not my supportive friends who are more like family.

It's my wedding day.

After countless awful dates, I never thought this day would come. Even the night Oliver proposed, and I said yes, I didn't believe it.

But it wasn't because I've ever doubted his love for me. It was because the last nearly year and a half since I met him has been surreal with a few challenges and snags along the way.

Although Bill and the board weren't thrilled to learn a teacher was involved with her superior, they only asked us to sign a waiver and sent us on to our happily ever after.

On the other hand, Nancy and Karen had plenty more to say, as expected. Nancy sneered in my direction more times than Karen made jabs about the disrespect for our handbook.

With plenty of meditation and sending positive thoughts out into the universe, I've survived. Of course, Oliver has been a huge help. His supportive nature has zero limits, and I've taken advantage of his reassurances.

Fortunately, Nancy latched her talons into an unsuspecting soul she met at her sister's engagement party a few months ago. Since then, she's loosened her jealous grip on the unofficial "ruin Erin's life" plan.

To add, Karen dispersed her efforts to maintain an orderly workplace among the rest of the faculty after she was announced as the new vice principal.

Most of us weren't thrilled, but she certainly deserved it. Selfishly, it was also a win for me since it gave her more responsibilities to distract herself from my love life.

The other teachers have warmed up to the idea of Oliver and me. In fact, they grew so excited that they threw us an engagement party at the school.

As for Tommy—he apologized to Oliver for the cold shoulder soon after he and I got back together. They've become close friends, and Tommy is even a groomsman today, along with Carter, Ian, and the guy Bree surprised us all with.

While the shock over Bree Finley falling in love took time to wear off, her man and Oliver frequently hung out and formed a bond in the meantime. They have more of a heavy bromance going, actually.

As for me, the last six months of being a fiancée and planning a wedding have been a dream.

"Oh my goodness." My mother appears in the doorway of the cabin and covers her mouth with both hands, her red eyes filled to the brim with joyful tears. "You're stunning, baby girl."

My face is not strong enough to contain my wide grin—the one I've been wearing all day as an accessory. It matches perfectly with my sparkling veil and elegant, slim gown.

"Your father is going to have a hard time giving you away," my mom says as she enters the room and walks toward me. "Oliver better deserve you."

I reach out to squeeze her hand, my stomach fluttering. "He does, Mom. I promise."

"We can attest to that," Bree speaks up. "I personally checked him out, did a deep dive on the internet into his background, and asked him several intimate questions while he was toasted on tequila."

"Bree!" I give her a warning glare to stop there.

"What? Everyone knows you can only get the honest

truth out of someone while they're drunk. It's why I enjoy margarita nights so much." She shrugs and looks to Tessa and Madison for backup.

"There is a lot of weight to that." Tessa nods while Madison says, "She has a point."

I roll my eyes and bring the veil over my bare shoulders.

I chose a spaghetti strapped dress with a deep heart-shaped neckline. Before I'd even finished trying the dress on at a boutique in New York, I knew I had to have it.

It's perfect for my style, and I know Oliver will lose his mind over the way it hugs my form.

There's a high-pitched gasp from the doorway, and Katie rushes inside, her champagne-colored dress matching the other bridesmaids. "You look amazing!" she raves as she waves one hand over me.

"Thank you." I smooth my strap into place over my shoulder and meet each of my friends' gazes. "Let's do this!"

Another round of cheers echoes across the cabin, followed by shuffling and low murmurs as they retrieve their bouquets.

And they lead the way, one by one.

Once they're all gone, my mother and I are joined by my father, who instantly has tears running down both cheeks. It's the second time in my life I've ever witnessed him cry. The overwhelming emotions get to me, and we have to call Madi back in to touch up my makeup a third time.

It's a happy day, indeed.

"Ready." Madison squeezes my hand and gives me an air kiss.

After a few minutes, the beginning tunes of the "Wedding March" sound, and I loop my arms through my parents' to start our descent to the gazebo.

When Oliver and I first discussed venues, we locked eyes, and I could tell we had the same thought before we shared it out loud.

The camp.

We chose the camp where we got stuck last year—the place where our love story took root like the trees by the lake.

It's the perfect place to make our vows and start our forever.

"I love you, honey." My mom kisses my cheek, and the coordinator shows her to her starting point, after which she ushers her to walk down the aisle.

Oliver's parents already walked, and little Malcolm and Rebecca are standing next to him at the altar.

At first, I was worried about the two worlds colliding, but Oliver got ahead of the situation and used it as an opportunity to bring the two sides of his family—and heart— together.

This is one of many examples where his controlling side came in handy.

Last Christmas, he sat Rebecca and his parents down, and Oliver insisted they meet.

Talk.

Find a way to get along, so we can all move forward with one less weight on our chests.

I made muffins and played with Malcolm in a separate room when things got too heated.

One conversation wasn't enough to solve everything, but it was definitely a productive start. Everyone walked out of the apartment a new person that day, and it was the beginning of something special. Although Oliver's parents are still working on their relationship with Rebecca and her son, I'm optimistic.

It's not in my nature to think otherwise.

The coordinator ushers for my dad and me to stand at the start of the aisle.

This is it.

My dad squeezes my arm, and I take a deep breath as the music changes to signal my entrance.

Peering down, I put one studded heel in front of the other and walk toward the man I love.

I slowly lift my gaze and meet his head-on.

Oliver stands tall in a khaki suit that was tailored to his muscled frame, a proud tug at the corners of his lips.

As I get closer, I note the slight gloss over his eyes.

And my own eyes sting once again with more tears building.

I always thought my day wouldn't come, but I never knew I'd be this emotional if and when it did.

As I've imagined several times over, my dad gives me away, and I stand on the other side of a man who's changed my life for the better.

A match better than if it were made in the stars. My soul mate.

"Hi, love." Oliver doesn't have to say anything else, and I still know he thinks I look beautiful as he immediately pulls me in for a kiss on the cheek.

My delicate heart melts.

Since the engagement, he's been more affectionate and attentive than usual—and I do mean *attentive*. Whether I'm rambling on about teaching, yoga, or my plants, he listens. If I'm in the mood at two in the afternoon or in the morning, he flips me onto my back and devours me.

Flowers. Romance. Love.

He showers me with it all, and when the time comes to say "I do" in front of our friends, family, and bouquets of dusty roses with splashes of carefully positioned greenery along the aisle next to us, I say the two words as if they're "I love you."

With enthusiasm. Meaning.

And happiness.

THE END

Want more of Oliver and Erin?
Download your FREE bonus epilogue here:
https://geni.us/SWTBossBonus

ACKNOWLEDGMENTS

Thank you, reader, for picking up this romantic comedy! It was such a blast to write. Oliver and Erin had me smiling from ear to ear, and I hope they offered you a fun escape.

To Bobbie Jo, Kelly, and Ana—thank you for reading early drafts of this book and helping me flesh out the weak spots. Your insight was invaluable, and I so appreciate you taking time out of your busy schedules to beta read. It means a lot!

To my KKSB girls—thank you for continuing to offer words of advice, encouragement, and memes that make me laugh when I feel like doing the opposite. You make this author gig so much more fun.

A huge thanks goes out to my mom, as always. Thank you for cheering me on and believing in me. I wouldn't be here without you.

I also wouldn't be here without my amazing husband. Thank you for your undying love and support. I love you more and more every day, forever and always.

ALSO WRITTEN BY GEORGIA COFFMAN

Stuck with You Series
Stuck with the Billionaire
Stuck with the Movie Star
Stuck with the Boss
Stuck with the Single Dad

Stuck with You Spinoffs
Stuck with a Date
Stuck with the Rock Star

Stuck with You Holiday Spinoffs
Stuck at Christmas
Stuck Under the Mistletoe

The Heat Series
Falling for a Stranger
Falling for a Player
Falling for a Bachelor
Falling for My Roommate

ABOUT THE AUTHOR

Georgia Coffman is an author of steamy contemporary romances and romantic comedies. She has a Master's in Professional Writing and loves the TV show *Friends*, as well as shopping. She and her husband enjoy working out and playing with their two pups. Georgia loves to connect on social media or through email, so feel free to reach out with any questions, your fave book recommendations, or even a funny joke!

Newsletter
www.georgiacoffman.com/newsletter

Website
www.georgiacoffman.com

Facebook
www.facebook.com/authorgeorgiacoffman

Instagram
www.instagram.com/authorgeorgiacoffman

Pinterest
https://www.pinterest.com/authorgeorgiacoffman

TikTok
www.tiktok.com/@authorgeorgiacoffman

BookBub
www.bookbub.com/authors/georgia-coffman

Amazon
amazon.com/author/georgiacoffman

Goodreads
http://bit.ly/georgiaonGR

Verve Romance
https://ververomance.com/app/authorgeorgiacoffman